Chapter One

CW01499981

The icy tarmac sparkled beneath the street lam   er. There was little traffic on the road, so he estimate   ven with the black ice slowing him down. He only hoped Hayley would be reasonably sober. Three Proseccos or more, and she would be spoiling for a fight.

And they fought more often than not lately.

She was expecting him at midnight, though he knew she would be late. She always took ages saying goodbye to all the people she spent the rest of the year bitching about. Although she hadn't been looking forward to it, he knew she would enjoy the belated Christmas party. She always did. Having an office Christmas party at the end of January made him shake his head. *Who does that?* The official explanation was that the office couldn't afford people taking time off before Christmas. In reality, Lester suspected what they couldn't afford was the Moorly Manor Hotel's December prices—or was it just serendipitous that the same party cost almost half the price a month later?

Up ahead, the glow of red brake lights made him groan. *Please, God, no!* As he got closer, he saw a police car parked across both lanes of the carriageway, its blue flashing lights blinding. He slapped the steering wheel with the flat of his hands and eased his foot off the accelerator.

Checking the dashboard clock, he muttered, 'damn,' through gritted teeth.

Just beyond the police car, he could see an ambulance and two other vehicles in the middle of the road. Squinting through the blur of lights, he could make out the crumpled bonnet of one car while a paramedic crouched down and spoke to the other vehicle's driver through the window. It was obviously going to be a while before the road was cleared.

Ten yards before reaching the queue of cars, Lester turned left onto Kelsey Lane, a slip road that joined Pendlebury Way after a mile. No one really used the old road anymore since the completion of the dual carriageway over twenty years earlier. *Twenty years, has it really been that long?* It seemed like only yesterday that his family used to drive up to the top of the hill and go hiking, enjoy picnics, and watch the paragliders circling above.

At the end of the slip road, Lester turned right onto Pendlebury Way. It wasn't long before he remembered why he rarely used the road. The surface was littered with potholes and debris, mainly clumps of foliage and broken branches from recent storms. There were no street lamps, though some light shone from the dual carriageway above, boosted by the eighty-foot wall of chalk that separated the two roads, although it was more of a glow than a visual aid.

On either side of the road, large trees seemed to close in around him and he instinctively turned up the volume on the radio. He tried to stay in his lane but found himself drifting into the centre, away from the reaching forest. Assuring himself that it was because the council had not trimmed the trees recently—and not that the forest was trying to get him—he continued up the hill, cursing every so often when he failed to evade one of the many obstacles in the road. He had just hit another pothole when a white glow manifested before him. He stared wide-eyed, but whatever it was had vanished just as quickly. His gaze snapped to the rear-view mirror. There was nothing discernible in the red glow of his taillights. He must have imagined it.

Fog? Even as he wondered, another, larger patch confirmed his suspicions. He expelled his breath with enough force to mist his windscreen. After wiping it with a chamois, he sank back into his seat and sighed heavily, wishing the glass surrounding him was thicker. Another patch of fog materialised before him like an impenetrable white barrier, and he turned off the full beam to make it seem less foreboding as he drove into it. Several long seconds passed before he emerged from the cloud. When he did, he puffed out his cheeks and exhaled the breath he hadn't realized he'd been holding.

Suddenly, bright green eyes reflected in his headlights. A fox. He instinctively slammed on the brakes, his Ford Fiesta skidding towards the left side of the road. He quickly turned his wheel in the same direction, even though logic told him to do the exact opposite. The vehicle began to straighten up, but he soon realised that he had over-corrected as it continued heading to the right, crossing over to the opposite side of the road before coming to a stop on a grassy bank.

'Jesus,' he said aloud, sinking back in his seat and turning his head towards the roof of the vehicle.

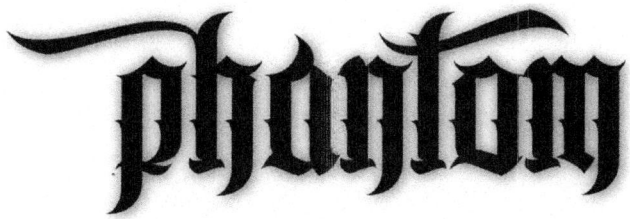

SHAUN SULLIVAN

For Mum & Dad

His heart pounded wildly, and for an instant, he feared it would explode. He pressed a firm hand to his chest. Several deep breaths later, he felt calmer and was able to reverse down the bank and back onto the road, cringing at the sound of debris scraping the underside of his car as he did so. Aware that his hands were shaking, he gripped the steering wheel firmly and continued up Pendlebury Way more slowly.

Lester put on his full beam again and turned the music down a little, the volume suddenly irritating as he concentrated on the road. *Thank Christ there was no traffic*, he thought to himself, imagining how badly things could have turned out if someone had been driving toward him. Twenty years ago, everyone used this road. Before the dual carriageway, it was the only means of crossing the Moorly Downs to Greyton and the towns and villages beyond. Since the end of the Second World War and the population explosion, the subsequent increase of cars warranted bigger, better, faster roads. Even the dual carriageway was at a standstill some days, especially during rush hour, so this road would have been gridlocked most of the time had it still been the main thoroughfare to the top of Pendlebury Hill.

A glance at the dashboard, and Lester's shoulders sagged. 23:59. He accelerated slightly, accepting that he was going to be late. Reaching into his jacket pocket, he grabbed his mobile phone and lifted it close to his face. It was too dark for facial recognition, so he tried to enter his four-digit PIN code with his thumb.

'Shit,' he cursed when he entered the wrong number.

He tried again, his eyes constantly switching between the screen and the road. The home screen suddenly glared up at him, and he selected the WhatsApp icon. His thumb pressed on Hayley's last message. Still looking from road to screen, screen to road, he started typing. *May be a few—*

When Lester glanced up again, his heart nearly stopped for the second time that night. She just appeared, stepping into the road right in front of his car, her head suddenly turning away from him. He knew it was too late, but he still hit the brakes hard. The sudden stop sent his car spinning across both lanes. For a moment, he was twelve years old and sitting in a cup and saucer ride at the fairground with his sister, Kat, beside him, a sadistic fairground worker spinning them mercilessly until he was sick to his stomach. He looked up, feeling just as nauseous, but all he could see through the windows was a haze of trees illuminated in his headlights as he spun around and around.

When the car finally stopped, Lester kicked the door open and tried to get out, only to be thwarted by his seatbelt. Trembling fingers blindly felt down the side of his seat for the release button. As soon as he heard the click of his seatbelt releasing, he stumbled onto the concrete, crawling a few feet before throwing up. He wiped his mouth on his sleeve and staggered around the car in search of the girl. In his mind's eye, he could see her profile vividly. Even in the gloom, she should have been easy to find in that white dress, but he couldn't see her anywhere.

'This isn't happening,' he told himself, hands on his head and eyes tightly closed, hoping that when he opened them again, it would all have been a dream. When he did open them again, the reality almost brought him to tears. She was nowhere to be seen. That meant there was only one place she could be.

Lester swallowed hard before getting down on all fours. He stared at the concrete beneath him for a few long seconds, trying to fortify himself, before reluctantly turning his head to check under the car. She wasn't there. *What the hell?* He jumped to his feet and walked around the car several times, widening the circle with each revolution. He looked along the grass bank and beyond, between the trees and even up into the foliage in case the impact had propelled her slight frame into the branches. He walked up one side of the road and back down the other, using the torch on his phone. Shaking his head, he returned to his car and dialled 999 on his keypad. The girl was nowhere to be found.

Chapter Two

01:17 Saturday, 27th January

It was over an hour before the police arrived and the absence of flashing lights and sirens suggested they were in no hurry.

The ambulance had arrived in eight minutes. Two paramedics rushed to Lester's aid, but after a fruitless search of the surrounding area, they stood in a huddle whispering to each other and eyeing him sceptically. Eventually, the female paramedic wandered over and looked up at him with an apologetic smile.

'I'm sorry to ask you again, Mr. Lester, but are you absolutely certain you hit someone?' She had asked the question twice already, although this time, she leaned towards him, her nostrils twitching as she awaited his reply.

'I haven't been drinking, Mandy,' he said, noting the name on her uniform and blowing out a breath of mist, which made her recoil. 'And like I said, I saw her step right out in front of my car. There was no way I could have missed her!'

She bit her top lip and watched him for a moment, her brow furrowing. 'But you said you didn't hear anything? Usually, when you hit something at thirty miles per hour, you would hear the impact and you would feel it. Did she roll onto the bonnet or anything like that?'

Lester shook his head. 'It all happened so fast. She was there one second and gone the next.'

The paramedic regarded him through narrow eyes. He guessed that she was in her mid-twenties, although her sickly sweet scent suggested she was younger.

'I had my music quite loud. I'm not sure I would've heard anything.'

'How loud?'

'Loud enough so I couldn't hear myself singing.'

Mandy continued watching him until his own unblinking gaze forced her to look away. It was obvious that she didn't believe him. Eventually, she nodded and walked back to confer with her colleague. They talked for a few minutes while her hand stroked her cheek in an attempt to cover her mouth. They both turned and looked back at him in unison before checking their watches. After a few minutes, the male paramedic got in the ambulance. Lester could hear him talking on his radio, although he couldn't hear what was being said.

He was about to call Hayley again when the police finally arrived. When the two officers got out of their squad car, Mandy beckoned them over and began talking to them in a hushed voice. All three of them turned his way several times, and his eyes looked skywards as he imagined what she was saying about him. It was several minutes before Mandy climbed back into the ambulance. He watched it head back up Pendlebury Way as the shorter of the two officers walked down the hill towards him.

He looked down at his notepad as he approached. 'David Lester?'

'Yes, and before you ask, no, I haven't been drinking.'

'That's good to know, sir. You reported that you had a collision with a pedestrian?'

'Correct. A girl in her late teens or early twenties.'

The police officer looked around the immediate area. 'So, where is this girl now?'

Lester shrugged. 'I honestly don't know. I got out of the car and looked all around, but I couldn't find her.'

'I see. So you're quite certain there was a girl. It wasn't a trick of the light?'

'What light?' Lester asked, turning his palms towards the black sky and looking around them.

'Your headlights, catching a patch of fog, perhaps? This hill is notorious for it, and we drove through a few patches on our way here. You'll be surprised how solid a patch of fog can appear with a full beam on it. You described her in a long white dress?'

'Yes,' Lester replied with a frown, starting to question himself. Maybe it was only fog.

'Is it at all possible that you could have imagined what you saw?'

Lester closed his eyes and tried to recall that instant, no more than a second. 'No,' he said adamantly. 'I can see her now. She was pale and wearing a white dress, but I can see her brown hair, parted down the centre and pinned at the back. She had thin, natural lips and pert nose that just rose at the tip. I could even see the fear in her green eyes before she turned away from me. There was no way I imagined all that.'

'That's quite a lot of detail, Mr.Lester, considering you only saw her for a split second.'

He shrugged; it was clear as day in his mind. 'That's what I saw.'

'I see,' the officer said, his index finger probing the cleft in his chin. 'So you definitely hit her?'

'How could I have missed her? I looked up, and she was right there in front of me. She was as close to my car as you are to me.'

'You said you looked up, sir? Looked up from what? Were you on your phone?'

'I just looked down at the time, on the dash. I was supposed to be picking my wife up at midnight.'

'I see,' he said, making a note on his pad. 'And how fast were you going, sir?'

'About thirty-five, maybe forty.'

The policeman raised his eyebrows and jotted it down.

'Sorry. I know it's thirty miles per hour up this road, but I was running late because of that accident on the dual carriageway and no one uses this road anymore.'

'Funnily enough, my colleague, Trev, and I were actually attending that accident,' the officer said with a wry smile. 'We had to leave it to come here. I was glad actually. It was a multiple fatality. A family of five, mum, dad, two teenage girls and a young lad, wiped out in seconds.'

'Jesus!'

'Any guesses what caused that crash?'

Lester felt his stomach turn over. He had a pretty good idea what was coming.

'It was some guy texting his girlfriend whilst travelling double the speed limit.'

He closed his eyes and shook his head. 'Here,' he said, offering the policeman his smartphone. 'You can check it.'

The officer took it and touched the screen. 'What's the PIN code?'

'9892, my birthday.'

Lester watched as the shorter man typed in the numbers and started tapping away on the screen. 'Saves me asking the question later.'

As the policeman interrogated his phone, he was aware that he needed to swallow. The build-up of saliva tickled the back of his throat, and his neck twitched as he fought the urge, knowing how unnaturally loud it would sound. He had deleted the text that he started writing to Hayley, deciding he needed to call her to explain what had happened, but he wasn't certain if there was a way of tracing his phone activity.

'All good,' the officer said, handing him back his phone.

'Thanks,' Lester managed to say, the word coming out strangled as he swallowed at the same time.

'Do you know what the worst thing of all was? The driver survived that accident without so much as a scratch. At worst, he's got a sore chin where the airbag caught him, otherwise he'll probably spend a few years behind bars, and then he'll be free to live out the rest of his days, whereas the five people he killed don't get that choice.'

Lester looked down at the ground, a fresh wave of shame washing over him. 'I'm sorry if I was going a little over the speed limit, but this road was deserted.'

'Apart from you and this girl you claim to have hit. What do you suppose a teenage girl would be doing along this road at midnight? There's nothing around for at least three miles.'

'I don't know.'

The policeman stared at him for a moment, his head moving from side to side. 'She would have been able to see your headlights a mile off. Why wouldn't she have just given you a wide berth?'

He shrugged.

'Did you feel an impact when you hit this girl?'

'I didn't feel or hear anything.'

'Is that your car there, the Fiesta?'

Lester nodded, even though it was obvious that vehicle skewed across both lanes of the old road was his.

'Trev!' the officer called up to his colleague, who was leaning back against the squad car on his phone. Without looking over, the younger policeman raised his hand in acknowledgement and started to wander down. Just before he reached them, he ended his call and looked up.

'Can you do a breathalyser test on Mr. Lester while I give his vehicle the once over?

'Sure,' he replied. 'Follow me, sir.'

Lester guessed he was in his early twenties. Leaner than his colleague with several days' stubble. He followed the officer up to the police car where he opened the boot and began rummaging inside. Lester stood with hunched shoulders, hands tucked beneath his armpits, and his arms folded tightly across his chest while the officer gathered a black box with a digital display. He opened a plastic bag, pulled out a small tube, and inserted it into the device. All he could see on the display was the word 'ready.'

The officer handed him the device. 'Breathe into the tube, please, sir.'

Lester drew in a deep breath, eased the tube between his lips, and exhaled, turning his head to watch the other policeman as he ran a flashlight around his car.

The officer took the device back and looked at the display. 'Negative,' he said simply.

'So what now, a drug test?'

'Now, my colleague and I will go back to the station and file a report, and you can go about your business.'

'But he hasn't finished checking my car yet. And what about the girl? Aren't you going to try and look for her? She could be laying around here somewhere, bleeding to death.'

'You said this girl was in her early twenties and wearing a white dress?'

'That's right.'

The policeman shook his head. 'We won't find her.'

Feeling his frustration building, Lester's eyes narrowed. 'How do you know without even trying?'

'My colleague is just going through the standard procedure, but we knew as soon as we got the call that this would be a waste of our time. It always is.' The look on the officer's face didn't offer any remorse for the girl.

Lester opened his mouth to speak but no words followed.

'We won't find a body because we never do.'

'What do you mean, you never do?'

'How long have you lived in this area, sir?'

'Eleven years.'

'So you've never heard the legend?'

'What legend?'

'Here comes my partner now,' the officer said, gesturing to the other policeman. Lester's gaze followed his. 'See him shaking his head? He's checked your vehicle and can't find a mark on it. No dented bumper, bonnet, or wing where you would have hit her. Nothing.'

'There's no sign of damage to your vehicle, Mr. Lester,' the shorter officer confirmed as he joined them. 'I can see in the road where you went for a bit of a spin and the tyre marks where you did your emergency stop, but I'm pretty certain you didn't hit anyone. I would conclude that you're just another victim.'

Lester looked from one officer to the other, his brows furrowed in confusion. 'I'm a victim? A victim of what?'

'Like I was telling you, sir,' Trev chipped in, 'the legend. You're just another victim of the phantom of Pendlebury Hill.'

Chapter Three

David Lester knew he was in trouble the moment he turned into his driveway. The outside lights were switched off, casting a foreboding darkness over the front of the house. He'd have to be quiet as he stumbled about blindly within. If he woke Hayley, his punishment would become even more severe. *Does she ever consider that I might fall and break my neck?* he wondered as he tried to line his front door key up with the scratched brass lock.

After adding several more scratches, Lester stepped into the porch. Closing the sun warped uPVC door quietly was almost impossible, but he managed it with some brute force. The next challenge was opening the porch door into the living room but there was nothing he could do to prevent it creaking. He winced as the protest sounded ten times louder than usual in the silent house. He could almost hear Hayley's voice reverberating inside his head with those familiar words, 'When are you going to oil those bloody hinges' as he removed his coat and shoes before entering the darkened living room.

The stale odour of his fish and chip takeaway dinner clung to the air, overpowering a multitude of diffusers that Hayley had dotted around the house. His bed for the night, the settee, was just visible on the opposite side of the room with a neatly folded duvet and pillow, but first he headed upstairs to use the bathroom. His wife was a light sleeper, so completing his ablutions without waking her was unlikely, although the alternative of peeing in the kitchen sink was even less appealing. He remained hopeful that she was 'three sheets to the wind' and 'out for the count,' as his father used to say.

As he slowly headed up the stairs, Lester listened for the snorting and grunting that had often been the cause of his own sleepless nights. He had once joked to his work colleagues that it was like sleeping with Miss Piggy. A bit of banter with the boys in the office was one thing, but if Hayley ever found out about her snoring, she would be devastated, and so would their marriage.

'£40.00 that taxi cost me.' Hayley's voice sliced through the silence like an alarm the instant his right foot touched the landing.

He padded over to their bedroom and stood in the doorway. He could just make out his wife sitting upright against the headboard. '£40.00? That's extortionate. It's only six miles.'

'It was twice the normal cost because it's after midnight.'

He winced at the annoyance in her tone. 'I'm really sorry about that, but as I mentioned on the phone, it was beyond my control. How was your evening?'

'I'm £40.00 out of pocket, David.' Even in the dim light, he could see her disapproving expression. 'And I had to wait for almost twenty minutes for the taxi. God knows what everyone must have thought of me standing there like a lemon. It was worse than being the last kid to be picked up after school.'

'I'll give you the £40.00, Hayley. Aren't you going to ask me about my evening? Did you hear what I said on the phone? A girl ran out in front of the car.'

'Yes, but I assumed, as you couldn't find her, that she was a figment of your imagination.'

Lester let out a rueful laugh. 'Well, she seemed real enough to me, so I reported it to the police and then had to wait an hour and a half for them to arrive. I couldn't leave the scene of an accident.'

'So was there an accident or not?' Hayley's tone remained unyielding.

'Officially, no.'

'Great,' she sighed. 'So you cost me £40.00 and left me stranded outside that hotel in sub-zero temperatures in front of all my colleagues for nothing. Not to mention wasting police time!'

'She was a phantom.'

'I'm sorry, what?'

'That's what the police told me. I looked it up on Wikipedia and it said, ghost, the soul or spirit of a dead person or animal that can appear to the living.'

'And I thought I was the one who had been out drinking all night.'

'I agree, it sounds a bit farfetched, but apparently, this girl has been running out in front of cars for years.'

'David, I'm tired. I've got a headache, and I'm really not interested in your fanciful stories.'

Perhaps you should give me a lie detector test, go one better than the police! 'Okay, so you don't believe me.' *So what else is new?* 'Do you think I called the police just to give credence to my story?'

'Given the choice between believing you saw a ghost or you fell asleep or simply forgot to come and pick me up, what do you expect?'

'I expect you to believe what I say, Hayley.'

'Well, that hasn't exactly worked out too well for me in the past, has it?'

Lester sighed, the weight of his guilt and her resentment pressing down on him. His head dropped forward, as if it were too heavy to hold up, and he could imagine her smug smile as she sat back against the headboard with her arms folded across her chest. He was grateful for the darkness, sparing him *that* look. After a few seconds of contemplation, he turned and walked into the bathroom.

He had no desire to argue with her, especially an argument he could not win, so his best recourse was to retreat and hope that time would eventually heal her pain. He couldn't change the past. He had exhausted using the time machine cliché for his indiscretion four years earlier, but throwing it in his face at every opportunity was not healthy. How could they move forward when she constantly dragged them back to the past? In her defence, she had given him a second chance, and he knew he didn't deserve it, so he was reduced to skulking away whenever the matter arose, hoping that with time, their wounds would heal.

Lester finished in the bathroom, glad that Hayley was awake purely because he didn't have to agonise over whether or not he should flush the toilet. Usually either decision was wrong. He headed back down the stairs, half expecting her to have the last word—'don't let the bedbugs bite'—but for once, she remained silent.

Despite the time, sleep eluded him as he lay on the sofa. He tried to sleep, but every time he closed his eyes, his mind replayed that scene a few hours earlier when he had glanced up to see the girl stepping out into his path. His only escape was opening his eyes into the darkness of his living room. He tried staring at the standby light on the TV until the bright red light multiplied and faded beneath his eyelids, but no matter what he did, she soon reappeared. She was inside his head.

Abandoning the idea of sleep for the time being, Lester reached over and grabbed his phone off the coffee table. If Hayley didn't believe him, he would give her proof. While asking the police officers to speak to her didn't seem feasible, searching online seemed like the next best thing. Google was his best friend. He only hoped this phantom had made it to the internet.

He opened Google and typed in the words 'Pendlebury Hill phantom.' Over 445,000 results were returned. His eyes widened as he scrolled through the first page. He quickly scanned two more pages before returning to the top result. Swinging his legs off the sofa to sit upright, he clicked on the link.

Phantom Hitchhiker Strikes Again!

Kent is home to Pluckley, reputed to be the most haunted village in England, but it is in the lesser-known village of Pendlebury where ghostly activity is picking up, quite literally. Phantom hitchhikers have been reported worldwide for years, but Pendlebury boasts one of the most prolific sightings of any recorded cases. The most recent sighting came on the night of 14th May when Stuart and Emma Hazeldine were returning from a meal out at their favourite restaurant.

'We were driving up the old Pendlebury Hill road when Emma spotted a girl frantically waving her arms in the air. She was wearing a wedding dress, and we both wondered if she was running out on her own reception. We pulled over, and she asked for a lift to an address in Greyton, which happened to be on our way. It seemed like no trouble, so she got in the back and we continued up the hill. By the time we got to the top, I had plucked up the courage to ask her about the wedding dress, but when I looked in the rear-view mirror, she was gone. I stopped the car and searched for her, thinking that she must have opened the door and jumped out without us realising. We even drove back down the hill to look, but it was like she just vanished into thin air.

'I wanted to go to the address that she had given us, but Emma insisted we make an official report, so we drove straight to the police station instead. That's when we learned about the phantom hitchhiker.'

The Hazeldines' encounter with the phantom hitchhiker is just the latest of many reported cases over the past fifty years, but who is this spectral bride? Local researcher, Paul Brotherton, has been investigating this particular haunting for over thirty years. 'I have no doubt that this is the ghost of Sarah Kendall, who was killed on Pendlebury Hill in 1970, in a head-on collision on the eve of her wedding. The address she gives was her mother's house in Greyton, so I believe she wants to let her know what has happened to her. The trouble is, Sarah always vanishes before the address is reached. Unless she completes her journey, I think she will go on haunting Pendlebury Hill for eternity.'

Although reported sightings of the phantom hitchhiker have dwindled over the past twenty years due to the opening of a new dual carriageway, it seems Sarah is still trying to thumb a lift on the old Pendlebury Hill road. Just something to think about the next time you're travelling home late at night!

Christ! How have I never heard of this before? Lester went on to read several more articles, all along the same lines as the first report on *Kent Online* dated May 2020. His own encounter had been very different to the reports he had read, but even so, he felt vindicated by them. Until that moment, he wasn't sure if the police were just humouring him. Now that he had something tangible to show Hayley, to prove to her that he wasn't lying, maybe she would start trusting him again.

Chapter Four

Lester walked into Greyton Police Station and screwed his face up at the strong stench of body odour that greeted him. He surveyed the small waiting area.

'Can I help you,' the desk sergeant asked, a woman with a closely shaven head.

You would look so much more attractive with long hair. Damn, stop judging people! Perhaps this woman had cancer and was having chemo. Either way, she has the right to have her hair however she wants it!

It was the only one of his New Year's resolutions to survive as he was determined not to make snap judgements about people. He had three lines of text written on a Post-It Note on his screen at work: *Give everyone a chance. Give everyone the benefit of the doubt. Don't judge a book by its cover.*

'Hi, my name is David Lester. I was involved in an incident last night.'

'And you were asked to come in today to make a statement?'

Now who's being presumptuous? 'Actually, no. The officer said he would write up a report, and there was no statement required or any further action.'

'Do you have further information that you want to provide?'

'Not exactly. It's just that the officer said there had been a number of similar reports of,' Lester looked over his shoulder at the girl and man sitting behind him and lowered his voice, 'the phantom of Pendlebury Hill.'

The desk sergeant stared blankly back at him.

'Have you heard of her?'

'Yes, I've heard of her. What is it that you want exactly?'

'Would it be possible to look through the other reports?'

The woman laughed. 'This is not a library, sir.'

'I know, but aren't your files public records?'

She laughed again. 'No, they're not available to the public, sir. Do you think people can just waltz in here off the street and say, "Can we read your file on that murder last night, take a look at the photos"?'

'No, but what about the older crimes, closed and archived, can't these be accessed? Don't they become public records after twenty-five years or something?'

'I'm sorry, sir, but the only information available to the public is what is given in our press releases. Perhaps you need a library after all.'

Lester smiled tightly at the woman, unable to keep the annoyance from his face. 'Thank you for your help,' he said before turning and walking towards the door. Then he stopped and paused for a few seconds before turning back to the front desk.

'Was there something else?'

'I just wanted to say, you'd look so much better with longer hair.'

10:03

When Lester opened the porch door and stepped into the living room, the negative atmosphere was as tangible as the fog he'd encountered the night before.

'Where've you been?' Hayley asked as he walked into the adjacent dining room, her eyes fixed firmly on her watch.

'Would you believe, I went down to the ATM to get that £40.00 I owe you?'

'No.'

Lester put his hand in the back pocket of his jeans and took out four folded ten pound notes and put them on the table beside her.

She looked from the table to him, her eyes narrowed. 'That took thirty-four minutes?'

'I went to the police station.'

'Why?' she asked. 'I thought that was all sorted?'

'It is. I just wanted to see if they would let me read their records.'

She looked at him as she always did lately, with her head slightly tilted and arched eyebrows. It warranted no words.

Feeling the need to explain himself, he said, 'I wanted to see what the other victims had reported, what address she gave them, and just to find out more about this girl and why she's haunting that location.'

Hayley continued glaring, her head tilting from right to left.

'She's dead, Hayley. You don't need to worry.'

'Like that would stop you!'

He forced a smile, ignoring her remark. 'So there you have it. That's where I've been.'

'I don't understand why you're going to all this trouble, even if you did see a ghost.'

To prove to you that I'm not lying. To turn things around. Instead, he said, 'I did see a ghost.'

'Whatever. She's dead, gone, forgotten.'

Lester sighed and looked down at the ground. The conversation had reached a familiar crossroads where he had the option to go forward into an argument, turn left or right to appease her, or turn back and let her win.

'She might be dead, but she's not gone or forgotten. She appeared to me for a reason.' Once he said the words, he knew it was true. He'd started his search to prove to Hayley he wasn't a liar, but the phantom *must* have shown herself to him for some greater purpose.

Hayley's narrow eyes reduced to thin slits until he could barely see her deep blue irises. 'What reason?'

'I don't know. That's what I need to find out. It could be a cry for help.'

'Help? It's a bit late for that, isn't it?'

Lester rolled his eyes as Hayley grabbed the underside of her chair and shuffled around so that she was facing him directly. He knew it wasn't going to be a straightforward conversation. 'Isn't a ghost just like a projection of the past? From what I'm hearing, you're crediting her with some intelligence.'

'According to a few reports I've read online, she's spoken to some people and got into their cars. That's more than just a projection.'

Hayley closed her eyes and shook her head.

'Okay, so what would you do if it happened to you?' he asked.

'If she's a ghost, probably nothing. She's dead! Why waste time on her?'

'That's easy for you to say. It didn't happen to you. You can't settle when you get a call from a number you don't recognise. I thought I'd killed someone. Don't you get how traumatic that was for me?'

'Not really. You should be relieved that she was already dead, David.'

Lester looked back at her, knowing that he was wasting his time and energy. 'Well, I'm afraid it's not that simple for me. I need to understand why she appeared to me. I have to find out.'

He could see from her unyielding glare that she wasn't convinced. 'And what about your chores?'

He stood with his mouth agape for a moment. 'My chores? What am I, ten?'

'You know what I mean. You've got to clean the car, fix that leak in the bathroom I keep telling you about, oil the door in the porch. Do you want me to go on?'

'No, I really don't. And what's stopping you from doing these chores?'

Hayley was stunned into momentary silence. 'I'm not cleaning the car. That's your job!'

'Why's it my job?'

She held up her hands like Wolverine, revealing long pink fingernails. 'That's why not!'

He watched as she turned away from him and manoeuvred her seat back to focus on her magazine.

'Have I done something to upset you? More than usual?'

Without looking up, Hayley pointed to the local paper that was open and facing him. He stepped forward and read the headline below where her finger hovered.

'Mayor Dering is opening the newly refurbished Greyton Town Hall at eleven o'clock today.' He shrugged. 'So? What am I missing here?'

'I thought it would have been nice to go, that's all.'

He laughed. 'When have you ever been interested in the mayor or the town hall?'

The look she gave him was laden with disappointment. 'It doesn't hurt to be seen at these events.'

Lester closed his eyes momentarily. 'Why didn't you mention it before?'

'Last night or over breakfast this morning, you mean, while you were off on your wild ghost chase?'

'Before that,' he said, getting his mobile out and looking at the time. He turned the phone round to show her. 'We can still make it. We've got half an hour.'

'Just forget it, David. I need at least an hour to get ready. As long as you're happy, that's all that matters.'

Happy? Remind me what that is.

He went to speak, but she held up her hand to silence him. As far as she was concerned, the conversation was over.

He stood watching her for almost a minute until he started to feel like a ghost himself. Eventually, he turned around and headed up the stairs to the office. He had some more investigating to do.

Chapter Five

The pink walls of Lester's office were a constant reminder of their little girl, Carla. Hayley had picked the colour. It was a shade between puce and that awful cough mixture the doctor prescribed him when he was growing up. He could almost smell it when he walked into the room, and the hazy memories of the surgery and waiting room that it evoked made him cringe. Even though Carla never took a breath, suggesting that they repaint the walls would have been like suggesting painting over the Sistine Chapel's ceiling.

He sat down at the desk and powered up his laptop, then started searching for 'Phantom of Pendlebury Hill.' He scrolled down until he found new links he hadn't visited yet. After reading from several different webpages, he decided to open an Excel spreadsheet to make some notes about the phantom bride.

It was nearly two hours later when he heard steady footfalls on the stairs and sat back in his chair, rubbing his eyes. Hayley walked in and placed a mug of coffee on his desk, leaning over his shoulder to look at the monitor as she did so.

'Are you still wasting time on this ghost thing?'

'Thanks,' he said, picking up the mug and putting it down again when it burned his hand. 'I don't know why we haven't heard about her before. It seems she's somewhat of a local celebrity. A couple of these websites are American, so she's actually internationally renowned.'

Hayley rolled her eyes. 'More people with too much time on their hands.' She read through his notes on the screen. 'There were four of them in the car?'

'Yes. The bride and her three bridesmaids were killed instantly.' He scrolled down the page on his screen to show her a black and white photo of the crash scene with a crumpled Mini and a white transit van.

'Jesus!'

'The driver of the transit van walked away without a scratch. He was over the limit.'

Hayley shook her head. 'Paul Fenwick,' she said as she scanned his notes. 'He got ten years but was released after seven. How is that not murder?'

'Murder has to be premeditated.'

'Isn't getting behind the wheel of a van knowing you've had too much to drink the same as picking up a gun?'

'Now, perhaps, but back in 1970, it wasn't. Fenwick got convicted of causing death by dangerous driving, but driving a three-tonne vehicle when drunk should have been manslaughter.'

'Well, at least the government got there in the end, and you've completed your investigation.'

'What do you mean?'

Hayley stabbed the screen with her index finger. 'You've found out all about her, so you don't need to spend any more time on it.'

'I've found out what happened, yes, but that's only the beginning. I still need to find out why she's haunting that particular location and why she appeared to me.'

Hayley rolled her eyes, her expression filled with frustration. 'It's a shame you can't pay more attention to the living.'

He frowned back at her, her words like a slap.

'Me!'

Not wanting to take the bait, Lester looked down at the carpet.

'You've already wasted enough time on this. Cleaning the car would be more productive.'

'Even if I clean the car today, it will need cleaning again tomorrow. That's what I call a waste of time.'

'Taking pride in one's appearance is not wasting time.'

Lester just looked back at her, his fingers stroking his bristled chin. 'So if I have a shave, put on my suit, and clean the car, you'll be happy?'

'Now you're being ridiculous. I just think it would be nice if you made more of an effort, that's all.'

'Because of the neighbours?' he said, recalling a similar conversation, before Carla, or even any talk of babies at all, when Hayley had pushed him to take accounting classes so they would have more money. *'All the neighbours who lived here when we bought this house have long since moved on to bigger and better homes,'* she'd said. *'We should be looking to climb that ladder too. If we don't do something soon, we'll be stuck on the bottom rung for the rest of our lives. Is that what you want?'*

24

'No, for my benefit.'

'Fine. As soon as I've drunk my coffee, I'll get out there,' he said with a steely smile, which she returned before leaving the room.

Lester flicked back to Google and continued scrolling down the page until he reached a photo of Sarah Kendall posing in the wedding dress she never got to marry in. It was poor quality, scanned from an old newspaper, he assumed, and as he leaned in for a closer look, the image became a mass of grey dots of varying shades. He then sat back in his chair. The image was much clearer from a distance, and he stared at it through narrow eyes. Soon his forehead corrugated, and he shook his head slowly. There was one thing he was certain of. Sarah Kendall was not the girl he had seen the night before.

Chapter Six

It was mid-afternoon by the time Lester was able to continue his research. Cleaning the car turned into waxing and then vacuuming. Hayley would have been happy with him just giving it a quick hose down to remove all the winter dirt that sprayed up from the roads, but he didn't want to give her any room for complaint.

By the time he'd finished, his fingers were so cold that he could barely type. He may as well have been wearing boxing gloves. He had missed lunch, so he made them each a cheese sandwich and a mug of tomato soup, which he cradled in his hands until the ache in his fingers eased. They sat in the lounge and ate in a familiar silence whilst watching an episode of 'The Walking Dead.' As soon as it ended, he washed up and headed back to his office, eager to confirm whether or not Sarah Kendall was the girl he'd seen.

An hour of trawling through more than twenty websites failed to produce a different picture of the bride-to-be. There were pictures of her bridesmaids, two brunettes and a redhead, so he was immediately able to eliminate them as the girl he saw. *So who was she?* Although the question remained, he continued working his way through the many websites that referenced the words 'phantom' and 'Pendlebury Hill.'

One name kept coming up again and again, Paul Brotherton. He seemed to be a local investigator who had a similar obsession with the phantom hitchhiker. Lester typed his name at the top of his spreadsheet as Hayley poked her head round the door and remained there until he looked round.

'Want to go into town or watch a film or something?' she asked.

He knew she was bored. It was always the same whenever he had to work weekends, which was often. She would amuse herself for a couple of hours by reading a magazine, messaging everyone she knew, checking Instagram, pottering around the house, moving ornaments by several degrees, and then she would come up and disturb him.

'Not shopping,' he said, turning and looking out at the steely sky. It was already getting dark, and the chance of more showers, or even snow, was high judging by those clouds. 'Why don't you pick out a film, and I'll be down in a bit.'

The corners of her mouth turned up, and he smiled back.

'How are you getting on?' she asked.

'Okay. There've been multiple sightings of this woman in white,' he told her. 'Many witnesses claim she wears a bridal gown. Some say that she steps out in front of the car, like she did to me. Others say she gets in the back seat and gives directions to a house in Greyton.'

'I'm surprised you didn't stop and let her get in the back of your car,' Hayley said, her words laced with sarcasm.

Lester closed his eyes momentarily, feeling as though he'd just been sucker punched.

'So, who is she?'

'One theory suggests she *was* Sarah Kendall. The bride-to-be we were looking at earlier. She was killed in a car crash on her way back from her hen night, along with two bridesmaids. The third one died in hospital two days later.'

'Yes, tragic.'

Lester nodded, sitting back in his chair with his hands behind his head. 'Apparently, she flags people down and gives them an address in Greyton, but she always vanishes before they arrive. She didn't get that far with me, but it still feels like she's asking for my help.'

'Oh, that's made me go all cold.'

'I thought you didn't believe in ghosts?'

'I don't, but it still gives me the willies.'

Lester held his breath for the inevitable quip, *'Not the same way that you gave Harmony the willy,'* but she missed the opportunity, and the relief caused him to expel the air more noisily than he intended to.

'But if she's a ghost, how can you possibly help her?'

He wanted to laugh, such was his frustration. It was either that or scream, and that never ended well. Instead, he took some deep breaths while he considered his answer.

'I did some research on ghosts and spirits, and many people believe that they're still here because they need to complete something before they can move on to the next world. Heaven, if you believe in that sort of thing. They're trapped between two worlds, a bit like the undead in the 'The Walking Dead.' If that's the case, maybe I can help.'

Hayley stared at him for several moments, squinting as though his own glare was blinding. 'Are you really serious about all this?'

Wow, the penny's finally dropped! 'Of course. Do you think I'd walk into the police station and ask to see their records if I wasn't?'

'So you actually did that?'

'Yes. I told you that's where I'd been.'

She scoffed. 'Well, you'll forgive me if I take a lot of what you say with a handful of salt.'

There it is. She never went long before finding another way to remind him of what he'd done. Lester sank his face into his hands, resisting the urge to scream. He sighed heavily instead. His eyes welled beneath closed lids as he tottered precariously on the precipice of tears. He was usually more resilient to her constant jibes but lack of sleep had left his defensive walls wafer thin.

After sucking in a deep breath and blinking the moisture from his eyes, he looked up. 'Which part are you struggling with?'

Hayley shrugged. 'The whole thing is a little farfetched, you have to admit. And now you're throwing zombies into the mix.'

Lester took another breath. *I'm going to be a zombie before the end of this conversation.* 'I'm not asking you to believe in zombies. That was a bad analogy,' he said. 'I guess if our roles were reversed, I'd struggle to believe it too. I'd probably try to find a logical explanation for what happened, like the police did.'

'And what did they say?'

'At first they suggested I imagined it. That it was just a patch of fog.'

'Well, there you go.'

'Fog patches don't move into your path, you move into theirs. Fog patches don't have human features and fearful expressions. I know what I saw, Hayley. Once they told me about the phantom I was certain.'

'Maybe you saw what you wanted to see.'

He laughed humourlessly and looked down at the floor, clenching his fists until his fingernails sank into his palms. 'I didn't want to see her. I didn't know anything about the phantom until the police told me about her. Whether you choose to believe me or not is up to you.'

He studied her for a moment, trying to read her expression, but she gave nothing away.

'I've decided what film I want to watch,' she said with a grin. '*Ghost.*'

Lester just stared at her, knowing that she was making a joke at his expense. 'Fine. I'm going to phone this guy, Paul Brotherton,' he said, pointing to the image of a man with long silver hair and a beard. 'I can put it on speakerphone if you want to listen in?'

Hayley glared back at him, uncharacteristically silent, before walking off.

17:21

Lester had been searching Google for over half an hour, trying to find the right Paul Brotherton, when he finally stumbled across a LinkedIn account. His progress was delayed briefly while he agonised over whether to compromise his ideals about social media and create his own LinkedIn profile. He continued surfing for another twenty minutes before conceding that he had no choice. Even with his own LinkedIn account, he still had to search through forty-nine Paul Brothertons until he found one located in Geshley.

When he opened Brotherton's page, it read: Paul Brotherton Owner of the Bridal Falls Public House. There were no contact numbers or email addresses, just a 'contact Paul Brotherton directly' button. Instead, he hit the back arrow and typed 'Bridal Falls Geshley' into the search box. Several search results were returned and he quickly located the official website and entered, finding the number under Contact Us in the top corner.

His stomach felt uneasy as he dialled the number and waited for it to be answered. *Why am I so nervous? I call complete strangers every day! Perhaps it's excitement rather than nerves,* he told himself.

'Bridal Falls,' a deep, cold voice answered.

'Can I speak to Paul Brotherton, please?'

'Speaking.'

'Hi, Paul. My name's David Lester. I've read some of your articles about the phantom of Pendlebury Hill and just wondered if you had a few minutes for a chat?'

'Actually, no. I'm done with all that. Sorry.'

Lester heard a click and then the phone went dead. He pulled the mobile away from his face and stared at it as though it were faulty. He rang Brotherton again, but there was no answer.

Undeterred, Lester returned to his laptop. He scrolled down the search results and stopped. 'That's why I don't recognise the name of the pub, it was previously the Poacher's Arms,' he said aloud.

He swiped his phone and looked at the time. 17:34.

'I can be there in twenty minutes.'

Chapter Seven

Pendlebury Hill seemed just as ominous in the early evening as it had at midnight. With the fine drizzle dripping onto his windscreen, visibility was poor. At least the clouds clinging to the summit kept the temperature above freezing. Lester was relieved that he wasn't driving up that far. Even so, he was aware of his stuttered breathing as he weaved in and out of the potholes and tried to take slower, deeper breaths. *She's not going to appear*, he told himself. *Ghosts only come out at night . . . don't they?*

Still, his heart raced quicker than usual.

He'd convinced Hayley to let him go by promising her he'd grab a takeaway on the way home. They could have a proper movie night, then. Even so, he'd half expected her to appear at his window while he sat waiting for the windscreen to clear, having had a change of heart. He was surprised she didn't.

Ironically, the cold, damp gloom outside felt less oppressive than the environment he had left behind.

The drive to Geshley took a little longer than expected. He took it slow through the dark grey veil, only increasing his speed when he approached *the spot*. He held his breath and readied his foot to hit the brake if necessary.

A pheasant emerged from the left and ran in front of his car. He hit the brakes as the bird darted one way and then the other. A long blast of his horn sent it scurrying back into the undergrowth from where it came as his car stopped diagonally across the road.

'Stupid bird!' he cried into the woods after it.

Once again, he was grateful that there were no other vehicles on the road. He could hear his own heartbeat in the silence of the car. He'd stopped in the same place as the night before. *Coincidence?* Lester decided it was before continuing up the hill at a crawl, wondering if scares of that nature did actually reduce life expectancy.

The Bridal Falls Public House appeared desolate. An empty carpark sat out front, with tufts of grass growing in sporadic clumps. The large, darkened windows on either side of the door resembled lifeless eyes, watching Lester as he steered the Fiesta into the first space beside the disabled parking bays.

Lester stepped out of the car and stared at the old building, noting the year 1771 etched into the concrete above the entrance. He had never frequented the pub, not even when it was the Poacher's Arms. Contrary to the image its name evoked, it lacked the cosy charm of a traditional country pub. It was more like a spit and sawdust saloon. White window boxes once meant for colourful flowers were now overgrown with weeds, and paint flaked and peeled from the old wooden frames, exposing signs of rot. The bottom of the front door was crudely bordered up, as if someone had kicked it in at some point, and the letterbox was crammed with rolled up papers and junk mail. The entire place appeared devoid of life. Lester suddenly felt a powerful urge to jump into his car and drive back home.

Steeling himself from the temptation, Lester walked up to the door and hesitantly pushed it open to enter a small porch. The orange glow beyond the glass door ahead looked a little more promising, and he continued on with more gusto.

He opened the inside door and walked into the saloon bar. It was dimly lit and appeared deserted. Twelve empty stools faced him, running half the length of the room in either direction, while shelves of glasses stretched from head height to the ceiling. Rather than the roaring fireplace he'd imagined, amber lights provided the welcoming glow he'd seen from the porch. Several square tables were pushed up against the front wall whilst a section of more secluded booths graced either end of the bar.

It was from a booth in the far left-hand corner that a man looked up from his half empty glass of merlot and gave a nod of his head. Lester guessed that he was in his late sixties, or from the sixties, with a mass of silver hair that made his head appear disproportionately large. When he stood, with his thin six-foot plus frame, he had a mop-like appearance. He wore blue-rimmed spectacles, a black turtleneck jumper, and a grey herringbone blazer, reminding Lester of his old physics teacher, Mr. Cameron.

Lester walked over to him. 'Paul?' he asked, extending his hand.

The man frowned and tentatively shook his hand. 'Yes?'

'I'm David Lester. We spoke on the phone.'

The older man's eyes closed beneath circular frames, and his nostrils flared. 'I told you on the phone, I'm done with all that stuff. Unless it's a drink you want, I'm afraid you've had a wasted journey.'

'But why?' Lester asked, his brow furrowing. 'You've spent so much of your life invested in this topic.'

'Exactly! And it's been a waste of my time so I'll thank you to leave before I waste a second more.'

Lester's gaze lowered to the floor, and he focused on a set of dried mud footprints on the ceramic tiles. He felt certain that he could reignite Brotherton's interest once they were talking face to face. There had been unmistakable passion in his writing, the same passion driving him now, but several years on, there was no trace of it.

When he looked up, Brotherton sat watching him with his glass in his hand. 'What happened to you?' Lester asked.

'I stopped looking for answers when I realised there were no answers.' He took a sip of merlot and gently swirled the glass, mesmerised by the dark liquid inside. 'The best advice I can give you is quit now before you waste precious time and money on what is, inevitably, a fruitless pursuit.'

Lester took a step towards him. 'I saw her.'

The older man's eyes slowly moved from the glass to meet Lester's.

'Last night, about a mile down the road.'

'What did you see, exactly?'

'A girl, late teens, early twenties, with short brown hair and a white dress. She just appeared from no-where. I was convinced I had hit her, but when I got out of the car, she was nowhere to be seen.'

Brotherton emptied the remnants of his glass and stood up. 'How about that drink, David?' he said, edging out from the booth. 'You look like a lager drinker to me,' he called as he stepped behind the bar, poised ready with a pint glass beneath the Foster's tap.

'Good guess,' Lester replied.

The bar owner pulled the tap back and started filling up the tilted glass. 'You get a sense for these things after a few years.'

'Why Bridal Falls? There are no waterfalls around here, at least that I know of.'

Brotherton shook his head. 'No, but by God I wish there were. The number of enquiries that I've had over the years from tourists popping in to ask that exact same question. Most of them leave disappointed without even buying a drink. Sometimes, after a heavy downpour, there is something akin to a waterfall on the chalk cliffs as the excess water runs off the moor, but I think that's a bit of a stretch.'

'So why then? It just sounds so out of place for round here.'

'And yet it's not. What's the reason you're here right now? Isn't it because of the phantom bride?' Brotherton walked back to the booth with a pint of beer in one hand and a wine bottle in the other. He handed Lester the lager before taking the seat opposite and filling his glass up to the brim. He took a long sip, emptying a third of the glass before sitting back. 'It's a play on words, Bride will fall.' Brotherton bit down on his bottom lip. 'Maybe I should have just stuck with the phantom bride or the phantom hitchhiker, as others call her. If you have to explain something that often, it's obviously too obscure.'

'Sorry.'

'So, did she speak to you?' Brotherton asked before picking up his glass and taking another sip.

Lester shook his head. 'No, it wasn't like the reports I've read online where she waves you down and gets in the back of your car. I just saw her for an instant as she stepped out in front of the car.'

'And disappeared?' he said, his focus still elsewhere.

'Yes.'

Brotherton smiled weakly, his gaze returning to Lester. 'Shame. I was hoping that your encounter may have . . . answered a few questions.'

'Sorry,' Lester said again as he sat back with his arms folded.

The older man gave a gentle shake of his head. 'This is why I got out of the game. Every new sighting offers hope but then always manages to fall short of the mark. Over the years they've become less and less. One day, they'll stop altogether.'

'What exactly were you hoping to hear?'

Again he shook his head and refilled his wine glass. 'I don't know really. Maybe that you picked her up and took her to the address she gave you, and when you got there, she got out and her mum raced down the drive to embrace her. That they all lived happily ever after . . . so to speak.'

Lester was thoughtful for a moment. 'I'm not sure she was hitching a ride. I mean, it happened so quickly, but I got the feeling she was running from something. I thought I saw a look of panic on her face.'

Brotherton looked suddenly pale, as though the blood had drained from his face.

'Paul?'

'Sorry,' the man said, picking up his glass again with a surprisingly steady hand. 'So what is it that you do, David? For a living, I mean.'

'I'm an accountant.'

'Another profession of repute,' Brotherton said with an assured nod. 'Many of the reports over the years have come from people of a certain ilk. One of the first to have claimed to see her was a copper. Usually, when it's a policeman or a doctor or a lawyer, let's say anyone with a reputable profession, the stories tend to gain more credibility.'

'I can't imagine it would have been easy for anyone of that stature to report it. They may have given the story credence, but they could just as easily lose their own credibility.'

'Of course. It begs the question, how many more have seen her and not reported it for fear of ridicule?'

Lester nodded. 'And what about you, how did you get involved?'

'Now there's a story,' he said, swallowing the remaining half of his wine in a single go. 'Best get a refill,' he said, standing and pointing to Lester's glass.

'Still working on this one.'

Brotherton walked off, returning moments later with another bottle of merlot. He sat back in the booth and filled up his glass. He picked it up and cradled it in his palm with the stem between his middle fingers. 'It was the 14th of May, 1987. I was on my way back from London after watching Wimbledon winning the FA Cup. Hands up, I had one or two pints more than I should have, but after catching the train back from Victoria, I only had a few miles to drive home from Greyton station, so I took the risk. I was coming down the hill, a mile down the road from here, when I saw a girl in a wedding dress standing by the road. She looked so out of place that I found myself braking. The clock on the dashboard read 11:11. I didn't realise it was significant at the time, but it just stuck in my head. Anyways, I pulled over and asked if she was okay.

'She was a very pretty girl, long blonde hair with black smears around her eyes. It's a tired cliché, but she did look like a panda.

'She bent down, her face almost as white as her dress, and told me she needed to get to her parents. I could see how stressed she was and thought it best not to engage in any banter, like had she been to a fancy dress party or worse, had she been jilted?

'I was still a little merry, but I felt I had no choice but to offer her a lift. I just hoped they lived close by. That's when she told me they were in Greyton. I had just come from there, but I couldn't leave her stranded. What if someone came along after me who . . . wasn't so gentlemanly?

'I told her to jump in and expected her to get in the front seat, but she opened the back and got in behind me. I found that a bit strange. No matter, I swung the car around and headed back up to the top of the hill.

'When I asked her what the address was, she didn't reply. I looked in the rear-view, and she was just staring straight ahead like she was in a trance. She was clearly distressed. I asked her again, and she told me 127 Kerberly Terrace.

'I didn't have a clue where that was, so I asked, "Would you be able to direct me when we get to Greyton?" She didn't answer, so I looked up and saw her nodding in the mirror. I kept trying to talk to her, but it was difficult to get a conversation going. "You really shouldn't accept lifts with strangers. There are some bad people out there."

'She made eye contact in the rear-view mirror and just said, "I have to get to my parents." She seemed a little less hyper, so I just kept driving.

'We carried on without a word until we reached Greyton, and that's when she began directing me. It was easy enough to find. I turned down her street and started looking for 127. It was hard to read the numbers in the dark, plus most of the houses were set quite away back from the road.

'"Let me know when you want me to pull over," I said but she didn't reply. I looked in the rear-view again, but I couldn't see her. I looked over my shoulder thinking she'd ducked down to get something out of her handbag and nearly crashed the car. She wasn't there.'

Lester stared back with wide, transfixed eyes.

'I thought she must have opened the door and jumped out, but there's no way I would have missed that. I wasn't that wasted. I stopped and opened the back door and double-checked. I even opened the boot. I know, it sounds stupid, but at the time I was frantic. I looked down the terrace in case she had got out and was lying in the road, but there was no one around anywhere.'

Brotherton sat in quiet contemplation for a moment.

'So what did you do then?' Lester asked, leaning almost into the centre of the table as if Brotherton was a vacuum, sucking him in.

'I left the car in the middle of the road and went up the nearest driveway, checking the numbers as I went until I found 127. All the lights were off, they were in most of the houses, but that didn't stop me. I ran up to the front door and knocked. They had one of those letterboxes with the knocker built in. I stepped back and waited, watching as one of the first floor lights came on. The door opened, and a woman appeared in a pink dressing gown. When she saw me standing there, she immediately stepped back and pulled it tighter around her. "Can I help you?" she asked.

'I knew it was her mother, I could see the resemblance. She was small and hunched and looked, dare I say it, haunted. I really wasn't sure how to explain what had happened, so I just blurted it out. "I've just given a lift to a girl who gave me this address. She said she had to get to her parents, but when I went to ask her how far up this road we need to go, she had vanished."

'The woman looked back at me and smiled. I tried to read her eyes, but all I could imagine was that she thought I was some kind of maniac and half expected the door to be slammed in my face. When I told the mother what had happened, she said "I've been expecting you. Her name is Sarah. She's my daughter, at least she was."'

'I shivered at that; it was that feeling of someone walking over my grave.

'You can imagine how strange that sounded. Then she told me that Sarah died eighteen years ago that very night. She and her three bridesmaids were killed as they were coming back from her hen night."

'I found myself walking backwards down her pathway. I was so shocked.'

Brotherton fell silent, and his gaze lowered to his wine. Again, he lifted the glass to his lips.

Lester leaned forward. He was quite literally on the edge of his seat. 'What happened next?'

'She told me the driver was drunk. He walked away without a scratch and only served seven years for four counts of dangerous driving. She said, "Sarah and her friends were given death sentences. Where's the justice in that?"'

The older man's eyes had welled with tears and he paused to take another sip of wine.

'My knees almost buckled listening to her going on like that. She told me that a number of people have seen her daughter over the years and given her a lift, but she's always gone by the time they arrived. Her eyes looked beyond me, into the night, and she said, "I would so love to see her one last time." When she asked me how her daughter looked, I said, "Beautiful," but it didn't seem enough, so I corrected with "Angelic in her wedding dress." The woman smiled. It seemed to give her some comfort.

'She told me her daughter wasn't wearing her dress that night.

'I can't deny that I found the whole thing fascinating and was interested to hear more when she apologised for jabbering on and invited me inside.'

'Did you?' Lester asked.

Paul shrugged and took another drink from his glass. 'I was tempted to. I had so many questions for her, but in the end, I declined and asked if I could visit again to discuss it further with her. I think she found my suggestion a bit weird, so I never pursued it. She was just in the moment and probably felt close to her daughter through my connection with her. I don't think she had any real wish to open up old wounds, so I bid her farewell and drove home.'

'I can see how that incident sparked your interest.'

The man nodded, a far-off look in his eyes. 'I became somewhat obsessed by the whole thing.'

'I can understand your obsession,' Lester said, feeling a sort of kinship with this man. Here was someone who had a sense of what he'd gone through. Someone who didn't think he was mad. 'I feel like this encounter is taking over my life.'

'It's natural. As human beings we love stories, and we are curious creatures. We need answers. We need to understand things. Until that night, I had no concrete convictions about the afterlife, but I became an instant believer after that. I had a mate from school who was a copper at Greyton, and I asked him if he could get me copies of any reported incidents surrounding a hitchhiking bride on Pendlebury Hill. He gave me the original files. Most reports mentioned a girl in a white dress who steps or runs out in front of their car.'

'Like my encounter!' Lester had not meant to be so emphatic.

Brotherton nodded. 'Yes, two very different types of accounts. That has always puzzled me,' he added, his eyes focused on the empty wine glass.

'But you never got all of the answers you were looking for?'

The man remained fixated on his wine glass. There were a few moments of silence before he shook his head and replied, 'No. In the end, I gave up searching.' He poured himself another glass of wine.

Lester was thoughtful for a moment. 'Did you ever try to enlist the help of a medium?'

The other man's eyes glared back at him through thick lenses. 'Thieving bunch of charlatans! I'm willing to open my mind to some form of life after death but not to the possibility of anyone being able to communicate with them. Anyone who believes otherwise is a fool.'

Lester sat upright in his chair, realising the subject was a closed book. He watched as Brotherton quickly drank the whole glass of wine in one go, wondering if he had outstayed his welcome.

'You say she had long blonde hair?' Lester asked.

Brotherton frowned back him.

'The bride. Sarah.'

The man nodded.

'The girl I saw had short brown hair, pinned up at sides and the back. I'm so used to seeing all these twenty-something girls with long blonde hair and fake eyelashes that I suppose it's the one thing that stood out for me. Her look struck me as being rather old fashioned.'

Again, Brotherton went deathly white. He emptied the contents of the wine bottle into his glass, shaking it to get every last drop. 'I thought you only saw her for a split second?' he challenged, swishing the wine around in his glass.

'I did, but it's amazing what the brain sees in that short space of time. She was wearing a white dress, as well. But . . .'

Brotherton's eyes narrowed behind the electric blue frames. Lester opened his mouth to speak but then thought better of it. 'C'mon, David,' Brotherton urged. 'Don't hold back. What's going on in that head of yours?'

'I know you're the expert, so I may be going out on a limb here, but have you ever considered that there might be more than one phantom?'

Chapter Eight

Lester headed back down Pendlebury Hill, the steady back and forth of the windscreen wipers threatening to send him into a trance. His mind drifted to the tatty Bankers Box full of manila folders Paul Brotherton had given him. All the research the man had done on the phantom bride. It was more than Lester had hoped for.

Two minutes later, he saw black rubber tyre marks illuminated in his headlights and found himself pulling over. Part of him hoped to see the girl again, to dispel any doubts that he had just imagined her or that she had been a misshapen wisp of fog conjured up by the contrasting darkness and light. He shook his head, certain that there were too many coincidences for her to have been a figment of his imagination.

After calling Hayley to apologise for taking so long and asking her dinner preference, Lester got out of the car. The chill evening air embraced him, making his body tense. The drizzle had stopped, and the clouds were dispersing to reveal star-scattered patches of clear sky.

'Hello?' he found himself saying. 'Are you there?' He walked in a circle, his gaze darting all around. 'Sarah?'

He expected to feel stupid or embarrassed talking to an empty road, but he didn't. It was as though she was there, hiding just beyond the shadows, but she was too scared to step into the light.

'I know you're here,' he continued, turning around to project his voice. The darkness felt almost tangible, like a shroud enveloping everything around him. 'Is there something you want from me? Is there some way that I can help you?' As he spoke, the night seemed to grow colder, and he folded his arms tightly across his chest and hunched over. The sensation of being watched sent goosebumps crawling along his arms.

'Sarah?'

Silence. Lester sighed, his breath forming a cloud before him. When he looked back at his car, he could see icy tendrils of frost beginning to spread across his windscreen. 'Sarah,' he called, louder than he had intended. His breath misted in an oval shape that, just for a fleeting moment, became a face. The girl's face. Then it was gone.

Unease swept over him like the rush of a passing train. He hurried to his car and jumped in, starting the engine with a quick twist of his wrist. He pulled away immediately, wheels spinning as they fought to get traction, and turned the heater on full blast to clear the windscreen. The wipers squealed, struggling to clear the thin film of ice that had formed on the glass, ultimately blurring his view. Still, he could see enough to put some distance between himself and the spot.

By the time he reached the roundabout at the bottom of the hill, his courage had returned and he was able to breathe normally once more. He called ahead to the Mandarin Chef and ordered their dinner to avoid having to wait and then headed home after picking it up.

By the time the time he pulled up to his house, it was 19:33. He got out of the car and locked it, grinning as he looked at the splashes of dirt around the driver's door and lower bodywork. At least Hayley had inspected it after he had cleaned it.

'An hour, you said,' Hayley's frosty greeting almost made him shudder as he staggered through the door with their takeaway balanced on the Bankers Box.

'I'm sorry. The guy I met with was so interesting that I just lost track of time. But look what he gave me?' he said, looking down at the archive box.

Hayley's eyebrow lifted. 'A filthy old box?'

'All his research on the phantom of Pendlebury Hill.'

'Another box of crap to go with your other boxes of crap,' she said with a roll of her eyes.

Lester ignored her comment. 'It's years of research and police reports. You should be pleased. It will save me a lot of time.'

Her face suggested she was anything but as he walked through the living room and into the kitchen, where he managed to offload everything on the breakfast bar.

'Don't put that there! We have to eat off there!'

Not literally. 'Sorry,' he said, moving the Chinese onto the breakfast bar and grabbing the box. 'I'll take it up to the office.'

'So, what now,' Hayley said, crossing her arms, 'you're going to waste even more time on this?'

Lester froze in the middle of the living room and sighed. It seemed he could never please her. 'What would you rather I did, Hayley?'

'You could spend more time with me, your wife. I wish you gave me as much attention as you're giving to this dead girl.'

He drew in a deep breath, and then another. 'Why don't you put on *Ghost* while I dish up? We can spend the whole night together.'

'I watched it while you were out.'

'*The Notebook* then? It's your favourite.'

'Okay,' she said, with a hint of a smile. 'But don't think we'll be spending the night together like *that.*'

Lester forced a smile to his lips before heading upstairs. *As if! I've got more chance of winning the lottery!*

Chapter Nine

It was still dark outside when Lester got up. He had lain awake for what seemed like hours, wondering what he would find in those files, before conceding that he wouldn't be able to get back to sleep. By contrast, Hayley was completely out. He figured he had a couple of hours before she turned the TV on in the bedroom, indicating that she was awake and ready for breakfast.

As he began looking at Brotherton's research, Lester quickly realised that a couple of hours would not be enough. It was clear that Brotherton had no organisational skills. Sorting his files into some semblance of order would take at least half a day. He decided to pull each file apart and put it back together in chronological order, noting on each cover names, dates, and descriptions so he could easily reference them later.

The first file he opened was a case similar to his own. Christian Collins reported a young girl stepping out in front of his Ford Sierra on the night of 9th September 1992, causing his to swerve and hit a tree. He scanned the report from top to bottom, nodding subconsciously as he related some of that experience to his own, and made more notes on the cover when he got to the description, 'short, lightish hair, pale dress, look of terror.'

The next file also had similarities. Russell Templeton reported a woman in a white dress running across his path as he drove down the hill. He stopped immediately and searched the area, but there was no sign of her. There was little information in terms of a description, but he noted Templeton's comment that she seemed 'out of place.' *What does that mean exactly?* Lester had to admit that there was something about her nagging away in the back of his mind, but he couldn't quite put his finger on it. Templeton's words, 'out of place,' resonated with him. He knew what the guy meant without actually fully understanding it or being able to explain it.

The incident took place on the night of April 25th, 1995, although, as he read the bottom line of the police report, Lester noted that it was actually signed and dated the following day. That didn't quite add up. He knew full well that failing to report an accident involving another person was an offence. One couldn't simply pop into the police station the next day and report it because it was late and they were tired or . . . drunk.

He pondered on that for a moment. It was the only thing that made sense. Even if he had seen a ghost and there was no actual victim, if Templeton had been drinking and was over the limit, he would have been prosecuted.

Lester allowed himself a smile, pleased that he had spotted the anomaly, particularly as he suspected that Brotherton had missed that fact completely. On the face of it, the older man didn't seem to be much of an investigator at all. He was about to open the third file when the sound of raised voices stopped him. It was the TV in the bedroom, which meant Hayley was awake. With a sigh, he closed the file and headed back to their bedroom to ask her what she wanted for breakfast, knowing his investigation was on hold for the time being.

13:39

The remainder of the morning was spent crossing off a mental list of jobs that Hayley had assigned him over the past few months. Most had been deferred with the words, 'I'll do that in the spring, when the weather is better,' but the bright empty sky had proved irresistible, even with freezing temperatures. The damp winter had left the patio tinged green, and it was satisfying to blast the algae with the jet washer, revealing the beige paving slabs underneath. Even though his feet and ankles ended up soaked and frozen, he enjoyed the alone time and the respite from Hayley's constant digs.

After cleaning out the shed and raking up the remnants of the autumn leaves, it was early afternoon, so Lester went inside and made lunch.

'Fancy going out for a drive this afternoon?' Lester asked as he handed Hayley a ham sandwich.

She screwed her face up and shook her head. 'It's too cold to go anywhere. Besides, I want to start my new book today.'

'I thought you wanted us to spend more time together?'

'Well, you can sit with me while I read if you like?'

'I think I'll pass. I still have loads of research to plough through. I was thinking of going to see the victim's mother.'

Hayley was about to take a bite of her sandwich, but she paused with it just beyond her lips. 'Excuse me?'

'I want to see if she can provide me with any more clues as to why her daughter is trying to get in touch with her.'

His wife glared back at him. 'Are you kidding me right now?'

'It could be vital to the investigation,' he said, trying to force away the guilt he felt at her disapproval.

'I don't think she'll thank you for going round there and raking up the past.'

'Who knows? Maybe she'll get some comfort hearing that her daughter is still trying to connect with her. She was receptive to Paul, the guy I saw yesterday, when he visited her.'

His wife shook her head, clearly exasperated. 'I'm not sure what you hope to achieve with any of this.'

He sat down in the armchair beside her. 'I've told you. I want answers, Hayley, just like you do when strangers try to befriend you on Facebook. You're always asking who are they and why do they want to be your friend. This is like that, but . . .'

'But what?' Irritation tinged her words.

'Different. Physical, for want of a better word. I just feel that this girl is reaching out from the other side because she needs my help. I'm not sure what I could possibly do, but my instincts are telling me I have to find out.'

From the soft, almost sympathetic, look in her eyes, Lester thought that she finally understood, until she feigned a yawn. 'I wish you'd put as much effort into helping me or getting a partnership at work.'

Rather than responding, he stood up with his plate in hand and started walking towards the stairs.

Her mouth fell open. 'Where are you going?'

'I've suddenly lost my appetite.'

He headed back up to his office, taking bites of his sandwich as he went. It was not so much his appetite he had lost as his resolve to carry on justifying himself to Hayley. There were always quips about his infidelity, which he took on the chin, but the mention of him becoming a partner at work meant that she would now start chipping away at him until his situation improved. She hated him having any kind of interest or hobby that didn't involve her. She craved attention, and it was eating away at her that she was playing second fiddle to a ghost.

In his office, Lester continued searching through Brotherton's files. Focusing was hard as his mind kept drifting back to their relationship. Gone were the days when he expected her to apologise for her comments. Sorry was not in her vocabulary. She believed that she was the victim and he was deserving of everything she threw at him. She couldn't see the damage that she was doing. Every remark was like a sledgehammer striking against the foundations of their marriage, and the cracks were there for all to see. She just either didn't want to see them or she was completely blind.

Lester shook his head as though it would empty all thoughts of Hayley from it. None of what he'd read so far had been digested, so he read the file again. It was a handwritten statement by Brian Thorne of Nestleford Brewery, who reported a woman with 'boyish brown hair and a white smock' crossing the road in front of him. He stopped the vehicle and looked around, but there was no sign of a body. Two officers carried out an extensive search of the area but were unable to locate a body. The incident took place at 10:27 3rd February 2000. Case closed, no action.

He checked his watch, 14:13. He decided to check one more file and then drive up to 127 Kerberly Terrace to interview Sarah Kendall's mother. On the cover of the manila folder was the name Michelle Blane and the date was 14th May 1974. Inside was another handwritten statement with small but neat penmanship. This one read much like Brotherton's.

Lester put the file back in the box and sighed. Since getting Hayley's input, he had been wrestling with the ethics of visiting Sarah Kendall's mother, but reading that last statement had made his mind up for him. He grabbed his raincoat from the back of the chair and took a fortifying breath before heading downstairs to face the inevitable resistance.

'I'm going to see the bride's mother,' he told Hayley as she looked up from her book. 'Shouldn't be more than an hour. Actually, best make it two after yesterday.'

'Have fun,' she said, her gaze quickly returning to her novel.

He stood there for a moment, wondering why she was suddenly so calm about him going to see her. Was this some kind of trick? He decided just to go before she changed her mind. Even then, he sat in his car for several minutes, unable to accept the ease at which he'd been allowed to leave. *What's she up to? Is it a test to see if I'll actually go, and if I do, will she make me suffer later?*

Lester pushed those thoughts aside and started the engine, blasting the windscreen with warm air to clear it before reversing onto Braithwaite Drive. As Rainbow's 'Stone Cold' started playing, he turned the volume up high and started singing along. It was his Hayley song.

At the roundabout, he found himself turning onto Pendlebury Way even though the dual carriageway would take half the time. He knew he was highly unlikely to see the girl again, but he felt drawn to her in a way he couldn't understand himself, let alone explain to Hayley. He believed that she had chosen him, and he had to find out why.

The sun was low in the sky as he made his way up the hill, and he found himself blinded by it when it snuck through the dense foliage. The phantom bride could have been standing by the side of the road, her arms waving frantically at him, but he wouldn't have seen it. All he could see was a bright spherical glow.

Lester's stomach churned as he turned onto Kerberly Terrace. It was different to the image that he'd built in his mind. He parked on the road outside 127 and looked up the long driveway. Now that he was there, doubts clouded his mind. *Perhaps Hayley had a point. How would I feel if I had lost a child and random strangers kept turning up at the door to remind me of the fact?* The idea of stirring up painful memories made him question his decision. He thought long and hard about it, waging a personal battle in his head, before his curiosity and need for answers drove him to turn off the engine and step out into the cold. He just hoped his reception would be a little warmer.

The walk up the slightly inclined driveway was laboured, as though he was wading through marshland, but he reassured himself that it was something that needed to be done. He could hear his dad's voice encouraging him— *'Nothing worth having comes easy'*—as he approached the front door. Before he knew it, he was pressing the doorbell and taking a step back.

The door swung open, revealing a rotund woman who he guessed was in her early fifties. She was clearly not the mother of the bride. 'Hello. Can I help you?'

'Hi. I was actually looking for Mrs. Kendall,' he said.

'Mrs. Kendall?' The woman's eyebrows disappeared beneath her fringe. 'Are you a relative?'

'More of an acquaintance.'

'I'm so sorry to have to tell you, but Joan died about twelve years ago. We actually bought this house from her so that she could move into a care home.'

Lester's shoulders sagged. 'Okay, in that case, I'm sorry to have bothered you,' he said, forcing a half smile to his lips.

He turned and started walking down the driveway when she called after him. 'Is there anything I can help you with?'

He froze for a moment, then retraced his steps back. 'Perhaps you can. Are you familiar with the story of Joan's daughter, Sarah?'

The woman's head lulled to one side. 'You're not a reporter, are you?'

Lester shook his head. 'No, more of a researcher.'

She looked over her shoulder briefly, then leaned forward. 'I'd love to help you, but my husband has had it up to here with all this phantom hitchhiker business,' she whispered, raising her hand high above her head.

'I'm not working for any newspapers or anything. This is purely for my own peace of mind. You see, I saw Sarah myself on Friday.'

The woman looked at him with a pained expression as she mulled over what to do.

'I've spent most of the weekend trying to find out as much as I can about her. Why does she keeping trying to contact her mother? What is it that she wants? It's become an obsession. I need to unravel the mystery, if only for my own sanity.'

She looked over her shoulder a second time. 'Can you come back tonight, around eight-thirty? I'll be alone then,' she added, with an unmistakable twinkle in her eye.

His breath whistled through clenched teeth. *Sure, if I want a divorce!*

'Bill plays darts at the Working Men's club on Sunday nights, so we can talk without being disturbed.'

'So you're happy to discuss it?' he asked, ignoring her provocative undertones.

'If you're not from the press and you're trying to help the girl, then yes, I'm all yours.'

Lester looked down at the ground for a moment, his brow furrowing. 'I would like to help her . . . if I can,' he replied. 'So yes, I'll come back tonight.'

'I'll be ready and waiting,' she beamed, dimples appearing in her plump cheeks.

Lester smiled back nervously, wondering what he was letting himself in for. Hopefully, whatever she had to say would be worth the cost—because there was no doubt in his mind his wife would make him pay for it later.

Chapter Ten

'How was the mother of the bride?' Hayley asked as he walked into the living room.

'You'll be pleased to know she's dead,' Lester quipped.

'Why?' she asked, her arms outstretched with her palms raised towards the ceiling. 'Why on earth would that please me?'

'Because it means I couldn't cheat on you with her.'

'I doubt her mortality would have stopped you.'

'She's been dead twelve years.'

'Getting fussy in your old age?'

Lester opened his mouth to respond but decided against it. Nothing good would come of this kind of banter. He chose to smile back at her instead. 'Actually, the woman who's now living in that house has asked if I can go back tonight.'

He could feel Hayley's eyes burning into him like the sun through two magnifying glasses.

'Why?'

'So that we can discuss the phantom.'

'Didn't you just do that while you were there?'

Lester cleared his throat. 'No, she wouldn't discuss it while her husband was there.'

Hayley stood up abruptly, her novel dropping to the parquet flooring with a thud. 'So, he's popping out, and you're popping in? Is that what you're telling me?'

Which idiot said honesty is the best policy? 'She's a fat woman in her fifties, Hayley. If you saw her, it wouldn't even cross your mind that something sordid would happen.' He couldn't keep the exasperation from creeping into his tone. 'She just wanted to wait till her husband was out of the house because he is sick and tired of this whole phantom business.'

'Well, that makes two of us!'

'Why don't you come with me?' he asked, making a last-ditch effort. 'You never know, you might find it interesting.'

'No, thanks! I'm not going, and nor are you.'

Lester's brow crumpled, and his smile became one of confusion. 'Sorry?'

'You heard me. If you go round that woman's house, then you're not setting foot in this house again.'

16:11

Lester put down *The History of Pendlebury Hill* by Paul Brotherton and sat back in his office chair. He'd read the dirty and dog-eared manuscript three times without absorbing any of it. He couldn't focus on anything other than Hayley's ultimatum. He'd sensed things were coming to a head, but he hadn't expected it to happen quite so soon or this way. Past punishment had come in the form of long silences, having to sleep on the settee, and a sex ban, but nothing quite as severe as being banished from his own home.

Part of him wanted to test her, in the same way that he had tested his parents in his early teens. Back then, his parents grounded him when he disregarded their edicts, and now that he was older and wiser, he could understand their reasons. But he wasn't a teenager anymore, he was a grown man. Even so, for the sake of keeping the peace, he decided to forget about seeing the woman.

He slapped his cheeks hard several times with the flat of his hands. 'Come on, concentrate!' he said aloud, reaching into the archive box and grabbing the next file. He opened the folder and started reading.

Sandra and I were on our way back from Wembley, having watched Wimbledon win the FA Cup.

Lester's face scrunched in a frown as he realised there was something very familiar about the statement. He continued, his brow furrowing further as he read.

He paused when he got to the section about the ghost getting in the car, then read it again.

Sandra tried talking to her, but all she would say is, 'I have to get to my mother,' so we drove in silence until we reached Kerberly Terrace. I started looking for 127, but it was dark and the houses were set quite away back from the road, so I asked her to let me know when she wanted me to pull over. There was no re-

ply, and I couldn't see her in my mirror anymore. I glanced over my shoulder and immediately stopped the

car. She had gone.

Sandra and I jumped out of the car and opened the back door to double-check that I hadn't missed her

somehow. I even looked in the boot! We walked back down the road, thinking she must have jumped out.

When we couldn't find her, we just left the car in the middle of the road and went up the nearest driveway to

check the number. It was eighty-something, so we ran up the road, checking a few numbers on the way, until

we found 127.

There were no lights on in the house. Not surprising as it was almost 23:30. We ran up to the front door

and knocked. I shook as we stood there waiting. A woman opened the door and asked if she could help us. I

guessed it was the girl's mother. When I explained what had happened, she just smiled. I thought she would

slam the door in our face, but to our surprise, she told us that she'd been expecting us and that the girl we

saw was her daughter, Sarah.

I felt as though someone had walked over my grave. 'She was *your daughter, past tense,' I asked. She*

told us how Sarah had died eighteen years ago along with her three bridesmaids. They were killed in a

head-on collision with a drunk driver on their way home from Sarah's hen night.

Sandra squeezed my hand so hard that she nearly broke my fingers. We both realised that we had just

seen a ghost. The woman seemed pleased that we'd come to see her and went on to tell us Sarah is often

spotted on Pendlebury Hill after eleven o'clock on the 14^(th) May, the anniversary of her death.

Robert and Sandra Wren, 14^(th) May 1988

Lester stared at the date until it went blurry. *Isn't that the same date as Brotherton's encounter? In fact,*

isn't that the same story that Brotherton told me, almost word for word? He stared at the report for a mo-

ment, trying to make sense of it. Something did not add up.

He shifted in his seat, a sudden feeling of discomfort coming over him, though it had nothing to do with

his chair. He'd already decided to put his marriage before his desire to talk to the woman at Kerberly Ter-

race, but this new information changed things. It only made him more determined to find answers.

He sighed, having changed his decision, but he knew Hayley would not be pleased.

19:47

Lester stood by the porch door, the sound of his keys jangling in his coat pocket echoing in the tense silence as Hayley continued reading her book. Her icy silence somehow cut worse than her sharpest words.

'I know you're not happy with me going to see this woman, so why don't you come with me?' he suggested again.

Hayley shook her head adamantly.

'If you can't trust me, what's the point in us being together?'

'I did trust you, and look how you repaid me.'

'We're not doing this now, Hayley. I've apologised more times than I can remember. I wish to God I could undo what I've done, but I can't. If you can't find it in your heart to forgive me, truly forgive me, then we need to call it a day.'

She looked up slowly and turned to him, her eyes filled with pain. 'You killed my baby. How do you expect me to ever forgive you for that?'

Lester hung his head momentarily and he sucked in a deep breath. 'She was *our* baby,' he reminded her gently, 'and you don't know that the affair was to blame for us losing Carla.'

He brushed his cheek as if he could feel her tears on his skin, then closed his eyes.

'*I* know,' she said, standing and stabbing her chest with her index finger. 'I know!'

'If you truly believe that, how can you still be with me?'

Hayley shook her head, more tears streaming down her face.

He watched her for a few seconds, his heart aching, before walking over to her. Just as he was about to embrace her, she raised a hand to stop him. 'Just go,' she said, her voice choked with emotion, 'if that's what you want.'

There had been times when he had ignored her attempts to ward him off and tried to wrap his arms around her, but she usually turned aggressive, slapping his face or punching him, so he always backed away. Even now, standing between his wife and the door, he agonised over whether or not he should go. He could give in and stay, but there would always be a next time. If he went, he risked being locked out of the house, but he wasn't entirely convinced that she would actually go that far.

After several seconds of deliberation, Lester opened the porch door and closed it behind him. He leaned back against it, the sound of his wife's heart-wrenching sobs audible on the other side, making his own eyes well with tears. There was still time to change his mind, do what she wanted in an attempt to right his awful wrong. *When would it ever end though*, he wondered. Sometimes it seemed like they were forever stuck in a cycle of pain and resentment. Nothing he did had ever fixed it.

Lester stepped out into the bitter January night and watched as his sigh became a swirling vapour before his eyes. In the few short hours since returning from Kerberly Terrace, a film of ice had covered his windscreen. Usually, a jug of lukewarm water would clear it in an instant, but he had no desire to go back inside. Instead, he got in the car and turned the heater on to blast the screen, bracing himself against the cold. He often despaired of his neighbours who started their engines and left them running for ten minutes to warm their cars up, pumping pollution into the air instead of spending a few minutes scraping ice off. Rather than become one of them, he took out his wallet, grabbed his AA card, and started scraping the ice off with it. His hands soon started to ache from the cold, but he believed it was better than destroying the environment.

He decided to take the quicker route via the dual carriageway. The less time he was out, the less hostile Hayley would be when he returned—in theory. 'Waiting For a Girl Like You' was still playing from his journey home, and he skipped to the next track, not wishing to hear the song that Hayley walked down the aisle to. When Poison's 'Every Rose Has its Thorn' began playing, the corners of his mouth turned up in an ironic smile.

Ten minutes later, Lester turned onto Kerberly Terrace and drove towards 127 just in time to see a white Audi A3 reversing down the long driveway. He looked at the dashboard to see that it was 20:02. Instead of pulling over, he continued up to the end of the road, waited for five minutes, then turned around and parked outside the house.

He headed up the driveway with a little more zest than earlier. The cursory glance over his shoulder as he rang the doorbell was habitual and had been for the past four years. Since his indiscretion, Hayley made it her mission to keep tabs on him. She tracked his phone, listened in on his phone calls, checked his texts, and read his emails. Although neither of them had ever mentioned it, he had spotted her on several occasions at events he told her he was attending. It had been more than two years since the last 'sighting,' but it was hard to break the habit of looking for her.

As he went to knock, the door opened.

'Hello again,' the woman greeted him, now wearing a silk dressing gown and bright red lipstick.

Shit! His eyes transfixed on her outfit. *Maybe Hayley was right to worry! I know I am!* 'Hi . . .' Lester managed to say, inwardly praying there was something beneath it. 'Sorry, I don't even know your name?'

'Karen,' she replied, standing aside to allow him to enter. 'Please, come inside.'

He held back for a moment, unsure if he should put himself in this position, before crossing the threshold. He followed her along the hallway and through to the kitchen. The warm house smelt of minced beef, and he guessed they'd had shepherd's pie for their evening meal.

'Can I get you anything, tea or coffee? Maybe something stronger?'

'I'm fine,' he said, his discomfort beginning to grow. 'I don't want to keep you.'

'Nonsense. Bill will be gone for a couple of hours. We have plenty of time,' Karen smiled, baring lipstick smeared teeth.

For what!

'Please take a seat,' she said, indicating to the dining room table and chairs. 'I'm going to have a G&T. Sure I can't tempt you with anything?'

'Mint tea would be great, if you have it.'

'Of course,' she replied, her smile fading as she turned and heading over to the kitchen units. 'So you've actually seen Sarah then?'

'Possibly.'

She looked round with a puzzled frown.

'The girl I saw stepped out in front of my car.'

'How terrifying for you. So she wasn't trying to hitch a ride?'

Lester shook his head. 'From what I've researched, there are two very different reports that people give. One is about a hitchhiking bride, Sarah Kendall, and the other is like my encounter. They have a couple of commonalities, like the location and their appearance, but I'm not even sure about that now. One has long hair and the other has short hair.'

Karen walked over with a cup of steaming tea in one hand and a glass with a paper umbrella in the other. She leaned across the table and placed his tea down on a placemat in front of him, exposing her ample cleavage in the process. He looked away as gravity allowed her breasts to escape the confines of her flimsy silk dressing gown.

'Oh, pardon me,' she giggled, attempting to pull the lapels of her dressing gown together with one hand.

Lester continued to look away as she fumbled awkwardly to cover herself up while her gin and tonic swished around in the glass she held in her other hand.

'Thank you for being a gentleman,' Karen said, once she had composed herself and sat down opposite him. 'Some men may have taken advantage of that situation.'

'I'm like my dad in that respect, old fashioned.' Lester turned to face her, his cheeks more flushed than hers. 'I can come back another time if it's more convenient?'

'Nonsense. We're both adults and it's nothing you haven't seen before…right?'

He forced a smile to his lips as his cheeks continued to burn.

'I've not heard anything about another ghost,' her words filled the awkward silence. 'Is she dressed like a bride as well?'

'The reports say she wears a white dress, which is probably why people have always assumed that they're the same person, but it's not a wedding dress.'

'So the reason you're here now is because you want to know if we've had any strangers asking about Sarah?'

Lester nodded. 'Yes, exactly. I've read online that the sightings have continued long after the research material that I have. I'm trying to fill in the gaps in his research.'

'In the fifteen years we've lived here, we've had four visits, not including you, of course. That's four visits too many for Bill. I'm not saying he's scared, but I think this sort of thing makes him very uncomfortable. He even talked about moving a few times. He doesn't want anything to do with it. I'm into all that sort of thing.' She leaned forward, her dressing gown threatening to come undone again. 'I'm a bit psychic myself, you see.'

'Really? I know it's not everyone's cup of tea. It wasn't mine until Friday night!' He picked up his mint tea and took a sip, immediately regretting it when he burned his tongue. 'So when was the last visit?'

'The last couple to come knocking, before you, was on the 14th May 2019. I believe it was on the forty-ninth anniversary of Sarah's death. Since then we've had Covid, of course, so Bill was happy at least.'

Karen lifted the glass of gin and tonic to her mouth and he watched with bemusement as the umbrella kept getting in her way. After several failed attempts, she grabbed it and threw it in the air, before taking a long sip. The umbrella landed on the table beside him and rolled off onto the floor. 'Sorry,' she said, shaking her head, 'would you be a love and fetch that for me?'

'Sure,' Lester said, pushing back his chair and ducking down under the table. As he looked up, she parted her legs, and his breath locked in his lungs. *The Sarlacc!*

'Can you see it?' she asked.

I can't unsee it! He quickly snatched up the umbrella and sat up, red faced. 'So, where were we?'

'Are you hot, dear? Do you want to take your coat off?'

Lester held his hand up and smiled back at her. 'I'm fine. So you were telling me about the last couple to visit. Did they give Sarah a lift here?'

'They tried to.'

'So she vanished before they arrived?'

'Yes. It's a pattern, from what I can gather. Joan never mentioned that we would be getting visitors. I think she assumed that they would stop once she moved out of the house. We got our first visit about fourteen months after we moved in. I remember their names because they were both the same, a husband and wife. He was Joe Smith, and she was Jo Smith. Quite comical really. I mean it wasn't at the time. The pair of them were physically shaking when they arrived here, and by the time they left, Bill was too.' She laughed.

'Did they talk to her at all?'

'All Sarah said was that she had to get home to Mum and that it was a matter of life and death. She gave them this address, but she actually disappeared just before the couple turned onto this road.'

Lester nodded. There didn't seem to be much variation with the story or the conversations people had with her.

'After the Smiths visit, I went and saw Joan in the nursing home. She was naturally upset to think Sarah was still trying to visit the house and that she would no longer be there to greet her if she actually managed to succeed. That's the main reason she didn't want to sell us this house, but she really couldn't look after herself by then.'

'I can't understand why Sarah gets this far and then disappears. What's stopping her from taking that final step?'

'It's very sad.'

Lester reached for his tea again and took a tentative sip before two mouthfuls. 'So there were three more visits after that?'

Karen nodded, her head turned towards the ceiling. She frowned.

She was clearly distracted by something so he followed her gaze but all he could see was a cobweb hanging from the kitchen light. *Please don't get on the table to dust it!*

'Were they all pretty much the same?' he asked, a little louder to regain her attention.

'They were in the sense that Sarah always disappeared en route. In one case, she never even made it to the top of Pendlebury Hill. The one I remember most was a horrible man called Ron Croft. He was quite angry when he arrived here. I'm not exactly sure why, but Bill had to come to the door as he was getting quite aggressive, thinking he was the victim of some practical joke. I think that was the last straw for Bill. There was another married couple and a girl on her own who couldn't stop crying. Apart from that, all the details and conversations were pretty much the same. Sorry, I haven't been much help, have I?'

'On the contrary! You've been a great help. More than you realise.'

'Well, I'm afraid we may have missed some callers. Bill was so upset by Ron Croft's visit that he refuses to let me answer the door now if anyone knocks on the anniversary of Sarah's death. It's the same at Halloween. We get a few unwanted callers then as well.'

'I'm sorry, I shouldn't have come.' Lester said, picking up his tea and taking two more mouthfuls before standing up. 'But I'm glad I did, so thank you.'

'Are you?' The woman stood up opposite him. 'I don't get many visitors. Especially young gentlemen.'

Lester's eyes widened as she toyed with bow of her dressing gown cord.

He swallowed loudly. 'As much as I'd love to stay and chat, I promised my wife I wouldn't be long.'

Her jowls drooped as her smile faded. 'Shame.'

'Thank you so much for the tea, Karen,' he said, hurrying towards the front door, almost tripping in his haste as he opened it and stepped outside.

'Good luck with your research. I hope you can find a way to help Sarah and find some peace yourself.'

Lester looked back at her with a quizzical frown, but she just continued to smile.

He pondered her words as he walked towards his car, wondering if they had more meaning than him simply finding peace with his investigation. It was the knowing way she had said it and the glint in her eye that made him curious, but it was soon forgotten once he was back in his car and driving home.

The dashboard display read 20:29, which meant his evening out would have taken less than an hour. He grabbed his phone and dialled Hayley's number and sat back while it rang. It continued ringing for about thirty seconds before a recorded message announced, 'The person you are calling is not available to take your call. Please leave a message after the beep.'

Lester hit the red phone icon to cancel the call. Hayley was ghosting him. For the first time, he realised that there was a very real chance that she had locked him out of the house.

Chapter Eleven

'I take it things with *her* are no better?' his mother asked, unable to speak her name.

Lester closed his eyes momentarily. He had dialled Hayley's mobile after leaving the office. Walker, his boss, had a strict 'no mobiles' policy at work. It had rung for a few seconds and cut off with no option to leave a voicemail, which meant she had declined his call. 'They've gone from bad to really, really bad.'

'Why do you put up with it, David? You know I don't agree with what you did, but she can't go on punishing you forever. You're miserable, she's miserable. What's the point of going on like that?'

He sighed. 'I'm sure we'll have that conversation soon enough.'

'But why do you insist on putting everything off till tomorrow? You're just like your father, God rest his soul.'

'She's not actually talking to me at the moment, so it's a bit difficult.'

'You sound just like him,' she said, shaking her head. 'He was a good man, but he would find any excuse not to do something. If he had gone to the doctors when I told him to, things might have turned out differently. He kept putting it off and off until it was too late.' Her eyes found a photo of them on the mantelpiece, and she smiled. 'Did I tell you I saw a spiritualist?'

'No. What for? A psychic reading or something?'

She nodded.

'To contact Dad?'

'Amongst other things.'

'So what did he or she say?'

'She was a lovely girl, David. She would be perfect for you.'

He laughed. 'Okay, so two minutes ago, you're telling me that I was wrong to cheat on Hayley, and now you're trying to set me up with a complete stranger?'

'I'm doing no such thing. And even if I was, there are certain ways of doing these things.'

Lester smiled to himself. 'So what did this lovely girl say?'

'Well, your father did come through, but he didn't say much, as usual. He just confirmed that it was him by mentioning Peugeot and hammock.'

He nodded, wondering how the 'clairvoyant' picked those two words out. His dad always bought Peugeots and liked nothing more than lying in his hammock reading a book, so they did sum him up very well. He wasn't as sceptical as Brotherton, but Lester was still not fully convinced that these people could do what they claimed. 'Anything else?'

'Just that he's happy. No more pain.'

He returned his mother's smile. Even if these people were charlatans, there was no denying that they had the ability to make people feel better.

'He said he wanted me to move on and find happiness with someone else, but I don't know if I can be bothered with all that at my age,' she giggled.

'I've been telling you that for years, Mum.'

'I took some notes,' she said, reaching for the A5 pad on the coffee table. 'Nana came through and had plenty to say for herself, of course, mainly about you.'

He tilted his head curiously. 'Really? Such as?'

'That you're miserable at home and miserable at work.'

Lester raised his eyebrows. 'So basically, I'm miserable. Anything else?'

'Things are about to change. She said your light has gone out, but soon it will burn brighter than ever.'

'Well that sounds more positive. Why couldn't you have led with that?'

'But be careful, David. You will start treading on toes with a project you're working on and you could put yourself and others in danger. I'm not sure I like the sound of that.'

Lester laughed at her concern, though her words made him think. Apart from treading on Hayley's toes and almost being devoured by a horny housewife, he could not see where his investigation could be dangerous. 'I'm an accountant, mum. The worst hazard I face is a paper cut.'

'Hmmm,' his mother gave him *that* look.

He stood up and feigned a yawn. 'I think I might have an early night.'

'What about pudding?'

'Thanks,' he said, patting his stomach, 'but I'm still full from dinner.'

'Are you okay, dear?'

'Just tired.' He smiled then headed towards the metal spiral staircase in the corner of the living room. As he was about to ascend, a thought occurred to him, and he looked round to meet her gaze. 'Actually, do you have that spiritualist's number, please? I might give her a call.'

'Of course,' she beamed, taking a piece of paper out of the pocket of her apron and waving it in the air.

He walked back over to her and took it from her hand. 'You just happen to have it on you?' He looked at the name and then the mobile number. 'Her number ends in 666, that's not a good omen, Mum.'

'She's a lovely girl, David. You're going to love her!'

'Yes, I think we've already established that,' he managed to say without rolling his eyes.

As he headed up the stairs, she called after him, 'Call her now, David. Don't put it off like you usually do!'

In his old room, Lester lay on the bed staring up at the ceiling. There was still a faint beige stain close to the uplighter where he had sprayed coffee from a syringe because Katie had dared him. It was the only time his mother had ever raised her hand to him. His father had painted over it a couple of times, but the stain still it came through. It was a constant reminder of his beloved sister.

As he looked around the walls, he realised that nothing had changed since he'd moved out. It was like a shrine to him. His old monochrome pictures still adorned the wall, a series of pouting ladies with rouge lipstick in black frames, stark against the white walls. There was even a Shrek poster behind the door from when he was ten. He didn't know whether to smile or sigh, knowing that Katie's room, across the landing, was also virtually untouched since Thursday, 12th February 2009.

He reached down and grabbed the manila files from his laptop bag. On top of the pile was a piece of lined paper with a torn edge, suggesting it had been ripped out of a notepad. It had a single word written in the centre with three question marks: Coldwell??? Lester stared at it for a while. *Was it a place? A company? A name?* Eventually, he put it to one side and turned his attention to the police reports.

He opened the first file, noting that the paper inside was starting to dry out. As he flicked through the pages, his eyes narrowed. The format of the police report was noticeably different from the previous ones he'd read. Even the musty smell of the old paper differed. He checked the cover page.

'That's interesting,' he said aloud, squinting as he brought it close to his face.

There was no mistaking it, but even so, he thumbed through to the last page, which was signed and dated. Lester sat up and stared at the date he had seen on the front of the report: 12th April 1929.

He turned to the statement of the witness, Reginald Wallace, and started reading.

My encounter occurred whilst cycling home from my place of work, Frobisher's in Greyton.

Well, that's different, Lester thought. He skimmed down until he found what he was looking for.

About halfway down the hill, just beyond the Poacher's Arms, I noticed a girl by the side of the road. She looked a bit anxious, so I slowed down to ask her if she was all right, but she hurried off down the road. She kept looking back, but not at me. I turned to see if anyone was following her, but there was no one else around. What struck me as odd was her hair. Although it was short, it remained completely still despite the wind, whereas I was struggling to stay upright.

Lester quickly read the rest of the account and then sat back, staring at the page until it became a blur. Wallace's encounter was much like his own. *1929?* That was over forty years before Sarah Kendall was killed. This was irrefutable proof that there was more than one ghost. If Brotherton read this, why had he dismissed a second ghost so readily?

Lester tried to push his concerns about Brotherton from his mind, knowing they would be a distraction, and updated his spreadsheet with the date and the description. He closed the folder and put it on his bedside table, a sigh escaping his lips as he looked at the number of folders left to be reviewed. He grabbed the next file and read through it.

Sally Burns 14th May 1971.

Lester shuddered as he noted the date. It was exactly one year after Sarah Kendall's fatal accident. If she only appeared on the anniversary of her death, Sally Burns must have been the first person to see the phantom bride. With his eyes growing increasingly heavy, he decided to review one more file before calling it a day.

The last folder was tattered, almost falling apart, and the smell of mildew reminded him of wet socks. It was thicker than the others, and as he thumbed through the contents, he realised that it was made up of three separate police reports, each held together by a mini bulldog clip.

He flicked to the back of the first file, gently prising the papers apart. His gaze shifted to the bottom line, and he read the words aloud, 'Myles Jenkins, 1st June 1950.'

Intrigued, Lester took the next file in the bundle and turned to the back page. *Clive Faraday, 23rd December 1931.* He turned to the back page of the third police report. *Thomas Knott, 15th March 1919.*

'Wow, that's over a hundred years ago!' he told himself.

As anxious as he was to read them all, Lester reached for his laptop and quickly keyed in all the relevant information from each report before sorting the seventeen cases, including his own, into chronological order.

Date	Name	Home Location	
15/11/1919	Thomas Knott	Greyton	
12/04/1929	Reginald Wallace	Gatherford	
23/12/1931	Clive Farraday	Meadowhurst	
01/06/1950	Myles Jenkins	Greyton	
14/05/1971	Sally Burns	Greyton	
14/05/1974	Michelle Blane	Morton Finchley	
31/07/1976	Tom Fielding	Meadowhurst	
14/05/1980	Joe and Jo smith	Gatherford	
26/04/1984	Bryan Naylor (Policeman)	Brenton	
14/05/1988	Robert & Sandra Wren	Grove Marsh	
14/05/1989	Tom & Sharon Jordan	Meadowhurst	

09/09/1992	Christian Collins	Greyton	
25/04/1995	Russell Templeton (School Teacher)	Brenton	
14/05/1997	Ron Croft	Greyton	
03/02/2000	Brian Thorne	Nestleford	
14/05/2015	Stuart & Emma Hazeldine	Moreton Finchely	
26/01/2024	David Lester	Gatherford	

Thomas Knott appeared at the top of his list, and his own account, three days earlier, at the bottom. A quick analysis of the data highlighted four reported sightings of a ghost before Sarah Kendall's death on the 14th May 1970. Prior to that date, the sightings were sporadic. He quickly concluded that it was because there was only one ghost and less cars on the road. There had only been two reported sightings following the completion of the dual carriageway in 2003, which made perfect sense as the traffic on Pendlebury Way became heavily reduced.

When he looked for sightings occurring on the 14th May, it was clear that these were of Sarah Kendall. It made sense then that all other sightings were of a different ghost, the one he had encountered. His mind wandered back to Brotherton. The man wasn't stupid. He had to know there was another ghost. He had even grouped the three older files together, so he knew full well they were not related to Sarah Kendall.

For some reason, Paul Brotherton was hiding something from him.

Chapter Twelve

Lester's eyes flickered open, and he stared up at the ceiling, a lighter shade of darkness. Thoughts of Hayley, Brotherton, and phantoms played on his mind, having already lured him from his state of subconscious several times during the night.

Accepting that sleep was not an option, he switched on the bedside lamp and reached for his laptop, flipping it open. His bright white spreadsheet blinded him, and he closed his eyes, opening them gradually and squinting until they adjusted. He studied the data before adding a 'type' field and typing 'bride' against all the sightings on the 14th May. Then he sorted the spreadsheet so that he could study the two sightings more easily.

There were seven reported sightings of Sarah Kendall compared to ten of the other phantom. Sarah Kendall's appearances followed a clear pattern, while the other ghost sightings were sporadic. The latter had appeared in different months, on different days, and at different times. No pattern. As he reviewed the names of the other ghost's witnesses, his eyes narrowed. He looked down the list a second time and nodded to himself absently. They were all males.

Maybe it was merely coincidence, but Sarah Kendall's witnesses were a mix of people, even some couples. He could understand the witness list being male-dominated to start with, because there would have been more male drivers between 1919 and 1971, but even over the last fifty years, all five female witnesses were linked only to Sarah Kendall.

Lester closed his laptop. He believed he was onto something but decided to shift his focus to the remaining reports for now. His hope being that he may discover a common thread between all the witnesses. Reaching into his laptop bag, he retrieved the police reports and placed them on the bed beside him. He grabbed the top folder, a report made by a police constable who'd had a sighting himself. *Bryan Naylor. 26th April 1984.*

When Lester got to the last line, he froze. *Height, approximately 5' 8", weight I would estimate as 7-8 stone, Caucasian, light-medium brown hair, either short or pinned up. White uniform.*

He rubbed his chin with his thumb and forefinger. *White uniform? Yes, it may well have been.*

He was glad to finally close the file and throw it onto the floor as the musty smell was making him feel nauseated. It reminded him of the many hours he'd spent alone in a cold, dank basement, sifting through archives when he was an accounts clerk. Unfortunately, the next file was even worse, and he sprayed a mist of his 1 Million cologne to mask the odour.

Clive Faraday, Wednesday 23/12/1931

Faraday's account was another that mirrored his. After discarding the file, Lester reached for the last manila folder, the tattiest and mustiest of all. Once again, he found himself reaching for his eau de toilette spray, the fine mist stinging his dry eyes. He closed them until they watered, then opened them wide enough to read the final report, from one Thomas Knott. *November 15, 1919.*

He entered all of the new data into his spreadsheet, then sat back and looked at the description fields of the two women. There were similarities. They were both young women, late teens or early twenties, and both wearing white, although none of the reports for the second phantom suggested a wedding dress. There was an array of different interpretations, which might have been influenced by the amount of time they actually saw her. One of the girls had short hair and one had long hair, one stood by the side of the road and the other hurried along it before stepping into the path of the victim.

Satisfied that he knew all that he needed to know about Sarah Kendall, Lester decided to focus on the second ghost. She had stepped out in front of most of them, himself included, giving none of them a chance to stop. Was the intention to cause an accident, to harm her victims? From what he had read, the only ones to actually be harmed were the cyclists, as they lacked the protection of an encasement.

He was certain there must be a reason all her witnesses were men. He wasn't entirely sure how to go about finding that reason though. The girl in question died over a century ago. Finding out who she was or any records that could provide answers was going to be a challenge.

Until that moment, he'd been reluctant to involve a spiritualist. Knowing this particular one was a 'lovely' young woman and already vetted by his mother meant one aspect of his life could get harder. On the other hand, if her abilities proved to be real, it might be the easiest way to find out who this second phantom was. Either way, he decided it was an avenue he needed to explore.

Lester pulled the piece of paper his mother had given him from his pocket and read the name, Lauren Miller. He grabbed his phone and noted the time, 3:43. With a sigh, he put his phone down and turned the light off before sliding down beneath the duvet. *I'll call her tomorrow.*

Chapter Thirteen

Lester sat in his office, feeling like a goldfish. There was no privacy at Walker Financial Services. Craig Walker believed in transparency, and that included office walls. Luckily, Lester sat with his back to the one plaster wall in his office. Even surrounded by glass on three sides, this limited amount of privacy allowed him to continue his research without any of his colleagues seeing his screen. He was in the middle of a search on Thomas Knott when Duggie Fenton appeared in his doorway.

'Oh dear, I know that look. Problems with the old ball and chain?' he asked with a little jig.

Lester counted to five before reluctantly looking up from his computer screen. 'I've just got a lot going on.'

The sound of heavy footfalls down the corridor had Duggie looking back over his shoulder momentarily before leaning into the office. 'Walker's coming, and he looks pissed,' he said before continuing on to his own office.

Lester quickly switched his screen over to his work email just as Walker entered his office. His boss slammed three files down on his desk and leaned across it. 'Did you check these fees before drafting your letters?'

Lester's eyes narrowed as he opened the top file and scanned it, wondering why his boss was so angry. Then he saw the company fee at the bottom. He closed his eyes momentarily before checking the next two files, the weight of Walker's scrutinising glare like two hands pushing him down in his chair. He sensed the prying eyes of his colleagues all turning to him in his glass box, and he shrank deeper into his seat.

He raised his hands. 'I'm so sorry, Craig, I have no clue what's happened here.'

'And that's my concern. This is totally out of character for you, Lester. Usually you're on your game, but these are schoolboy errors. Had these letters gone out, they could have been very damaging for my company. We've lost clients for less than this.'

Lester scratched his itching cheek. He could feel them burning. 'You're right, I have no idea what happened, but I will get it sorted.'

'I don't want to hear that you have no idea. That doesn't fill me with confidence. Get it fixed now. And I want to review the letters before they go out.'

'I'll do it straightaway,' Lester said with a resolute nod.

'And I want to check all your letters until further notice,' Walker said, his piercing glare making Lester want to shift in his seat, as though he *were* a schoolboy. He certainly felt like it, being on the receiving end of Walker's ire. 'Till I feel I can trust you again.'

'Of course,' he said, maintaining eye contact until the older man finally turned and walked out.

Alone in his office, Lester opened the last file again and homed in on the amount his client owed, £3,725,000. 'Shit,' he muttered, sinking his face into his upturned palms. He could feel his face burn. *How could I be so stupid?*

His boss did not suffer fools gladly. It took an eternity to earn his trust and just a moment of madness to lose it. One mistake was enough to damage his standing at Walker Financial Services and probably would have cost him his job had it reached the client. Finding his way back into Walker's confidence would be a struggle.

As Lester searched on his computer for the first of the three invoices, he decided to abandon his investigation into the phantom. It was the only thing that made sense. It was distracting him so much that it had already affected his home life, and now it was affecting his work. *It's not worth the aggravation.*

When the invoice appeared on the screen, he almost laughed. *How could I have missed that?* He deleted the additional zeros from the final amount, changed the date, and printed off the letter again. He was sure the client would have seen the funny side of being charged a thousand times too much, but Walker was a perfectionist, and as he often liked to point out, 'This is my business, and I'll run it any damn well way I please!'

By 17:00, Lester knew he wasn't leaving on time. Everything he did was taking longer than usual as he found himself checking and rechecking in case he had made a mistake. Having taken the revised invoices and letters to Walker's office, along with several others, he realised his own confidence and trust in his judgement and ability was impaired as well.

It was 18:30 by the time he felt comfortable enough to leave. As everyone else had already left, he took his phone out of his jacket and dialled Hayley. It rang several times. He was about to cancel the call when she answered.

'Hello,' she said, her voice soft, barely audible as though she were getting over a cold.

'I didn't think you would answer,' Lester said.

'I nearly didn't.'

'What made you change your mind?'

'I think I've made my point.'

Lester paused momentarily. 'Does that mean that I can come home?'

'Do you want to? All weekend it felt like you wanted to be anywhere but.'

'I know, and I'm sorry. I just got so consumed with my investigation that nothing else seemed to matter. You'll be pleased to know I've decided to call it a day.'

'I am, but it's a shame it had to get to this stage before you realised.'

'I'm sorry.'

'So where are you now?' Hayley asked.

'Still at work.'

'Can you pick up takeaway on your way? I haven't eaten all day.'

The relief that filled him almost overwhelmed. His relationship with Hayley had been hanging by a thread. He was convinced that her picking up the phone, in addition to the spiritualist not calling him back despite leaving her a voicemail that morning, must be the universe telling him that he made the right decision. He would invest his time in his marriage and career, rather than something less tangible.

19:25

Without even looking up from her Chicken Korma, Hayley asked, 'So what made you decide to quit?'

He froze momentarily, his fork poised in mid-air, carefully balancing a pile of pilau rice. 'The phantom? I made some mistakes at work that didn't go down particularly well. A calculation in my spreadsheet was wrong, and I just typed out the figures without checking. They were so obviously wrong that a blind man would have spotted them.'

'So, not because I asked you to?' she said, finally turning her head to give him her full attention.

'To be honest, I looked at how it was affecting my home life and work life and decided it wasn't worth it.'

'Why isn't it worth it anymore?'

The interrogation was expected and resisting her questions was futile. He taught her a long time ago that if you ask why five times you eventually get to the answer you want, and she would not give up until he had admitted what she wanted to hear.

'I've been so focused on finding out who the phantom is that I took my eye off the ball.' He finally put his fork down and turned to face her. 'I'm sorry that I abandoned you for most of the weekend.'

He watched her face, but she showed all the emotion of a porcelain doll. Inside she was probably doing backflips. A gentle nod of the head was all he could expect or even hope for but even that was asking too much, and once 'Eastenders' started, her attention was lost completely.

They ate the remainder of their meal in silence, with the exception of a few gasps from Hayley when certain revelations were made by the show's characters. She looked so engrossed that he questioned if she realised it wasn't real. After the inevitable cliffhanger, Lester grabbed her tray and plate and took them over to the sink. 'Do you fancy watching a film?'

Hayley's nose wrinkled at his suggestion. 'No war, westerns, superheroes, horrors, or anything in space.'

A rom-com then! 'Do you want to choose while I wash up? Anything you like.'

There was a suggestion of a smile but from the angle and the dim light, Lester wasn't sure. Hayley scanned through Netflix for several minutes before announcing that she'd found one.

When he walked over with two mugs of coffee, he saw *Notting Hill* on the screen. 'Didn't we just watch this a couple of weeks ago?' He placed the mugs down on coasters on the coffee table and sat down next to her.

She fixed him with a sardonic smile. 'You said I could pick anything I wanted.'

'Indeed I did,' he said, ignoring the bite in her tone. 'I just thought you might fancy a change?'

'No, thank you,' she said, stabbing the play button with her thumb.

Twenty minutes into the film, Hayley had her head back with her eyes closed and her mouth agape. He knew she was gone for the rest of the evening. Even if he woke her, she would nod off again within a few minutes. She always did. Usually, at this point, he would either have to sit through *Notting Hill* for the umpteenth time or he could switch to a war, western, superhero, horror, or space movie instead. The only issue with them was they tended to be loud. The dialogue was always quiet, which meant turning the volume up high to hear what was being said, whilst the action scenes often involved deafening explosions that rattled the windows in their frames. The contrast was stark.

Hayley's eyes snapped open as his mobile rang, and she turned to him questioningly.

Lester looked at the screen and hit the decline button under the weight of her stare. 'Unknown caller,' he told her before putting the phone back in his shirt pocket. 'Probably a cold call.'

She continued to stare for a few seconds before turning back to the screen and continuing to watch Notting Hill as though she had not already slept through most of it. Lester did his best to try and look invested in the film, but his mind was elsewhere. The 'unknown caller' part of his statement was true. He didn't know her—but he did recognise the number ending in 666.

The spiritualist had called him back.

Chapter Fourteen

20:07, Tuesday, 30th January

Notting Hill became a blur with Lester's thoughts consumed by the spiritualist returning his call. Was *this* a sign? He wondered if he had been too hasty deciding to shelve his investigation. *Maybe I can meet with her without Hayley knowing. During my lunch break? Or I could leave work early?* Whilst he remained sceptical about the spiritualist's so-called abilities, if there was a possibility that she could provide clues to the identity of the second phantom, then he had to give it try.

Hayley was asleep again, so he lowered the volume on the TV and headed upstairs to call her from his office. He waited for the number to ring, his eyes fixed firmly on the door. It went to voicemail. He sucked in a breath around clenched teeth and cancelled the call, not wishing to leave another message and risk her calling him back again without warning. He decided to try again after a few minutes.

While he waited, Lester switched on his computer and eased into his desk chair. He looked at the most recently opened Chrome tab and clicked on it, not recognising the icon. It was the search he had started that morning on Thomas Knott, which had returned six and a half million results. He refined the search with the word Greyton and then added the year of the sighting, 1919, to reduce the results by more than ninety per-cent.

He quickly scanned the first page of websites and was about to click on the X in the top right corner of his screen when the words 'deathbed confession' piqued his curiosity. His eyes lit up when he saw the name Thomas Knott emboldened in the search criteria. He clicked on the link entitled 'Genealogy: Expect to dig up dirt, a skeleton or two, and a few secrets you may wish to leave buried' and started reading.

The article was written by Thomas Knott's grandson, and it detailed research he'd done into his own family line. but it was one particular section that jumped out to Lester.

I will never forget standing by my grandfather's deathbed—the stench of faeces, the gloom and the sweltering heat of his open fire. He was forever complaining that he was cold, and as his body weight diminished and his muscles wasted away, it became even worse. Despite the overwhelming nausea we all had from the scent of his decaying body, Dad made us kiss his bristly cheek. I almost vomited. Years later, I can still see him lying there. Still smell him lying there.

He had little breath left in his frail body, but he managed to summon the strength to say, 'There's something I need to tell you all. I'm sorry but it was me . . .' We all looked at each other, asking ourselves the same question, 'What was you?' but no one dared. My grandfather eventually broke the silence with three words that I could never have dreamt hearing in my wildest nightmares. 'I killed Lily. I drowned her upstairs in the bathtub. My ears were ringing with her ceaseless wailing about Harold. I couldn't stand the misery, the wallowing, or the self-pity any longer. I couldn't live with her.'

I know, you're not thinking anything right now that I've not thought myself for over half a century. How could any loving husband do that, especially to one so grief-stricken from the sudden loss of a sibling? You can bet we were all wondering the same thing. Some of us still are, those still living. It was the only time I'd ever seen my father cry. Time seemed to stand still as he stared down at his father. For a moment, I thought he was going to yank that pillow from under his head and smoother him to death. But he simply said, 'Goodbye, Father,' grabbed mine and my brother's hands, and led us from that awful room with Mum and our older sister following. We never spoke of it again.

It was another twenty years before I started researching my family's history. That deathbed confession had stayed with me the whole time, but out of respect for my father, I didn't act upon it until after he had sadly passed away in 1988. With my mother's consent, she never liked my grandfather anyway, I was first able to inform the police about this revelation. I'm not entirely sure what they did with the information, but I expect they have a protocol for that sort of thing.

Jesus! Did the phantom choose Thomas Knott because he killed his wife? Lester leaned back, absentmindedly tapping his bottom lip with his index finger. The name, timing, and location all matched. This was undoubtedly the same Thomas Knott who reported the first sighting of the phantom back in 1919. Is that what all these men had in common, they had all killed someone? He almost laughed. *I haven't killed anyone. Not yet, anyway. The worst thing I've ever done is . . . cheated on Hayley. Is that why she appeared to me?*

He sat for a moment, deep in thought, before leaning closer to scan the list of names. *I wonder . . .* He toggled back to Google and started a new search, typing in the name Reginald Wallace and Gatherford, his home town. Unfortunately, none of the results were relevant.

Clive Faraday was the third witness. The search returned three hundred results. After checking the first ten pages, Lester concluded that there were no records online. The same was true of the next three witnesses: Myles Jenkins, Tom Fielding, and policeman Bryan Naylor.

Lester's enthusiasm was starting to wane. He looked down the list, then entered Russell Templeton and the village of Brenton. Over one and a half million results. He slumped in his chair, rubbed his eyes, and yawned. His weary mind wanted to quit, but part of him fought to continue searching, and he sat there for a moment contemplating his next move.

Reaching for the pile of files, he quickly flicked through them to find the one with a Post-It Note marked Russell Templeton. Inside the folder, he scanned the police report, searching for any information that could be relevant. At the bottom of the sheet was a contact number, All Saints Secondary School, Greyton. Returning to Google, Lester added the words school, teacher, and Greyton to his search and entered. The second site listed made Lester straighten in his seat. *Retired school teacher found guilty of child molestation.*

'Bingo!' He clicked on the link and read the article.

Russell Templeton, a respected former history teacher at the All Saints Secondary School in Greyton, Kent has pleaded guilty to six counts of child molestation after former pupils came forward following the suicide of Kevin Norton in November 2001. Templeton, who previously denied allegations made against him in 1991 and 1997, broke down in tears and confessed to being a paedophile, saying 'he was broken and could no longer deny to himself or the world his guilt following Norton's suicide.'

Lester found that he was involuntarily shaking his head at the computer screen.

Templeton was sentenced to twelve years at Maidstone Crown Court for the offences that took place between 1979 and 1997. Clayford said of the verdict, 'no amount of prison time would be enough. A child had his innocence stolen, endured a tortured adulthood, and ultimately lost his life. Several other men have been left permanently damaged by this man's heinous acts. Justice can never be done but the truth prevails and if this can raise awareness and save other children in the future then Kevin's loss of life would not be completely in vain.'

Two of the eight phantom eyewitnesses were clearly bad men, three if he included himself. The nature of this girl's appearance, stepping out in front of speeding vehicles and bikes without warning seemed to suggest that she was intending to cause an accident. Perhaps she was trying to get justice for their victims by causing fatal crashes.

Thomas Knott had literally gotten away with murder whilst Russell Templeton had gotten away with eighteen years of child molestation before he'd been imprisoned. When he checked his spreadsheet again, he could see that Templeton's sighting was 1995, but he was not actually imprisoned until 2001.

There was a good chance that all eight of the eye witnesses had committed crimes that had gone unpunished, and Lester was certain that this was why they had been targeted. He still had a few names to search, but he wasn't confident of finding any more information. He was keener on identifying this girl and finding out what happened to her. If she had come back as a vengeful spirit, the chances are it was not a happy story, but that was a job for tomorrow. For now, he had to keep up the pretence.

With an ironic smile, Lester shutdown his computer and padded down the stairs just in time to see the last few minutes of *Notting Hill*. As soon as the credits started to roll, Hayley's eyes flickered open, and she blinked at the TV screen.

'I missed the end,' she said with her lower lip protruding.

Chapter Fifteen

Having left twenty minutes earlier for work than normal, Lester found himself turning into Greyton police station as if some magnetic force was drawing him. As long as he kept his actions covert, there was no reason why he couldn't continue investigating the hauntings of Pendlebury Hill without it affecting his work or home life. With his latest revelations, he was certain he was close to discovering the truth about what happened, at least closer than Brotherton had ever got. To give it all up now would be criminal.

He walked into the police station and almost spun on his heels when he saw the same duty sergeant sitting there that he'd seen on Saturday morning. Only because their eyes had already met did he continue walking up to the counter, wondering if she would remember him.

'Can I help you?' she asked, the sincerity in her voice failing to reach her eyes.

'Do you have a list of missing persons from this area?'

He watched as her eyes became narrow slits. 'Do you want to report a missing person?'

Lester shook his head. 'No, I just want to see if you have a list of missing persons from this area going back to . . . 1900?'

Her expression remained unyielding. 'Name?'

'David Lester.'

'Take a seat, David Lester,' she said, her eyes slowly moving over to the right to indicate where she wanted him to wait.

At 8:49, he stood up and walked back to the counter. 'Will someone see me soon? I'm supposed to be at work in ten minutes.'

Slowly the woman lifted her head, and he could see from the quiver of her lip that her smile was forced. 'Missing persons going back to 1900? Has the person in question has been missing for some time?'

'Since at least 1919,' he replied.

Smiling became a little easier for her. 'So it's safe to say this is not an emergency?'

'No, just an enquiry.'

'Perhaps you should come back when you have more time. I would hate to disrupt your day, sir.'

'No, that's fine. I just wondered if you had any idea how long I will have to wait?'

'We'll get to it. Once we've finished dealing with all the murders and robberies,' the duty officer said with a smirk.

Lester held her gaze for a few seconds before looking away, his eyes homing in on a framed award on the wall behind her. *I'm guess that's not for outstanding customer service,* he mused as he walked back to his seat. He knew he was already late for work and decided that a few extra minutes would not make much difference.

It was close to an hour later when a square-jawed officer appeared through a door next to the counter. 'David Lester?'

'Yes,' he said, rising from his seat.

'I understand you want a list of missing persons going back to the turn of the last century?' he asked with a deeply furrowed brow.

'That's right.'

'I'm sorry, we don't give out that sort of information. It's not public record, I'm afraid.'

Lester's jacket almost slipped from his shoulders as they sagged. He looked past the man to the duty sergeant, who was grinning behind the counter.

'I'm sure if you Google it, you'll find a several websites with missing persons, but we can't help you. Sorry.'

Lester nodded and remained there for a moment while the man disappeared back through the door. He looked at the time on his phone, 9:54, and then slowly walked up to the counter to the duty sergeant, who seemed to be expecting him.

'This is about the hair, isn't it?' he said, then turned and headed towards the entrance.

'Have a nice day, sir!' she called after him.

Lester hurried along the glass-panelled corridor to his office, his feet gliding silently across the carpet tiles.

'Morning, Dave!' a voice called out.

He closed his eyes momentarily. *Why don't you say it over the PA in case someone didn't hear you?* He stepped into his office and froze in the doorway.

'Good of you to join us, Lester.' Walker was sitting in his chair looking at his watch, an array of files opened on his desk.

'Sorry, Craig, I had to attend to some urgent personal business on my way here.'

'What's going on with you, Lester? I thought you were someone I could rely on, but you keep fucking up. You walk in halfway through the morning without letting me know. I had Maitland's here at 9:00 for their annual review meeting. I had to wing the whole fucking thing because their account handler had gone AWOL! Now, is there something you want to share with me? Help me to understand the reason I looked a complete arsehole in front of one of our biggest customers.'

Lester swallowed hard. The 9:00 meeting had completely slipped his mind. 'I am so sorry,' he repeated, his eyes briefly meeting Duggie's in the next office. *I'll bet he's enjoying this!* 'I promise it will never happen again.'

'You're damn right it won't, because if it does, you're out of here. Do you understand me?'

Lester nodded slowly, shifting his weight nervously.

'You're supposed to be an asset, not a fucking liability!'

As Walker got up, Lester took a step back from the doorway. He knew his boss would have pushed him out of the way otherwise. He had seen it before. The sound of stomping feet echoed down the corridor as Walker returned to his own office. Then there was silence. Lester let go of a breath he hadn't realised he'd been holding. He could feel all his colleagues in the fishbowls opposite peering over their screens at him. His cheeks burned.

Lester kept his head down the rest of the day and focused on his job, working right through lunch and only stopping to make a quick call to Hayley to explain that he would be late, again.

'So what are we having tonight, KFC?' she asked.

He ignored her dig. 'I was hoping you might rustle something up. I think we could both use a home-cooked meal.'

'I agree, but I'm not cooking. That's your job.'

'Okay, but we won't be eating till eight.'

'And whose fault is that? Why do you have to work late again anyway?'

'I'm just trying to keep everyone happy.'

'Does that include me?'

That would be a first! 'Of course.'

'And you think working late every night will achieve this?'

'I need to find a happy medium,' he said. 'I'll try and be home on time the rest of the week.'

After putting the phone down and deciding to head home, Lester reflected on his words: 'I need to find a happy medium.' *That's exactly what I need!*

From the car park of Walker Financial Services, Lester dialled the number his mother had given him and reclined in his car seat as the phone started to ring through the Fiesta's speakers.

'Hello,' a voice said, upbeat and younger than he had expected.

'Hi, is that Lauren?'

'Yes, speaking.'

'My name's David Lester. I left you a voicemail, and I think you tried to call me back last night?'

'Oh yes, hi, Dave. We seem to keep missing each other, don't we?'

'My mum gave me your number. She said you're a clairvoyant?'

'Are you interested in having a reading?'

Lester paused for a moment. 'Not exactly, but I would like you to connect to the other side for me as part of an investigation.'

'Okay?' Lauren's response was more of a question.

'Have you heard of the phantom of Pendlebury Hill?'

'Of course.'

Am I the only person on the planet who hadn't heard about her? 'Have you ever done any spiritualism work up there?'

'Actually, no, although it is on my wish list. It's supposed to be very active.'

'Do you want to tick it off your wish list?'

The phone went quiet for a moment. 'What exactly do you have in mind?'

'I had an encounter up there on Friday night.'

'Oh cool! What happened?'

'A girl stepped out in front of me and then vanished into thin air. I've been investigating all week to try to get to the bottom of who she is and what she wants. It's become a bit of an obsession.'

'I've heard that story. So you want me to try and contact her?' Lauren asked.

'Yes. And maybe one other. My research suggests there are two ghosts. I think they both have a message to give.'

'Perhaps they're lost souls who need to be directed to the light.'

'Yes, I think they both need closure, but so do I. This incident has kind of taken over my life for the past week; it's starting to impact my work. I feel I've gone just about as far as I can go on my own. Do you think you would be able to help?'

Silence.

'Lauren?'

'Sorry, I was just consulting my guides. So you're wanting to help these spirits, then?' When he replied yes, she said, 'Okay, you've definitely got my interest, although I can't promise anything. What are you thinking to do?'

'I'm not sure really. I think the logical thing would be to drive up to the spot where I saw her and see if we can make contact there. I appreciate that it's not the normal sort of reading you give so I'm happy to pay more.'

'Okay, cool, I'll give it a go. Just tell me where and when.'

'As soon as you can.'

'Is tomorrow soon enough?'

Lester was thoughtful for a moment. 'Perfect! Are you available at five thirty?' he asked, knowing he could not be late again.

'Yes, no problem.'

'That's great. I can pick you up if that will make it easier.'

'If it's not going out of your way. I don't really like driving at night.'

Lester took Lauren's address and agreed to collect her at 17:15, after enquiring how much it would cost. Arranging the spiritualist was much easier than he had been expecting, though he wasn't convinced that this wasn't just a waste of money. The £40.00 fee was what he'd expected to pay for a normal reading, not a paranormal one, so he was pleased not to have to pay an exorbitant price. At least not monetarily. His marriage was another thing entirely.

He sensed, somehow, that the hardest part of his investigation was still to come.

Chapter Sixteen

The office was deserted as Lester walked slowly from the reception desk to his fishbowl, waiting for the automatic lighting to detect him. He sat down and logged into his computer, wondering why his colleagues didn't get in earlier. Walker religiously checked the time and attendance records of his staff. If they were smart, they'd get in before him. It might not get them on his good side, but Lester was sure it wouldn't hurt.

That was exactly why Lester was there. To try and repair some of the damage he'd already done that week. Well, that and he was hoping he'd be able to leave early without recrimination. Plus, he had about half an hour before any of his colleagues arrived. It was the perfect time to carry on investigating without anyone knowing.

After making himself a coffee, Lester began searching online for missing persons in Kent. He quickly narrowed the search by adding Pendlebury Hill, but there were still more than three thousand results, and none of them had anything to do with Pendlebury Hill. The closest match was for someone posting a blog about their missing cat.

Lester changed the search criteria to Greyton, Meadowhurst, Gatherford and then Brenton but none proved successful. He checked the clock in the bottom right-hand corner, 8:17. Walker would be in soon. A little disillusioned, he started going through what he knew of the ghost he'd seen. Short, 'boyish,' light to medium brown hair. *Not helpful!* White dress, coat, smock, or uniform, the latter being mentioned twice in the witness statements—one from the policeman, Bryan Naylor. His observations might be a little more reliable than others purely because policemen were trained to be vigilant. The other report was from the wife murderer, Thomas Knott, who mentioned a uniform or nightdress. Lester's own recollection of her dress was a blur, although he felt certain he would have remembered a nightdress, even from that era.

He quickly Googled 1916 nightdress and sighed when the images appeared on the screen, unable to discount the long-sleeved, high-necked garment. Whilst it was possible, Lester decided it was more likely to be a uniform, especially as All Saints Hospital was just two miles from the spot he had seen her. In that moment, he made his mind up that it must have been a nurse's uniform.

He reached for his coffee and took a sip. It was tepid. The clock showed 8:31. Immediately, he heard footsteps coming down the corridor, and as he tried to guess who it would be, Alice stepped into the office beside him and waved through the glass. He raised his hand and smiled, then quickly returned his attention to the screen. He typed 'missing nurse Kent 1900' in Google and hit enter. The link for a website he had seen earlier, *Gone But Not Forgotten,* was still in blue, meaning that he had never opened it. He had dismissed it twice already because he assumed that it was a memorial site. Accepting that this would have to be his last search of the day, Lester clicked on the link. A scan of the homepage suggested that his assumption had been correct, but it was an American site with a list of different states. He scrolled towards the bottom of the page and saw a link for the UK.

Still doubting that it was a good investment of his time, he clicked on the link. The format was identical to its American counterpart, the site listing all the counties in the UK, and he lazily clicked on Kent, ready to concede that he was never going to discover the identity of the second phantom.

The screen listed decades, going all the way back to 1900, and there was even a link at the bottom to go back further still, from 1800-1900. Without getting his hopes up, he clicked on the 1900-1910 link. A list of names appeared in chronological order, twenty-seven in total. There were just four women among them, and he opened each link in turn. Only one had a photo, and her black hair swiftly eliminated her as a possibility. The next woman lived in Margate. She was about the right age, but her location made him rule her out. The third woman was in her fifties and lived in Gravesend. The final option was a schoolteacher in her thirties, but her description mentioned that she had red hair and that she'd gone missing from Orpington.

Lester went on to the next decade. A list of eighty-five names appeared. His initial surprise at the high number faded as soon as he saw the photos of men in uniform, soldiers who had gone off to war and were never heard from again. Of the ten women, eight had photos. One image, in particular, sent a shiver down his spine, as though fingers were raking down the centre of his back. He leaned in closer to the screen, his hand covering his mouth. Nausea swept through him like a hot flush, and he released a stuttered breath. His heart raced as he stared at those hypnotic eyes. Although he'd only seen her for an instant, he recognised her immediately.

He clicked on the link.

Frances Alice Coldwell 1895-1916

Frances Coldwell's story is shrouded in tragedy. More than a hundred years on, the mysterious disappearance of the twenty-one-year-old nurse remains a haunting enigma. She was reported missing on the 3rd October 1916 by her mother, Florence, when she failed to return home from her shift at Greyton's All Saints Hospital. Frances usually walked home with best friend and fellow nurse, Margaret Winter, but Ms. Winter recalled Frances was detained in surgery that evening and told her not to wait.

On the night in question, witnesses at the hospital claimed Frances left around seven fifteen, just quarter of an hour later. Her journey home, down Pendlebury Hill to the village of Morton Finchley, should have taken around ninety minutes. Yet she never arrived. A police search commenced the following morning, when Frances failed to show for her shift at the hospital. Leading the investigation was Police Sergeant Alfred Dering, who connected Frances's younger brother, George, to Frances's disappearance. He alleged that four scratch marks on George's face were evidence of a struggle between the two siblings.

A search of George Coldwell's bedroom uncovered blood-stained shackles, the blood type matching his sister's, and undergarments believed to have been owned by Frances. George Coldwell, described by the prosecution as a retard during the trial, was found guilty of his sister's murder and sentenced to capital punishment. Despite his mother pleading that George idolised his sister and was incapable of violence, he was hanged at Greyton Gaol on 14th March 1917. Sadly, Florence died two months later, 11th May 1917. Frances Coldwell's body was never found.

Lester shivered. There was no question that Frances Coldwell was the woman he had seen that night.

It was all he could do to stop himself from shouting 'Eureka, I've found her!' at the top of his lungs, but he didn't want to attract any more unwanted attention to himself. Instead, he bookmarked the website and Googled her.

'Frances Coldwell,' he said her name aloud, wondering why it sounded familiar.

He wracked his brain, but it was a pointless exercise. He was already booked to meet with Lauren later so he decided to focus on his work until then.

17:15

Lester pulled up outside 15 Boxley Drive exactly on time, having left the office uncharacteristically early. His fingers drummed on the steering wheel as he waited, unsure if tooting his horn seemed too pushy. After a few minutes, the tempo of his drumming increased, and he leaned across the passenger seat to look at the house in time to see the curtains twitch in the front room.

Nice house, he thought to himself. He and Hayley had looked at several houses around the Meadowhurst estate when they first decided to move in together. They opted for the cheaper estate of Gatherford, just the other side of the A300. It seemed like a lifetime ago now.

A few moments later, he watched as Lauren stepped out and waved, before locking the door behind her. In the glow of the street lamp, she appeared as lovely as his mother said, which was a surprise. Her assessments were usually as reliable as the weather with a vast array of ages, sizes, and shapes in what she judged to be suitable matches for him. Even with her mauve quilted coat, he could see she had a slight frame, and with fur cuffs and knee-high boots she looked very girly. She shuffled down the path and opened the car door, ducking down and asking, 'Dave?'

'Hi, Lauren,' he said, offering his hand as she climbed in. 'Pleased to meet you.'

Her dark chocolate eyes smiled as she grabbed his fingers in her mitten-clad hand and shook gently. The smile extended to natural, thin lips that complimented her caramel skin, which suggested she had brunette hair hidden beneath her lilac bobble hat. Perhaps she had no hair—that would have been criminal and something his mum would probably have mentioned as he, like his dad, preferred long hair.

As he continued to stare, the dimples in her cheeks faded and she instinctively looked down at her coat and then back up at him.

'Sorry,' he said, with a shake of his head. 'You're just not what I expected.'

Her frown remained. 'Okay, is that a good thing?'

'Definitely! I thought spiritualists were old . . . er.'

'Well, I'm sure some of them are, but I'm actually a medium.'

'What's the difference?' he asked as his phone vibrated. He opened it, wondering who had just sent him a WhatsApp.

'A medium's like a conduit. Someone who can communicate with spirit. A spiritualist can't usually communicate with the other side and often use mediums to make contact for them. Spiritualism is a religious order who believe that life exists on two planes, the physical plane and the spirit plane, and that the dead interact with the living and can come back in different incarnations. Mediums also dance around naked in sacred places.'

Lester looked up from his phone with round eyes.

'Just making sure you're paying attention,' she said with a grin as she fastened her seatbelt.

His laugh was delayed, awkwardly so, but he liked that she had a sense of humour. It took the edge off. His mum was right. From everything he could see, Lauren was perfect.

Lester quickly read Hayley's WhatsApp message. *What time will you be home?*

B47, he replied and put his phone away.

'Sorry,' he said, still smiling. It was infectious. Her smile lit up her face and extended to those deep brown eyes with sincerity.

'So, tell me about your experience on Pendlebury Hill?' Lauren asked as he pulled away from the kerb.

Lester nodded, a slow assured bob. 'It happened around midnight on Friday. I was driving up Pendlebury Way when this girl just stepped out in front of me.'

'Wow, that must have been terrifying.'

'It was. I thought I'd killed her. I jumped out of the car right away, but there was no sign of her. I dialled 999. The paramedics helped me look for her for about half an hour, but she was nowhere to be found. When the police eventually showed up, they just asked me a few questions, breathalysed me, checked my car and left.'

'So this is the girl you want me to get in touch with?'

Lester nodded as he pulled up to the roundabout and waited for two cars and a lorry to pass. 'One of them, yes. I mentioned there were two ghosts on our call? One is known as the phantom bride.'

'Yes, I've heard about her.'

'She only appears on the anniversary of her death. From what I understand, she's trying to get a message to her mum to tell her that she's been involved in an accident. She actually died on the eve of her wedding along with her three bridesmaids.'

'Oh my God! How awful. I didn't know they actually knew her identity.'

'It's pretty conclusive,' he said, turning off the roundabout and onto Pendlebury Way. 'I've discovered two things so far. Firstly, the ghost I saw is not the phantom bride, though they haunt the same place, and she's appeared to others over the years too. Secondly, these reports actually date back to 1919. The bride-to-be died in 1970.'

'Do you know who the other girl is?'

Lester was about to say her name, but he held back. 'I have a theory about who she is, or was. I'm ninety-five percent certain, but I'd rather not say. I'll be further validation of your abilities if you come up with her name.'

'So I'm on trial?' Lauren asked, her face deadpan. He was about to stammer an apology when the corners of her mouth turned up. 'I'm just messing with you. Most people want some sort of proof the first time they see a medium. It's completely understandable. I can't promise I'll come up with her name or even make contact with her, but I'll give it my best shot.'

'Thanks, I appreciate that. The validation is just so I can confirm her identity. I only discovered who she was this morning. I've been a bit obsessed with my research.'

Her eyebrows shot up to her lilac hat. 'Why's that?'

'This girl chose me,' Lester said with a shrug. 'At first I thought she was reaching out to me because she wanted my help.'

'And now?'

'Now I think it's because she wants to exact revenge.'

He could feel those brown eyes staring at him as he negotiated the potholes in the road. 'Revenge for what?'

'All of her eyewitnesses were men. One of those men was a murderer and another one was a paedophile. I couldn't find any information on the other five, but I think she only appears to men who are bad in some way.'

Lauren's silence spoke volumes, the unspoken question hanging in the air like exhaust fumes.

'So, here we are travelling along a deserted road in the middle of nowhere, and you're about to tell me that you're a serial killer?'

Lester laughed. He felt at ease in the medium's presence. 'I had an affair four years ago,' he said, opting for honesty being the best policy.

'Phew!' Lauren said, her head falling back against the headrest. 'Not that I'm condoning it or anything, but that's way preferable to rape or murder.'

'I don't know what the other five men did. If they had only had affairs, then it wouldn't have made headlines. I'm pretty much all researched out. I can still see my computer screen every time I blink.'

'So that's why I'm here? You want to go straight to the source?'

'Exactly. I have trouble contacting some members of the living.'

He was rewarded with Lauren's laughter. He was aware that his gaze was lingering too long and made a conscious effort to look away. She was good company, and he enjoyed having a conversation in which he didn't have to overthink every word to avoid saying the wrong thing. It felt right, the way it was supposed to. The way it never really had with Hayley, even in the early years.

He cleared his throat. 'I want to find out what happened to her and what she wants. Her brother was convicted of her murder, but I don't believe he did it. He was unable to defend himself.'

'Why?'

'He was a retard,' Lester said, parroting what he'd read in the article without thought. He paused briefly, when he saw Lauren frowning at him, and added, 'sorry, it was an old article. Not very PC.'

Lauren wagged her finger at him and tutted. 'No, it's not PC. You need to translate. What you meant to say was, he had a learning disability.'

'Sorry. Her brother had a 'learning disability' and was unable to defend himself. They didn't say that in so many words, but that's what was implied in the article. Reading between the lines, I believe someone took advantage of his disability and made him the fall guy.' He told her what the article he'd read said.

'So you want me to contact this girl to find out what really happened to her?'

'Yes, and the phantom bride, too, if possible. I think they are linked somehow. I have a feeling that both girls are stuck here and need help to move on.'

'Both stories are so tragic. Even though I'm a medium and I don't see death with the same finality as most people, it's still making me well up. For us, death is a new beginning.'

Lester swerved around an object in the road, and Lauren yelped, her hand clutching her chest.

'Sorry, I thought it was a hedgehog. It was just a rock.'

She sighed heavily. 'I'm glad I'm not driving. It's so dark up here!'

'It's creepy as hell, especially when someone suddenly appears in front of you!'

'You would have definitely needed new seat covers if I'd been with you.'

'Really? Don't you talk to the dead all the time? Am I allowed to say *the dead?* There's not a PC term like living impaired, is there?'

She laughed. 'Yes, that's allowed. I do talk to them, but I don't see them in the flesh, so to speak. I get a sense of what they look like, just like you do a character in a book. An interpretation, I suppose. I'd definitely pee my pants if I saw one like you did.'

Lester smiled.

'We're almost there,' he said, slowing down slightly as they continued up Pendlebury Way. 'As these two girls are haunting this hill, does that mean that they're stuck between life and death?'

'Pretty much. They can't move on or be reincarnated until they cross over. That's where I can help.'

'Pendlebury Hill has a history rife with bloodshed. It will be interesting to see what you get. I'll pull over just up ahead.'

Lester parked exactly where the incident had taken place a few days earlier, his landmark being the skid marks left by his Ford Fiesta.

'Here we are,' he said, feeling like he was reliving one of his teenage dates as he turned off the engine. 'So how do we do this? From the car? Or do we get out and walk around?'

Despite the temperature being -2°, Lester felt somewhat relieved when Lauren replied, 'Let's get out and see what happens.'

He zipped up his jacket as far as it would go and stepped out into the inhospitable February evening. The concrete road had scattered patches of black ice, although it wasn't as obvious as on tarmac.

'Be careful,' he warned, sliding his foot back and forth on the silky surface. 'This is where I stopped,' Lester said, squatting down to illuminate the rubber tyre marks with the flashlight app from his smartphone.

Lauren looked but remained silent, her attention elsewhere. He studied her as she circled the area, her eyes darting around as though she were seeing things that he could not. His head buzzed with questions, but he held back, not wishing to break her concentration.

The cold was already penetrating his clothes and shoes, and he clenched his fists inside his jacket pockets. He trailed behind her as she wandered down the hill a short distance and stopped to look into the foliage to her right. She raised her hand and waved it in a circular motion, as though cleaning an imaginary window. Then she turned around and walked back up the hill, expelling deep breaths in bursts like a steam train.

'There's a lot of activity up here,' she said eventually. 'It's like being in a big hall full of people all talking at once. It's hard to separate one voice from the next. So much pain and anguish. I don't know why, but I definitely get a sense that something went on over there,' she said, pointing into the hedgerow close to the skid marks.

Lester continued to hold back his questions and just watched her as she stood with her eyes closed, her expressions suggesting that she was hearing things or seeing things that made her uncomfortable. She scrunched her face up at one point and hunched her shoulders momentarily before relaxing once more. Then she smiled.

'I have a lady here. She's quite short and broad. Silver rounded hair. She says exactly what she thinks.'

Lester shook his head at her. Maybe he was right to be sceptical. 'No, the woman I saw was slim, medium height, with light brown hair and green eyes.'

'This lady's here for you, Dave,' Lauren said.

'For me?' He frowned.

'She's saying to me, "Tell him he doesn't have to put up with it and you don't owe her anything." Do you understand what that means?'

Lester could have sworn his heart stopped. He stared at her in astonishment.

Eyes still closed, Lauren said, 'Dave?'

Shaking himself, as though he could shake the shock from his body, he said, 'It sounds like my nan.'

Lauren smiled. 'She's nodding.'

Lester looked down at the ground, the skid marks blurring into four curved lines.

'She's here for you. In the same way as if you had come to my house for a reading.'

He didn't respond, his thoughts whirling in his mind.

'Earth plane to Dave.'

He looked up, blinking as his vision blurred. 'It was the last thing she said to me before she died. Here she is, eleven years later, saying exactly the same thing. Sorry,' he said, pinching his eyes with his index finger and thumb. 'I've never really believed in all this sort of thing.'

'It's quite normal, especially for men. To disbelieve, that is.'

He smiled. 'So she's here? You can actually see her?'

'Not like I see you, in the physical sense. I can hear her really clearly though. She's very forthright, no beating about the bush with this lady. She says exactly what's on her mind.'

'Yes, she did. No grey areas where Nan was concerned. So, is she okay? Is she with my grandad?'

'She's with Os . . . I want to say Oscar, but it doesn't feel quite right.'

'Oswald. That was my granddad's name,' Lester said with a grin.

'She's smiling, although she has a tooth missing here,' Lauren said, pointing to one of her canine teeth.

Lester rolled his eyes. 'She fell over on the patio putting out the washing. She sometimes whistled when she spoke. We used to tease her about it.'

Lauren nodded, a grin playing at the sides of her mouth. 'She's happy and pain-free, apart from watching you tiptoeing around "that witch," she says.'

Lauren opened her eyes finally as his hand swept across his face and rested across his mouth.

'Is there anyone else there who wants to speak to me?' he asked.

Lauren closed her eyes for a moment, her chest rising and falling as she drew in deep breaths. 'I'm not getting anyone else. Just your nan.'

His smile failed to disguise his disappointment. 'Is she able to help us find this girl?'

The medium closed her eyes and was silent once again, her long, deep breaths visible in jets of white cloud as she expelled warm air into the frozen night. Eventually, her eyes flickered open, and she gave a single shake of her head. 'Shall we walk a little way up the road? Maybe she'll come to us.'

'Good idea. Some of the reports said that she was coming down the pavement on this side of the road.' He pointed to the right as they walked up. 'Although you can't actually see it because of the overgrown bushes.' He cupped his hands and blew warm air into them, then rubbed them together vigorously. 'I'm glad we're moving. I was beginning to seize up.'

'Don't you have a scarf or gloves?' she asked, taking his hands and rubbing them.

He looked back at her in surprise but allowed her to continue.

'Better?'

He nodded, unable to keep the smile from his face.

'So, will they follow us, the spirits?' he said as they walked up the hill.

Lauren laughed. 'Don't think of it as us being a tour group walking around London. They are all around, all the time.'

'It's amazing. My whole life I just . . . dismissed it.'

'Seeing is believing, and so is hearing. Some people are only convinced once they get a message that the medium couldn't possibly have known unless they had been speaking to someone in the world of spirit.'

'Well, I'm getting there. Quicker than I ever imagined. My nan was convinced that I was marrying the wrong woman. She kept asking me, are you happy, is this really what you want? She would never say it in front of Hayley, my wife, though. She was in a care home, following a stroke, and my mum called me and

95

said that they didn't think she had long. I was in Stone on a training course, a three-hour drive away. She managed to hold on till I got there. That's when she said, "You don't have to put up with it, David. You don't owe her anything, and she'll never make you happy." She died that evening.'

'I'm so sorry,' Lauren said, stopping and taking his hands again. She squeezed them gently. 'So I take it you're still with this Hayley?'

'Yes,' he said, unable to hold her gaze any longer.

'I wasn't going to say anything, but your aura is mostly grey.'

'My aura?'

'You've never heard of an aura?'

'I've heard of it, but if I'm honest, I'm not exactly sure what it is.'

'An aura is a field of spiritual energy that encompasses all living things. Humans, animals, trees, and plants.'

'And you can see them?'

Lauren nodded. 'Since I was a little girl. A lot of children can, but it fades as they get older, like imaginary friends.'

'Imaginary friends?' Lester laughed. 'Are they real as well?'

'Of course. They're just spirits. Children are very spiritual. It's only when they're told not to be silly or tell lies that they learn to block them out, like most adults.'

'Huh.' Lester's eyebrow disappeared into his fringe. 'This is fascinating. It's like a whole other world I never knew existed.'

'Seeing is believing,' she said with a shrug. 'The spirits are around us all the time, but you need to train your mind to see them once you've lost that natural ability. The way I explain it to people, mainly because I work on an IT helpdesk, is think of it like a Wi-Fi signal. You can't see it, but you know it's there, otherwise you wouldn't be surfing the internet on your tablet.'

'You work on an IT helpdesk?'

Lauren giggled. 'I'm finding it harder and harder to understand you.'

'Sorry. My lips are frozen,' he said, pointing to his mouth. 'They're not doing what I want them to.'

Again she laughed, dimples appearing in her cheeks and her nose wrinkling.

'Is it just me? Can you whistle?'

She tried and failed, instead bursting into laughter once again. 'Warm hands, cold lips.'

Lester found himself looking at those lips and then up into her eyes. This was the best time he'd had in a long time. Lauren was a pleasant surprise.

'Come on,' she said, taking his hand. 'Let's get you back in the warm.'

Lester hesitated for a moment, the thought of wasting an opportunity difficult to bear, but he was so cold and his fingers ached. 'Okay,' he relented.

They walked down the hill in relative silence until Lauren said, 'I know you're disappointed, but I have no control over who comes forward. Usually, those who are most determined find a way. At least you got a message from your nan. No one was getting in front of her!'

'Absolutely. No, that was amazing. My mum will be thrilled when I tell her. I just felt this girl was so determined to be heard that she would have fought her way through the crowd.'

'Well, let's keep our fingers crossed for next time.'

They stopped just before reaching his car, and he looked at her curiously. 'So there's going to be a next time?'

'We're not just going to give up at the first hurdle, are we?' Lauren asked with a playful smile.

'No chance.' He grinned and unlocked the car with a press of the key.

They got inside, and he turned on the engine, followed by the heater. A thin film of ice was beginning to build up on the inside of the windscreen, and he began wiping it with a chamois leather when Lauren grabbed his arm. He looked round sharply, straight into her eyes.

'She's here.'

Chapter Seventeen

18:32, Thursday, 1ˢᵗ February

Although it was no more than a few minutes that Lauren had sat with her eyes closed and head tilted ever so slightly towards the roof of the car, to Lester, it felt an eternity. Twice he'd gone to speak, but his inner voice told him to be patient, and he duly complied.

'I have Fran here,' the medium said finally.

Lester's eyes and mouth opened wide in astonishment. If he had any doubts about Lauren's abilities, even after Nan, this erased them all. Not only that, but it meant that his research was correct. Frances Coldwell was his phantom.

'Look around you, Fran. Do you see a light?'

'Don't we want to ask her some questions first?' Lester cut in, worried that he was about to lose that opportunity.

She held her hand up to silence him.

'Do you see a solitary bright light?'

Lester opened his mouth to speak again but held back.

'I just wanted to find out if there was a light first,' Lauren said, her eyes blinking open. 'A light means they're ready to cross over but just need a bit of guidance. No light means they have unfinished business. Fran says there's no light, only darkness. She's so faint and distant that I'm struggling to make sense of what she's saying. I only hear snippets. She talks of betrayal . . . injustice. Sanctum of God. And I think she said, lies beneath the barrow.'

They locked eyes for a moment, each waiting for the other to speak.

'Do you have any idea what any of that means?' Lauren asked. 'It definitely sounds like this is the girl who disappeared rather than the bride-to-be?'

'If she said her name was Fran, then it's definitely the one who disappeared. Frances Coldwell.' Lester drew in a deep breath and turned down the blower. 'Injustice, I assume she means her brother, who was hung for her murder. Betrayal . . . no idea,' he said with a shrug of his shoulders.

'What about the rest?'

'Sanctum of God. That's a holy place, I assume. Sorry, I'm not religious at all. The barrow bit, I have no idea. Maybe whoever killed her dumped her in a wheelbarrow or moved her in one. I'll have to research it.'

Lauren nodded, the bobble on her hat bouncing back and forth.

'Is she still here?' he asked.

She shook her head. 'If she is, the connection is so weak that I'm not picking her up anymore. It wasn't great to begin with. If you think of her like a mobile phone signal, then I only had one bar at best.'

'You really do work in IT, don't you?' he said with a chuckle.

She nodded. 'Is that so hard to believe? You're not a chauvinist, are you, Dave? That would be disappointing on top of the infidelity.'

Lester stared at her for a moment, at a loss for words, until she punched him playfully on the top of his left arm. 'I'm just messing with you. I get that all the time, but I like to bite back sometimes.'

'You got me,' he said, exhaling in relief. He was still trying to figure her out. 'No, I'm not a chauvinist. I find it quite refreshing, actually, to hear that you work on a helpdesk since it's one of those male-dominated professions. One of the few left. You don't see many female builders or bricklayers, for instance.'

'That's true. There are still female-dominated professions too. Dental assistants, secretaries, and supermarket checkouts technicians or whatever they are called these days. I don't think we'll ever get away from it.'

'And, at the risk of getting a slap, I would say most mediums are women?'

Lauren nodded. 'You're probably right, although it wasn't something that I'd always wanted to do. I've had the gift since I was a little girl, and it's just got stronger over the years.'

Lester stared out through the windscreen at the skid marks on the concrete surface. 'Does their signal fade over time? It has been over a hundred years since she disappeared.'

'I'm not sure. Fran may be the oldest connection I've ever made. They don't have the same concept of time as we do. Some spirits are strong and determined and can make themselves heard quite easily.'

'Like Nan?'

'Exactly. Others struggle, and I guess there are some that never come through. No one truly knows how it works, and the only way we'll find out is by crossing over ourselves.'

She was so matter of fact. To her, there was no question that this unseen world existed. Lester found himself whisked away, as though he were on a magic carpet soaring high above the world, looking down on it with a totally new perspective.

'I don't think we're going to get anymore tonight, and it looks like we have some investigating to do,' Lauren said with a smile, placing her hand on his knee.

We?

His smile was immediate, and he felt it light up his face. Placing his own hand on top of hers, he said, 'Thank you for tonight. You've been amazing.'

For a moment, they held each other's gaze. It was the *moment*, usually the point at which he would lean in for a first kiss, and he was painfully aware that his look had lingered far beyond that of a casual conversation. He could tell when someone liked him, recognise the signs, but it wasn't an exact science. There had been occasions in the past where he had misread signals and had made propositions only to discover that he was way off base.

Lauren was definitely giving off signals. Sultry looks, holding his hand, touching his knee, and that playful punch, but he had only known her for two hours. Maybe it was just her personality, the way she naturally behaved. For all he knew, she was happily married with kids, and she was just a genuinely nice person who was acting the same way with him as she would with anyone else. He had to constantly remind himself that Hayley was not a stereotypical woman but an extreme case and that anyone who showed him any kind of attention was not necessarily looking to hook up. Making a wrong assumption could cost him a friend and ally, not to mention a wife.

Instead of leaning in, Lester looked away, removing his hand to lower the handbrake, and proceeded to complete a three-point turn. During the manoeuvre, he noticed that her radiant smile had faded. It wasn't enough to suggest disappointment, but his instincts told him otherwise. Perhaps she had felt the connection too, but would she have expected him to act upon it knowing that he was married?

As they drove back to Meadowhurst, a cluster of tiny white and orange lights at the bottom of the hill, the silence was tangible.

'When you said I have a grey aura, what does that mean exactly?' Lester asked, relieved to be able to re-ignite a conversation. 'What colour should it be?'

'It all depends on what's going on in your life and what type of person you are. Most auras I see are vibrant colours. There are often different layers of varying colour, a bit like a rainbow, but there's usually a predominant colour or two from which I can make a quick assessment. Mine is very girly, violet and pink. Violet is spiritual.'

'And pink?'

'Love,' she replied, the pigment of her irises were almost swallowed up by her pupils.

'So what about grey,' Lester persisted. 'That doesn't sound good.'

'It's not just grey. Mostly, but I saw blue and green layers as well.'

'But what do they mean?'

'Grey is, as you would expect, fairly negative. Depression, low self-esteem, low energy, exhaustion, sadness, emotional. A bit like how you feel when you look out into a miserable rainy day, although, personally, I love the rain.'

Of course you do! Lester grinned as he slowed down at the roundabout at the foot of the hill.

'Blue means you're spiritual as well, otherwise you wouldn't have seen Fran in the first place. The green is a healing colour.'

'Healing?'

'You've heard of spiritual healing, right?'

Lester shook his head, his bottom lip jutting out.

'That's a conversation for next time! I have a lot to teach you.'

He drove across the roundabout and took the turn for Meadowhurst, wishing they had further to drive and deliberately reducing his speed to prolong the journey. Moments later, he turned off onto Invicta Drive. 'So how do I change my aura from grey to one of the pretty colours?'

'That's something you need to figure out on your own. Find whatever it is that's making you sad or depressing you and change it.'

Like it's that easy, Lester thought to himself as he pulled up outside Lauren's house.

'Thank you so much, Lauren. I probably have more questions than before we started, but I feel we've made some real progress tonight. Which reminds me, I owe you some money,' he said, searching inside his jacket for his wallet, but her hand reached out to pin his arm against his chest.

'That won't be necessary.'

He met her eyes again, trying not to get caught in them like before. 'Why not?'

'This experience has been very educational for me too. I almost feel like I should be paying you.'

He grinned and held out an upturned palm, but her hand came down and slapped it away.

'It's been an adventure, Dave,' she said as she unfastened her seatbelt. 'You've got my number, use it.'

Lester was about to speak when the medium leaned forward and kissed him softly on the lips. He was so stunned, he barely had time to register what was happening before she pulled away.

He stared at her in a wondrous daze. 'You have nothing to feel guilty about. I kissed you,' she said, opening the car door and stepping out into the icy darkness. Before she closed the door, Lauren ducked down and laughed at his frowning face. 'Did you think that was the only thing your nan said to me?'

Chapter Eighteen

Lester guided the key into the lock and held it there, his other hand resting against the uPVC door frame as though he needed it for support. He endured the cold a bit longer, -3° according to the display on his dashboard. After a moment, he took a deep breath and turned the key.

The warmth was welcomed, along with the scent of lavender from the porch diffuser, but the atmosphere itself was noticeably toxic. He closed the door behind him and stood in that confined space, reflecting on the past two hours. The thought of Lauren made him smile. He had almost forgotten how gratifying a relationship could be. It must have been that way with Hayley in the beginning. It was hard to remember now.

Tonight had opened his eyes, in more ways than one, and he knew things couldn't continue the way they had been. If his marriage had failed, then he accepted responsibility, but should he go on being punished for all eternity? The only relevant question, when he thought long and hard about it, was did he still love Hayley and did she still love him?

'Why do you stay with her?' his mum would often ask.

'Because I made a commitment. Till death us do part. I don't want to be one of those couples who throw in the towel at the first sign of trouble.'

'What commitment? You've already broken one of the most sacred vows,' she reminded him.

Lester hung his head as hypocrisy stared him in the face. He had truly believed in every vow as he recited them at the altar from memory. He'd been certain Hayley was *the one* as they had set off on the road of married life together. What he didn't realise was that the road ahead curved and twisted, that it had ups and downs and was scattered with potholes and other obstacles.

The affair, four years earlier, had been the start of the darkest period of his life. Harmony showed interest in him at a time when Hayley had stopped. Once she was fell pregnant, he was no longer allowed to touch her. 'I don't want to risk hurting the baby,' was her automatic response to his romantic advances, despite assurances from the hospital that it was perfectly safe. Harmony was not the love of his life. She was just a stark contrast to his wife, effervescent, fun-loving, and easy-going. She made him feel alive in the same way that Lauren had that evening. That was what he missed. That was what he craved.

Bracing himself, Lester slowly pushed open the lounge door. 'Hiya,' he said as Hayley looked round from the settee.

'I thought you were only going to be a couple of hours?'

'Sorry.'

'So what's the excuse this time?'

He remained silent, wondering if now was the right time. He knew what would happen if she found out he was back on the case, but he also knew not telling her now could be worse.

'Well?'

'I went to see a medium,' he admitted, sighing internally. 'I found out the phantom's identity and wanted to try and make contact.'

She glared back at him. 'Are you fucking kidding me? You're still wasting time on that?'

Lester nodded.

Her eyes narrowed at him. 'So you lied to me?'

'Not intentionally,' he said, but he knew it wouldn't matter. 'I did quit but then this medium got in touch.'

Hayley shook her head like a disappointed schoolteacher. 'And what did he say?'

'Not a great deal. She confirmed the name that I had found.'

Her eyebrows shot up to her forehead. 'She?'

'Yes. And mentioned injustice, betrayal, sanctum, and a barrow,' he told her, counting each word with his thumb and three fingers.

'Well, she got the betrayal part right.' He felt the dig go straight to his chest, exactly where she wanted it, he was sure. 'And what does all that gibberish mean?'

Lester shrugged. 'That's what I need to figure out. Sanctum and barrow, I have no clue. Injustice, I think relates to her brother being falsely hung for her murder.'

'So you intend to pursue this after all?'

'I have to, Hayley. I'm so close now.'

'With this medium?'

His affirming nod was like lighting the blue touch paper.

Hayley was silent for a moment, but he knew what was coming. 'What's she like, this medium?'

'She was good. She also got a message from my nan.'

'Was she old or young?

'Mid to late twenties.'

'Of course she is.' Hayley rolled her eyes. 'Attractive?'

Lester sighed. 'Is that relevant?'

Her eyebrows arched.

Usually, he would have played down her age and beauty, but he had grown tired of the constant games they played. 'Yes, she was, but I don't see why that's important.'

'Because it's you, David. You're out on a date with some floozy while you should be here with me, your wife. That's why.'

Jesus! 'You're being melodramatic. First of all, it wasn't a date, and secondly she's not a floozy.'

'Is she more attractive than me?'

Lester laughed. 'I can't believe we're even discussing this. This conversation ends right here.'

'Is she?'

'This line of questioning is not healthy, Hayley. I can't go through this cross-examination every time I have to interact with a member of the opposite sex. Your behaviour is completely irrational. Neurotic.'

'And whose fault is that?'

He sighed, feeling the weight of their marriage fall down around his shoulders for the umpteenth time. 'It's mine. I have never denied that, but you were like this even before the affair. Always jealous of any woman I worked with or spoke to. I couldn't go to female dentists or doctors. You wouldn't even let me watch some films or TV shows if there was someone remotely attractive in it, and God forbid that there's any nudity. I may have had an affair, Hayley, but it was you who drove me to it.'

She stared back at him, at a loss for words, something that he had rarely witnessed.

Lester felt an immediate sense of relief as he spoke the words aloud. Until that moment, he had been ver- bally constipated. He had played out this scenario in his head many times over the years, but his guilt had kept him from doing anything but accept her behaviour as his penance. Now that his words were out there, it felt as though a physical load had been shed.

'I'll sleep on the couch tonight,' he told her, trying to not revel in seeing her dumbstruck.

20:07

That's one small step for mankind, one giant leap for David Lester, he thought to himself as he sat on the sofa reflecting on the evening. The past four hours were a blur. He tried to recall his conversation with Hay- ley, but he struggled to separate what he had actually said from what he was merely thinking. Their ex- changes were often like that, which is why she typically had the upper hand.

Even though it was early, Hayley had taken herself off to bed. Heavy footsteps and the slamming of doors was to be expected. The silence was not. She needed time to process before they could talk like adults. Lester was mentally drained, but his head spun with everything that had gone on and what would happen next with his marriage. Deciding not to dwell on it, he grabbed his laptop. Research was a welcome distrac- tion.

Lester typed 'sanctum of God' into Google and spent the next hour and a half searching through the vari- ous sites, but he found nothing of any relevance. After rubbing his eyes and checking the time, he decided to give it another thirty minutes before trying to get some sleep.

He sighed when the search for barrow returned almost seventy million results, the first of which was a football club in the North of England. The amount of places named Barrow in England alone surprised him. There were few references to wheelbarrows or carts, although several sites mentioned earth mounds, which his instincts drove him to pursue.

It was the second entry, 'People also ask, "What is an English barrow?"' that caught his eye. The words ancient burial place made him tingle with excitement. He carried on reading about how bodies were buried in wooden or stone chambers and covered with mounds of earth. Sometimes stones were erected above or placed on top. The text said that this form of burial was common in England before Christianity. *Could this be what Frances was trying to tell us?*

After finishing the article, Lester Googled barrows in Kent. He was surprised by the amount of ancient sites located in his own county. He found one called Coldrum Long Barrow and scrolled down to a photo of some large stones atop a grass-covered mound, much like the standing stones he had visited in the southwest. There was also an artist's rendition of what it may have looked like when it was created. Not exactly on the same grandeur as the pyramids, but the idea was the same—a tomb for burying chiefs and elders.

He continued searching, this time narrowing his search to Pendlebury Village. As soon as he saw the name Raghlan Coe, he recalled Brotherton mentioning it. When the monochrome image appeared, he recognised it as the stone monument he'd seen at the top of Pendlebury Hill. It was made up of three tall standing stones with a large oval-shaped stone resting on them, like a roof. How they had managed to raise that stone eight feet to sit atop the others all those years ago, he could not even begin to imagine. He continued to study the image, wondering if it had become Frances Coldwell's final resting place.

As he read the article, the prospect of sleep became less and less likely. The visible part of the long barrow was called a dolmen or stone table, a Neolithic tomb. He remembered Brotherton also using the word 'dolmen.' It seemed too much of a coincidence not to be the barrow that Frances had mentioned.

Lester quickly picked up his phone to call Lauren when he noticed the time. 22:11. 'Damn,' he said through clenched teeth, opting to send her a text instead.

Hi Lauren I think I've found the barrow that Frances mentioned. Fancy a trip to the top of Pendlebury Hill tomorrow?

Within seconds, his phone pinged. He snatched it up from the coffee table.

I have readings all day. Tomorrow night any good? x

7 ok?

Lester held the phone in his hand, sensing she would text him straight back.

Perfect its a date x

He sat there looking at her message, trying not to read too much into it. Yes, she'd sent him a kiss, but people often did that without a second thought. He hesitated over his phone's keypad, wondering if he should reply or leave it at that. Whilst he was happy to stay up all night chatting to her, he didn't want to seem over-keen and needy. In the end, he relented and sent a final text, part of him hoping she wouldn't reply, and part of him wishing she would.

See you then

He stared at the phone for a few minutes, knowing that if she was going to reply, it would be almost immediately, but the screen remained black. *Probably for the best*, he thought, swinging his legs up onto the sofa and pulling a blanket over him. He repositioned the cushion beneath his head and nuzzled into it to get comfortable before turning off the light. Time for some much needed sleep.

It was over an hour later when Lester sighed heavily and sat up. Rather than sleep, his mind went round and round about Lauren and Hayley. Since he was wide awake, he decided he could at least be productive.

There had been one thing he'd been meaning to look up since discovering Frances Coldwell earlier that morning, but other distractions had got in the way. If George Coldwell didn't kill his sister, how did bloody shackles manage to get under his bed. He decided to start his search with the police sergeant who had discovered the shackles along with some of her underwear. Something didn't sit right with Lester about the man.

He powered up his laptop once again and searched 'Alfred Dering Kent.' The search returned just under four million results. Feeling weary, like his eyelashes were nails, Lester tried several permutations including name, occupation, location, and date, and it was over half an hour before a combination of Alfred Dering Police Greyton Kent 1900-1950 brought up a site that gave him hope. He clicked on the link from 2017 and opened up the page.

History in the Making as Dering Elected Mayor of Greyton

William Dering made history this week by becoming the fourth successive member of his family to be elected mayor of Greyton. This is the first time four generations of the same family have held office in the United Kingdom. Dering said of his appointment, 'It is truly an honour to carry on what has become a family tradition, started by my great-grandfather over a hundred years ago. Greyton residents know that the Dering name represents honesty and integrity, and I promise to continue serving the people in the manner that they have been accustomed to for the past century.'

Beneath the article were two photos. The first was of William Dering wearing his collar and other regalia. Next to this was a picture of a highly polished mahogany board listing the names of all the Greyton mayors in gold lettering going back to the first in 1837. In the top section, he could see the four Dering mayors.

William Dering	2017 -
Clive Phelps	2007 - 2017
Geoffrey Dering	1990 - 2007
Trevor Gaskill	1978 - 1990
Russell Turner	1962 - 1978
Alfred Dering, Jnr	1937 - 1962
Douglas Penfold	1916 - 1937
Alfred Dering, Snr	1906 - 1916

Lester stroked his chin as he studied the photo. Both the timing and location matched. It could have been a coincidence, but Mayor Alfred Dering must be related to the policeman who had discovered blood-covered shackles under George Coldwell's bed back in 1916. He squinted at the list again, wondering if the policeman was Alfred Dering II.

Even if he had to drive up to the town hall and make an appointment, he decided William Dering would be his next line of enquiry.

Chapter Nineteen

Lester was no stranger to butterflies. They were a constant companion whenever he went home and only ceased to flutter once he had gauged Hayley's mood. Even then, the slightest thing could send them soaring. As he walked up the garden path of number 227 Cobtree Road in Morton Finchley, the butterflies felt more like bats. It was making him nauseous, like he was about to give a big presentation at work.

The night before it had seemed like a good idea. He had searched for Dering online and easily found him—at least he hoped it was him. It was the only W.Dering listed in the BT Phonebook. The enormous detached house surrounded by beautifully maintained gardens was certainly befitting of a mayor.

He hesitated at the front door, knowing that this would probably be the most awkward of all of his house calls. With a deep breath held in his lungs, he rang the doorbell. There was no answer. He exhaled, the temptation to turn and leave growing stronger, but he fought it. He rang again, keeping his finger depressed a little longer. A few seconds later, he saw the silhouette of a broad figure coming towards him through a patterned glass partition. His heart raced inside his chest as he stepped back.

The door swung inwards, and Lester immediately recognised the steely-haired man from his photos in *Kent Online*, although his stern expression, silk dressing gown, and slippers were less familiar. The man looked Lester up and down.

'Can I help you?' he asked, the customary smile he'd worn in his photos absent.

'Mayor Dering?'

'Yes.'

'My name is David Lester,' he said, surprised by how steady his voice sounded. The bats in his stomach had multiplied. 'I'm researching the disappearance of Frances Coldwell and wanted to confirm if your grandfather was the same Alfred Dering who investigated the case back in 1916?'

Those unyielding eyes narrowed to slits. 'Can I see some identification?'

'I'm not the police,' Lester told him, 'or a reporter. I'm just trying to get to the bottom of a missing persons case that appears to have involved your grandfather.'

Dering frowned at him, one hand still on the door as though he might close it any moment. 'My grandfather has been dead for over sixty years. What possible motive would you have for going over such an old case?'

'Some new evidence has recently come to light. We believe that an innocent man was convicted of Miss Coldwell's murder, and we are close to discovering where her body is buried.'

'Don't you have enough current murders to investigate?' Dering hissed through clenched teeth.

Lester shifted his weight from one foot to the other and offered a weak smile. 'I'm not the police.'

'Then who the hell are you, and what business is this of yours?'

'I just want to find justice for Frances Coldwell and her brother, George. I believe someone got away with her murder, and I'm just trying to right a wrong.'

Their eyes locked momentarily, and Lester was certain Dering could hear him swallow nervously.

'Let me make something crystal clear to you, Mr. Lester. My grandfather was awarded the King's Medal for his exemplary work in the police force. This honour led to him becoming the second mayor in our family. The second of four, I might add. I would hate to have the Dering name defiled just because you read too many Hardy Boys novels as a kid.'

Lester went to speak but only got as far as opening his mouth.

'Rest assured, I will do whatever is necessary to safeguard it,' Dering said pointedly, the veins bulging in his reddening face.

'Wow, that sounded like a threat.'

For an instant, he thought the older man was going to spit at him or come out and hit him, but instead, he slammed the front door, the glass shaking in its frame.

Lester hurried down the driveway, feeling justified in his nervousness. Mayor Dering was a frightening man. He even made Walker look meek. He opened his car door and slipped behind the wheel, turning his head to look back at the house. Movement in the upstairs window caught his eye. The room was dark, but he couldn't shake the feeling that someone was watching him. If Alfred Dering had been the hero police sergeant that his grandson portrayed him to be, then why had he been so hostile?

The question of what to do next played on his mind. Lester looked at the clock on the dashboard. 8:41. He knew he had to head to work rather than risk being late again. With a sigh of resignation, he pressed the ignition key and slowly pulled away.

11:38

Gray Warren pushed past his father and walked down the long hallway into the kitchen, leaving the stench of stale smoke and alcohol in his wake. He opened the fridge door, grabbed a bottle of beer, and twisted off the lid.

'So tell me, Pa, what's so urgent that I had to rush over here?' he asked, putting the bottle to his lips and throwing back his closely shaven head. His father had called him and told him to come over right away. 'I have a situation that I need you to take care of,' he'd said. His father was always being cryptic.

'Rush? I called you three hours ago. Luckily it wasn't because I was having a heart attack.'

Warren looked towards the ceiling and took another swig of beer.

'There was a man here earlier. He said his name was David Lester, and he was asking questions about your great-grandfather. He said he's investigating the Coldwell girl's murder.'

'So?' When he was old enough, his dad had told him the family secrets, like his father did before him, and his father before him. It was the one thing that William Dering did that showed he thought of his son as part of the family. Not that it meant anything to Warren.

'So, we don't want people poking around in our past, opening up old wounds and ruining our good name.'

'*Your* good name. I ain't got one, remember?' He wasn't good enough for the Dering name—just their dirty secrets; if he was, his dear ol' pa would've been there when he was growing up. Instead, Warren grew up not knowing who his father even was. When he found out, he'd been so proud. It didn't take Warren long to track him down.

'Nevertheless, the Dering name means something in these parts. Four generations of mayor. Our reputation could be destroyed like that,' he said with a snap of his fingers, 'if people go digging around.'

'It was over a hundred years ago, Pa. What could they possibly find after all this time?'

'How about a body?'

Warren looked down at the bottle in his hand and brought it back up to his lips, draining the final mouthful. 'Don't tell me they've finally found her?'

'That's what this Lester guy was alluding to.'

Warren placed the empty bottle down on the counter, walked over to the fridge, and grabbed another bottle. 'So who is this guy, the filth?'

Dering shook his head. 'He says he's not. Not the police and not a reporter.'

'Then who is he?'

'I don't know, Graham, and, frankly, I don't care. I don't want strangers asking questions about our family.'

Warren laughed. 'I think you're worrying about nothing, Pa. Even if they find her body, what evidence are they going to uncover after a hundred years.'

Dering shrugged and held his hands out. 'I don't know, DNA? They have very sophisticated equipment these days. I don't want to take any chances.'

'Nah, there's no way they'll find anything now,' Warren said, twisting off the cap of his bottle and taking a long swig.

'You think all that time you've spent in police stations makes you some kind of expert?'

Warren took another swig, ignoring the sting of his words. 'I don't know why you're so worried about some murder that happened over a century ago when the biggest threat to your good name is your own son. I'm more of an embarrassment to you, Pa.'

'I'm not ashamed of you, Graham, and I don't blame you for the way you turned out. If anyone, I blame your mother. As lovely as she was, she came from different stock. You were the only good thing to come out of our relationship.'

'It's been a long time since I've been referred to as good. It may even be a first!'

Dering closed his eyes momentarily. 'Do I wish things had been handled differently? Yes, of course I do, but your grandfather took the decision out of my hands.'

'You know something,' Warren said, staring at the bottle in his hand. 'All I've ever wanted was to find a way that I could make you proud of me.'

Dering looked back at him for a moment and smiled. 'There is a way you can make me proud of you, son. Make this Lester guy go away.'

Warren met his gaze with wide eyes. 'What'd you want me to do? Make him disappear?' he asked, before emptying the second bottle of lager.

Dering looked down at his feet and sucked in a deep breath of air.

'Don't get all squeamish on me now, Pa. You called me for a reason.'

The Mayor looked up and expelled his breath in a heavy sigh. 'Just start by giving him a friendly warning,' he said. 'I don't want any more family secrets.'

'Any if he doesn't listen?'

Dering closed his eyes and pinched the bridge of his nose. 'Just make me proud, son.'

18:11

By the time Lester pulled up on his driveway, the butterflies were back with a vengeance. He was aware that his breathing was erratic. Turning the engine off, he sat there for a few minutes, taking deep breaths to calm himself. He looked at the front door, mentally preparing himself for whatever awaited him on the other side.

Nan's right. I shouldn't have to put up with this day after day. He closed his eyes and pictured her face. She was always smiling. Thin, almost translucent skin etched with laughter lines and surrounded by those never-changing tight white curls, like a High Court judge. She always had words of wisdom. She would have told him that his affair was like a cancer, slowly eating away at their marriage until all that was left was a husk. He had spent the past four years prolonging the agony; he had to accept that there was no chance of remission.

Lester's eyes welled, and he blinked rapidly to disperse the tears rather than allow them to spill onto his cheeks as symbols of his failure. *I tried to make amends*, he told himself before slowly opening the car door. He got out and cut across the neat square of lawn to the front door. As he stepped inside the porch, he was surprised at how cold it was and how strangely calm it felt.

He opened the porch door and stepped into the darkness. 'Hayley?'

There was no answer. He turned on the living room lights, then walked up the stairs, looking beyond the landing. Their bedroom door was ajar, but it was dark inside. *Perhaps she's got one of her heads*? He pushed the door open and peered into the gloom. It was empty.

His movement to the bathroom was more hurried, and he threw back the door. Not only was it empty, but it had the smell of detergent. He walked through to his office and looked through the shutters, just in case she was in the garden. He knew it was unlikely as it was about 4° out there. She must have gone out. *She never goes out.*

After checking his phone to make sure he hadn't missed a call or a message, Lester headed downstairs to see if Hayley's car was still in the garage. When he reached the foot of the stairs, he could see a pink Post-It Note on the breakfast bar, and he made a beeline for it. It read simply, *Gone away for a few days. I think we both need some space.*

His whole body sagged as he read the message again and then a third time. He'd been prepared to face the silent treatment or a barrage of questions, even to have things thrown at him, but her total absence was unexpected. As predictable as her behaviour had become, she still had the ability to surprise him.

He leaned up against the breakfast bar to think. Was Hayley just playing games? If so, hide and seek was a new one. She had milked his affair for every drop she could get over the years, knowing that he would do whatever she wanted to appease her. This week, things had not followed that familiar pattern. He wondered if running away was her way to up the ante. Did she expect him to go round to her parent's house to beg her to come home? He knew that's where she would be.

Since meeting Lauren, his whole outlook had changed. It had taken a voice from beyond the grave to make him see the light. Hayley was no good for him. If she wanted him to go and find her, then he would, but only when he was good and ready. Frances Coldwell had been waiting over a hundred years to be found, and she was his priority now.

Lester grabbed a pen and flipped the Post-It Note over. He wrote down two words and left the note there for Hayley to find before grabbing some things and heading to Lauren's.

Chapter Twenty

Hi Lauren, I'm outside when ur ready

Lester sent the WhatsApp message and lowered the driver's window, welcoming the fresh air. It felt pleasantly cold on the back of his throat, and he took a breath, convinced that it was helping fight the nausea that had been building all afternoon.

After tilting the rear-view mirror to face him, he bared his teeth to check there was nothing unsightly wedged between them from lunch. He exhaled into his cupped palm and sniffed, regretting not cleaning his teeth when he had the chance. *What if she tries to kiss me again?*

When the dashboard showed seven o'clock, he frowned. *Where is she?* He looked up at her house. There was a light in the downstairs window. He checked his phone, noting that she had read his message. *Why hadn't she replied? Had she changed her mind? Was she upset because he hadn't returned her X?* His heavy sigh misted the windscreen, and he cleared it with the flat of his hand. It was like being fifteen all over again.

While he waited, he scrolled through his MP4 player for some appropriate music to play on their journey. Some soft rock ballads in the background would give a nice ambiance, although he decided to steer clear of Air Supply, not wishing to bring out the big guns at this early stage. He settled on Foreigner instead, one of his dad's favourites.

As the music played, he closed his eyes and was transported back to the Fox and Goose, trying to line up a shot while his dad strutted around the table to his jukebox selections. Lester smiled as the thick end of the cue became a microphone and he grimaced as his dad sang along out of key. He was an entertainer, comically if not vocally. More like a friend than a father, until he had to be.

He jumped when the car door opened and Lauren slipped into the passenger seat.

'Hey, Dave,' she beamed. 'How are you?' she asked, patting his thigh.

'Hiya. I'm good thanks,' he replied, looking down at her hand. 'How are you?'

'Were you asleep just now?' She leaned in close to him, big round eyes staring back at him.

'No,' he said emphatically. 'I was just . . . lost in the moment.'

'I believe ya, thousands wouldn't.' She giggled, sitting back and fastening her seatbelt. 'I was really glad when you messaged me. I wasn't sure if I'd hear from you again.'

'Really? How come?' He put his foot on the accelerator and slowly pulled away.

'I don't know. This spiritualism stuff can be a bit much for some people. I wasn't a hundred percent sure about you, if I'm honest.'

'No, I'm totally into it. I was sceptical, but you've completely won me over.'

'That's a relief. I thought the whole aura thing might have been too much. It's looking totally different today, by the way. Has something happened since yesterday?'

'Kind of,' he said, looking sideways at her, 'although I don't really want to talk about that at the moment.'

'Of course. I wasn't prying. I just don't ever recall seeing such a drastic transformation in such a short space of time. Not without someone dying!'

'Really?' Lester grinned. 'So what colour am I now?'

Lauren looked him up and down. 'You're like a rainbow. Yesterday it was totally stormy, but today the sun is shining. I can see red and yellow and pink and green. Purple and orange and blue.'

He laughed as she broke into song.

'I can sing a rainbow. Sing a rainbow. Sing a rainbow too.'

Lester's hands left the steering wheel to applaud but quickly returned to straighten the car as they reached a junction.

'Thank you,' Lauren said, bowing as best she could in the confined space. 'From now on, I will call you Rainbowman. Like Rainman but with a bow.'

He laughed. 'I do feel totally different,' he said, breathing in her perfume, 'and I have you to thank for that. The message you gave me from Nan made all the difference.'

'I'm so pleased. That's when this job becomes truly rewarding. It's definitely not about the money.'

'Not when you won't even take any,' he said, slowing on the approach to the roundabout, then speeding up when he saw no one coming.

'So, are you going to tell me what's changed?' Lauren asked.

He looked at her briefly and raised an eyebrow. 'Are you going to tell me what else my nan said?'

'Touché!' She grinned. 'Perhaps we should save it for now.'

Not for the first time, he found Lauren's demeanour refreshing, and he turned to her and smiled, his gaze lingering. She had a natural look, that suggested little or no make-up. There was a subtle sheen to her lips, as though she had just licked them, and her brown eyes drew him in without the need of war paint or false eyelashes. She was not stunningly beautiful but effortlessly pretty, with olive skin and a with a hint of pink in her cheeks.

As Lester navigated the dark, pitted concrete road, he wondered if Lauren was having similar thoughts to his own. Perhaps the subject had not even entered her mind.

'What's the plan for tonight?' Her voice cut through his thoughts and almost made him jump again. In the background, 'I Want to Know What Love Is' was playing, and he smiled when she had sung along to the chorus.

'I discovered that there's a barrow right at the top of this hill.'

'Really? Do you know what a barrow is then?'

'It's basically a burial site. They dig a long chamber and lay a body or several bodies in it and then decorate it with stones or, in this case, a dolmen, which, before you ask, is a stone table. Three standing stones, which are the legs, with a capstone across them, which is the tabletop. It's a memorial.'

'Oh wow, so you think she might be buried there?'

Lester shrugged. 'Who would think to look for a body in a burial site? It'll be interesting to see what you can pick up, although if it is a mass grave, you could be inundated.'

The smile she gave lit up her whole face. 'Sounds exciting. I like a challenge.'

'I still haven't figured out the other part,' he said, breaking hard as something moved across his path and then closing his eyes momentarily when he realised it was just a leaf. *This journey is taking years off my life!*

'Which other part, the sanctum of God bit?'

He nodded.

'I'm guessing that Fran had a religious upbringing, otherwise she wouldn't have mentioned sanctum of God. Doesn't it then follow that she wouldn't be at peace if she was buried in a barrow rather than a church cemetery?'

'That does make sense. I didn't even think of that. Still, I can't help thinking that it's more than just religion keeping her here.'

As they drove past the skid marks in the road, Lester noticed Lauren shiver.

'Are you cold?' he asked.

'No, I just had that feeling that someone had walked over my grave.'

They continued to the top of Pendlebury Hill where the road levelled out and a layby appeared on the left-hand side. Lester pulled into it, parking at the far end.

'It's been a long time since I've been here,' he said, staring out into the darkness. He remained quiet for a moment until her hand reached across to rest on top of his. He turned to face her. 'Did anyone else come through for me last night?'

She met his gaze but remained silent for a moment. 'There was a man standing in the background,' she said. 'I sensed he wanted to come forward, but he may have felt it was not the right time.'

He thought of asking what the man was like, but he already knew. Feeling his eyes begin to well, Lester blinked repeatedly and then closed them tightly, but he couldn't prevent a single tear from escaping. Her mitten-covered hand swept across his cheek to gently mop it up. 'Your father?'

He nodded and then wiped his eyes.

'He's around you. I'm sure he'll come through when he's good and ready,' she said with a soft smile.

'Thank you,' he said, drawing in a deep breath. Her face was close to his, and he fought the urge to lean in and kiss those lips.

'Shall we go?' she asked, only removing her seatbelt when he nodded.

As they stepped out into the cold, Lester zipped up his jacket as far as it would go and blew out a stream of mist. 'It's even colder than last night.'

'That reminds me. I've got something for you,' Lauren said, reaching into her pocket and retrieving something dark and round. She threw it over the bonnet to him, and he caught the end of it as it unravelled.

'Y-you got this for me?' he stuttered, taken aback by her gesture. He raised the scarf to his face and sniffed it.

'Yes, but to wear, not to smell,' Lauren laughed.

He held it to his nose and drew in a deep breath. 'It smells of you. Which is a good thing, by the way.'

They stared at each other a moment before she grinned and said, 'I can't have you dying of hyperthermia out here. I need you.'

He looked into her eyes again, feeling himself fall deeper somehow. 'You do?'

'Yes, to drive me home!'

'Ah,' he let out a nervous chuckle, grateful for her easy humour. 'I knew there'd be an ulterior motive.'

'Just kidding. I took a wild guess that black would be your first choice?'

Lester looked down at his black jacket, jeans, and boots. 'Good call! Thank you, that is so sweet of you.'

'My pleasure, but please stop sniffing it. It's freaky,' she said with a cheeky smile.

He laughed, throwing his new scarf around his neck before securing a knot at the front. He noticed the difference immediately. 'Snug as!'

She beamed at him, then looked around the darkness. 'So, where to?'

Lester locked the car remotely as they started walking into the field beside the layby. 'I don't recall exactly where it is but it was near the top of the hill. My parents used to bring us up here for a picnic and hike, and I'm sure it was close by.' He took out his phone and switched on the Flashlight app. 'And then there was light,' he said, illuminating the area ahead of them.

'So how long was this hike?'

'A whole day, hence the picnic.'

'Hmmm, so theoretically, it could be anywhere up this hill?' Lauren asked.

'I'm pretty sure it was near the top, not far from where we are now.'

Her smile was invisible in the darkness, but he felt it nonetheless. 'Okay, I trust you,' she said, bumping him with her shoulder. 'Let's go find this barrow.'

Though it was a split second, he could feel her warmth permeate his layers. 'Do you trust any strangers that want you to follow them into a field in complete darkness?'

'Not usually, no. I think I'm a pretty good judge of character. You are strange though, especially the scarf sniffing thing, but I think you're harmless enough.'

Lester laughed. As they passed through a gap in the fence and into the field beyond, his attention was suddenly drawn to a blaze of lights behind them, and he turned to see another car pulling into the layby. They continued walking, but he couldn't help but be distracted by the other car. He kept glancing back, twice stumbling into Lauren.

'What do you keep looking at?' she asked.

'There's another car in the layby behind us.'

'So?'

'It just seems a bit unusual.'

'Are your Spidey senses tingling, or are you always this paranoid? Maybe the driver had to make a phone call, check the SatNav or answer the call of nature!'

Lester raised his eyebrows. 'I'm not hanging around for that!' he said, increasing his strides so that she had to run to keep up with him. 'You're probably right, but my instincts are telling me otherwise.'

'It's probably my husband, the butcher.'

He stopped and stared at her with wide eyes, wondering if he had to worry about a jealous man with a cleaver now too.

'I'm just kidding,' she laughed, slapping his arm playfully. 'He's actually in the SAS.'

She giggled as he rolled his eyes and shook his head, but he couldn't ignore his sudden unease thinking she was married. So far the subject had not come up, it was all about him or Frances. Asking 'what does your husband do' just felt too obvious. She wore mittens, so there were no tell-tale signs, but the way she behaved suggested that she was young, free, and single. Either that or she was just an outrageous flirt. He had been burned before, so he decided to tread carefully, at least until *that* question was answered.

'It's dark!' she said after a few minutes of silence.

'Wow, you have amazing powers of observation,' he said, for which he received a punch on the arm. 'Yes, maybe coming up here at night was not my best idea.'

'Can you try and find it on Google Maps?' Lauren suggested.

Lester felt stupid for not thinking of that himself. 'I knew there was a reason I brought you along.'

He found her giggling endearing. He entered Raghlan Coe into the app, surprised by how quickly the image appeared before him.

'It's just over there, apparently,' he said, pointing over to the right.

'Wait!' Lauren grabbed his arm to hold him back and pointed to a yellow sign with the image of a matchstick man falling beneath the words: Danger! Sudden Drop.

Lester scrunched his face up. 'I read something about these cliffs eroding,' he said, suddenly deep in thought. 'Maybe we should come back in the daylight. We can barely see twenty feet ahead of us. I would hate it if you had to use your super powers to speak to me in the future.'

Again she laughed. 'We just need to take it easy.'

'Are you sure? I'll understand if you want to come back another time, like July! We don't need to add to the body count.'

'I'm sure,' she said, grabbing his hand. 'Come on, before I change my mind.'

How can holding someone's hand feel so right? The question whirled in his head as she led him into the darkness.

The moon would have provided ample light for them to navigate in the dark, but it remained hidden behind a thick covering of cloud. The upside was that it kept the temperature above freezing, although it felt vastly colder with the wind chill.

'We're close,' Lester said after a few minutes. 'According to Google Maps, it's directly ahead of us.'

She squeezed his hand excitedly, and he returned the same pressure. The silence was comfortable as they focused on the ground ahead of them, aware that the edge of the chalk cliff and a sheer drop was precariously close by.

'There!' Lauren's voice was a shrill.

At first sight, it looked like a storm cloud that had fallen from the sky, only distinguishable from the blackness due to its lighter colour. But as they drew nearer, it began to take shape: three standing stones with a larger stone laid across the top. It was smaller than Lester remembered.

They continued towards it, their pace increasing steadily until they started jogging, only slowing to a stop when they could reach out and touch the cold stone.

Lauren looked up to the top of it, her head tilted all the way back. 'So this is a barrow?'

'Or dolmen. Like a giant stone milking stall.'

'It's more impressive than I was expecting.'

'The impressive part is its age. They estimate it's four to six thousand years old. Imagine how difficult it would have been to get that capstone up there without a crane or hydraulics.'

He turned to Lauren, but she had closed her eyes and was drawing in long steady breaths. 'I'm just seeing what I can pick up,' she said when he went quiet.

Lester circled the stone monument, illuminating it with his phone. His shoulders sank when he saw graffiti on the other side, someone having carved their name into the sandstone. *Mindless idiots! Why do people have to deface things.* There was also rubbish scattered around and within the stones. Plastic and tin foil containers, empty beer bottles, and some charred wood, the remnants of a fire.

His eyes fell to the grass mound within the dolmen's confines, and for a moment, Lester visualised Frances laying there beneath the earth. Even if Lauren did get a message from her, confirming that she was buried there, what then? They couldn't just get a shovel and start digging. That was a job for the police. He knew he was getting ahead of himself, but trying to convince them, when the time came, wouldn't be easy either—especially without concrete evidence.

He continued walking around the dolmen, marvelling at how long it had endured, defying time and the elements, although, unfortunately, not the vandals. He returned to Lauren, watching her breath cloud like hazy ectoplasm as she meditated. In his flashlight's glow, he saw her cheeks glisten, and when he looked more closely, he could see tears streaming down her face.

'Lauren?'

'Fran is here with us. Her voice is distant, like she's already fading away, but I can make out some of what she's saying. "Chained and imprisoned. Dark. Four days or for days. No food or water. Rodents gnawing on my flesh."' She screwed her face up as though she was trying hard to listen. 'I think she said, "How could I have ever loved this man?"'

'Christ,' Lester said as she wiped her face with her mitten-clad hands. 'That proves that it wasn't her brother.'

'Not unequivocally,' Lauren said, shaking her head. 'She could be referring to her brother just as equally as a lover.'

'I suppose. It just doesn't sound the sort of thing you would say about family.'

'Was she married? Did she have a boyfriend?'

'I don't know. There wasn't a great deal of information about her on the website. Just that she was a twenty-one-year-old nurse who never came home from work one evening. Is she still here? Can you ask?'

'She just came forward briefly and went. They flit in and out. They remind me of hummingbirds.'

He looked back down the hill at the distant wall of chalk, illuminated by the lights of the dual carriageway below it. 'I wonder where he kept her prisoner?'

'I got a sense of restriction and confinement. A stone dwelling rather than a wooden one.'

'I read that these long barrows can have either stone or wooden chambers. But I can't imagine that she would have been kept inside.'

'There's definitely a connection here.'

'By restriction, I assume you mean the shackles?'

Lauren nodded. 'She mentioned chains, which would have allowed some movement but not much.'

'They found blood-covered shackles beneath her brother's bed. They were likely chained to a wall or floor or something. I just can't imagine her brother could have done it.'

'You said he had mental health issues?'

'Apparently so. They used the R word.'

'It's possible that he had some sort of episode that led him to become violent. Maybe something she did triggered it. It could have been something as simple as getting a boyfriend. Who knows?'

Lester shook his head dismissively. 'Perhaps we shouldn't speculate. Shall we come back in the day-light?'

'Definitely. You've got me embroiled in this murder mystery now,' she said with a grin. 'But let me try again to see if I can get her back . . . or anyone else.'

'Sure,' he said, glad that she had suggested it.

She walked around the dolmen, stopping briefly before continuing for a few more paces. When she stopped again, she turned 360 degrees and then sat down on the worn grass track.

'Are you getting a better signal over there?' he asked.

'No, just getting out of the wind. I'm cold.'

He laughed and squatted down beside her, watching her intently as she closed her eyes and lifted her head slightly. He removed his scarf and gently wrapped it around her shoulders, his head rising and falling with her rhythmic breathing.

He shuddered with the cold as he studied her face, only now appreciating the benefit of his scarf. After a few minutes, the softness of her features shifted into a frown, a grimace, and even a snarl before she relaxed and her eyes flickered open.

'Did she come back?'

Lauren shook her head and looked up at him. 'You had a sister?'

Lester's eyes were suddenly wide. 'Katie came through?'

'She called herself Kat. She wanted you to know that she's sorry for leaving you all and hopes you can understand that she couldn't carry on.'

Her words hit him like a brick. He bowed his head and wept, unashamedly, into upturned palms. Shuf-fling over to him, Lauren put an arm around his shoulder and pulled him closer, until his face was cradled against her chest. They remained like that for several minutes until he finally pulled away and stood up, blowing out a sigh through puffed-out cheeks.

'I'm sorry,' Lauren said, getting up and wiping his cheeks with her mittens. 'I knew that was going to be difficult, but she was really insistent.'

'That sounds like Katie,' he managed to say, his voice breaking up. He cleared his throat. 'She was a lot like my nan, although she didn't have her strength, otherwise she'd still be here.'

'I know they say it's the coward's way out, but taking your own life takes real courage.'

'I'll never forgive myself for what happened.'

'You can't blame yourself. She didn't want you to know. She didn't want anyone to know.'

'I should have known. Imagine how miserable her life must have been for her to end it.' Lester bared his teeth. 'I thought we were close. We didn't tell each other everything, but we used to talk. Why couldn't she talk to me, her brother, about what was happening in her life?' Tears filled his eyes again, and he wiped them away with his sleeve.

Lauren's eyes softened as she watched him, and she grabbed his hand. 'She also said she's proud of you.'

He looked round sharply at the medium with narrow eyes.

'It took long enough, but you finally saw the light. She knows only too well how hard it is to see the light when you're blinded by darkness. She says she's around you all the time and that you often sense her.'

His eyebrows arched on his forehead, but he didn't speak. He couldn't.

'You sometimes feel her brush your cheek?'

Slowly his mouth opened to speak, but instead he smiled. 'That's her?' he said eventually. 'She used to do that to wake me up. She would come into my bedroom and trace her finger gently across my cheek because she knew it irritated me. It felt like a spider crawling across my face and sometimes I would just slap my cheek, and it would make her laugh. Once she laughed so hard, she wet herself.'

Lauren smiled softly.

'Now that you mention it, I still have that sensation quite often. Particularly at low points.'

'That's Kat.'

He stared down at the ground, remembering his sister with fondness while a hundred other thoughts entered his head.

'Are you okay?' Lauren asked after a while, her arms so tightly huddled by her side that she looked as though they were bound by invisible rope.

'Yes, thanks to you and your incredible gift. I'm just so overwhelmed by this whole thing. I feel like I've been walking around with my eyes closed my whole life.'

'That's why I do this, to help people. Even if they don't realise they need it.'

'Come on,' he said, taking her hand. 'Let's get you back to the car. I can see you're frozen.'

Lauren didn't argue. She allowed him to lead her back across the field. With the street lights ahead, the way back felt much easier to navigate. As they neared, he could see the silhouette of his Fiesta in the layby, and he lined up a direct route back to it.

They walked in silence for a few minutes until Lauren sidled up close to him, almost knocking him over.

'I'm so cold,' she said, nuzzling into him.

Lester pulled her in closer and rubbed her coat with his hand to try and warm her. When they reached the brow of the hill, he noticed that the other car was still parked behind them. He frowned, wondering what they could be doing, but didn't mention it to Lauren.

They continued walking, his attention locked onto the other vehicle. *I didn't think there were any of these left on the road,* he thought to himself, his eyes fixed on the battered blood-red Ford Capri. When they were just fifty yards away, he squinted, trying to see if anyone was in the driver's seat, but it was too dark. There was a chance that the owner was having a sleep, abiding by the 'Take a break' signs that flashed up on the electronic message boards up and down the dual carriageway. Unconvinced, he kept his gaze on it until he reached his own car and opened the passenger door for Lauren.

'A true gentleman. Who knew?'

She climbed inside and he closed the door before walking around to the driver's side. A quick glance at the windscreen of the other vehicle was enough to tell him that there was someone sitting in the driver's seat. Whether they were asleep or not he couldn't tell, but he still felt uneasy. *I watch too many bloody horror films!*

Lester got in the car and started the engine, stabbing the demister button and sitting back to rub his hands together, his fingers stiff and aching from the cold. As he shifted the car into first gear and pulled away, a blinding white light flooded the interior.

'Jesus,' he said. The vehicle behind had put on its full beam. Lester ducked below the rear-view mirror and wiped his sleeve across the windscreen to clear it faster.

'Where did he come from,' Lauren asked, looking over her shoulder and then shielding her eyes from the intense light.

'It's the same car that pulled in when we arrived,' he said as he turned onto the dual carriageway.

He watched in his rear-view mirror as the other car sped up to catch them. He could hear the engine roar and see the trail of white smoke left in its wake.

'Why are you so fascinated by this car?' Lauren asked.

He looked at her, their eyes meeting for an instant. 'You don't find it a bit strange that he turned up and left at exactly the same time as we did?'

She shrugged. 'It's probably just a coincidence.'

'Let's find out.'

Lester pushed down on the accelerator pedal and watched anxiously as the Capri sped up to maintain a distance of twenty feet behind them. Heart racing, he slowed slightly to pass a speed camera. As soon as they were beyond its range, he sped up to ninety miles per hour, closing his eyes momentarily when the Capri effortlessly matched them for speed.

'Still think it's a coincidence?' he asked as they came up to the roundabout at the top of the hill.

He slammed his foot on the brake as a lorry suddenly appeared to his right. The Capri changed lanes, drawing up beside him. He cast a sidelong glance through the passenger window, but the windows were tinted. All he could see was the silhouette of a head turned his way. Once the lorry had passed, Lester entered the roundabout in the inside lane.

'Okay, maybe you have a point,' Lauren conceded, her voice sounding strained, as the other vehicle circled the roundabout, sticking beside them like they were attached.

His grip tightened on the wheel. 'It's not your husband, is it?'

'It can't be,' Lauren said, clenching her mitten-covered fists. 'I'm not actually married.'

He allowed himself a smile, but it faded when he spotted their exit approaching. Panic surged through him. They were trapped on the inside lane. *He's not going to let me get off this roundabout!*

Lester floored the accelerator and shook his head as the other vehicle quickly caught up with them. He looked across, getting an eerie feeling that the driver was grinning behind that tinted window. As they reached eighty miles per hour, the Capri matched their speed, and despite struggling to stay in his lane, Lester pushed even faster.

'Hold on,' he warned, his eyes darting from the exit up ahead to the car beside him.

Before Lauren could ask why, Lester hit the brake hard and swung his vehicle into the space that opened up behind the Capri, its driver failing to react in time. Their turnoff appeared on the left, but he continued following the other vehicle until they had almost passed the exit. At the last possible moment, he veered hard to the left.

Lauren screamed in sync with the screeching of tyres as the centripetal force of the turn yanked her towards him. Lester gritted his teeth as he dropped down to second gear and steered the Fiesta away from the kerb.

'Sorry,' he said as she hauled herself upright with the help of her seatbelt.

Lester looked in his wing mirror to see that the Capri had pulled over just beyond the turning. He kept his eye on it, expecting it to reverse back and give chase. To his surprise, the driver got out and leaned back against his vehicle. He lit up a cigarette and watched as their taillights shrank into the distance.

'Wow, that was a bit scary!' Lauren said as he slowed to meet the speed limit.

Lester nodded. 'It seems someone doesn't want us poking around.'

Chapter Twenty-One

'You're quiet, Rainbowman,' Lauren said, her hand reaching out to rest on his thigh once again.

Lester raised a smile, his heart rate finally coming down after that chase. 'Sorry. My head is literally spinning. I'm still trying to process even seeing a ghost, and it seems that every day since then, something even more incredulous has happened.'

'You mean Kat?'

Lester shook his head, the guilt threatening to overtake him all over again. 'I know it sounds awful, but I've kind of pushed Katie to the back of my mind. It's almost like she didn't exist.'

'That's just your way of dealing with what happened. It's normal.'

He nodded. 'I know. I've psychoanalysed myself many times. Out of sight equals out of my mind, right? By pushing Katie from my thoughts, I don't have to deal with my own guilt.'

'She didn't want anyone to know. That's what she told me.'

'Why though? She could have changed schools! She could have dropped out! Anything would have been better than suicide!'

Lauren was quiet at his outburst, and he glanced over.'Sorry, I wasn't shouting at you.'

'I know. You're angry and frustrated.'

'It was all so unnecessary,' Lester said, running a hand over his head. 'I know it's not easy to talk when you're in the middle of these things, but if people just opened up, I think they would feel instantly relieved, just getting it out there. Bottling it up, thinking you're alone and helpless is just so wrong. No one should feel like that. I'll bet there are hundreds, maybe thousands, of people just like Katie who are going through something similar right now. I just want to shake them all!'

'I know what you mean. I often have to help them on the other side. When they take their own lives, it's not a natural passage over to the spiritual plane. They get lost in between the two worlds.'

'Was Katie okay?'

Lauren nodded. 'Yes, somehow she made it. I wouldn't be surprised if your nan went and dragged her over.'

'She was that type of person, all right. She would never have allowed it to happen in the first place.'

'It's easy to say that in hindsight, but our lives are so busy that we barely manage to keep on top of what's going on with ourselves, let alone anyone else.'

'Exactly. We never seem to have time for people anymore.'

'And yet here you are, trying to help a complete stranger.'

'For all the good it's done. It's cost me my marriage, almost cost me my job, and as for my sanity . . .'

'Long gone!'

Lester laughed.

She grinned at him, lightly punching him on the arm. 'That's more like it!'

'I needed that. It's so nice being around you. I can just be myself. There's no pretence. It's not draining.'

'This is your wife you're talking about?'

He nodded. 'I'm sure my nan has filled you in with the gory details.'

'Not really, but I get the gist of what's happened from snippets here and there. She sounds like a piece of work.'

'That's a polite way of putting it. Even if nothing else comes of our investigation, I will always be grateful to Frances for opening my eyes and making me see what everyone else has been able to see for years.'

'So, in a way, you're helping each other.'

'Yes, although I don't think that was her intention. I think she was trying to kill me. Like that nutcase back there,' he said, gesturing with his thumb back towards Pendlebury Hill.

'You really think that he was after us?'

His eyebrows raised involuntarily. 'You don't?'

Lauren looked back at him blankly.

'He was toying with us.'

'I just thought he was one of those boy racers who has to try and outrun anyone he sees as a challenge.'

Lester turned to face her as they pulled up to the roundabout at the bottom of the dual carriageway. 'Why would he see me as a challenge?'

'I don't know.' She shrugged. 'Because you're out with a stunning brunette and he's not?'

'Ah, so you *do* have hair under there. I was beginning to wonder.'

She punched his arm, and he pretended to be mortally wounded. 'We lose forty to fifty percent of our body heat through our heads.'

Lester shook his head as he cut across the roundabout and took the turning to Meadowhurst.

'No?'

'That's a myth. It's more like ten percent. It's all about the ratio of your head compared to the rest of your body.'

Lauren grabbed the bobble on top of her hat and pulled it off to reveal dishevelled hair, which fell down around her shoulders, framing her face.

'Perhaps you should put it back on,' he said with a grin. 'Now I know the real reason you're wearing it.'

She punched him in the same spot again and removed her mittens before combing her hair back with slender fingers. His eyes widened as he saw her properly for the first time. He looked away when she caught him staring.

'Have you seen your hair?' Lauren asked. 'Do you remember Jedward?'

He looked up at the rear-view mirror and his jaw dropped open. 'Bloody wind!' he said, trying to flatten it as best he could. 'You didn't think to mention it earlier?'

'Where's the fun in that? Perhaps that's what the guy in the Capri was trying to tell you,' she laughed.

Lester shook his head slowly.

'Seriously though, if by some miracle that guy wasn't simply jealous of you having a gorgeous brunette beside you, why would he be trying to stop you? This is a hundred-year-old investigation. Who would even care about it now? Who would even know you're investigating to begin with?'

Lester looked at her, unable to keep the concern from his face. 'I tracked down the policeman's grandson, the one who arrested Frances's brother. I went and visited him this morning. You'll never guess who it is.'

'No wonder your head is spinning. I can't keep up with what's going on in your world. So tell me, who is the grandson of this policeman?'

'Mayor Dering.'

Lauren stared back at him with narrow eyes, seemingly unmoved by his revelation.

'Did I say that out loud?' he quipped. 'Perhaps I should have said the current mayor of Greyton. He's the fourth generation of the Dering family to be elected mayor.'

'I was just going to ask why that was relevant, but my little brain has just worked out that this policeman would have been mayor as well?'

'Correct,' Lester said as he pulled up outside her house, checking the rearview mirror again to make sure they weren't being followed.

'Right, so in other words, this could turn out to be a high-profile cover-up?'

'I'm starting to think so. Mayor Dering was not particularly pleased to see me.'

'You don't have enough drama in your life already?'

'Nope. I won't be happy until I have complete and utter chaos.'

Lauren giggled. 'Looks like I'm home,' she said, looking at her house. She unfastened her seatbelt and just sat there looking at him.

What is she waiting for? Am I supposed to make a move? 'So tomorrow we'll go back in daylight? Unless things are getting a bit too . . . interesting,' he asked after the silence started to become awkward.

'I like interesting. What sort of time tomorrow?'

Lester had not thought that far ahead. 'How about eleven and then I'll buy you lunch to say thanks?'

'You've got yourself a date, mister.'

A date? He smiled and then rubbed the corners of his mouth. 'I don't think I've smiled this much in ages. My face is literally hurting.'

Her eyes softened, and he felt the butterflies come back. Though these were decidedly different than the ones he was used to. 'I'm glad to hear it,' she said. 'Sounds like you need it.'

Again the silence verged on the edge of awkwardness until Lauren leaned in and kissed his cheek. She lingered a little longer than a normal peck, and he wondered if she was waiting for him to turn his head towards hers, but he decided against it. Even if he was reading the signs correctly, everything was still too raw to add more complications.

'Goodnight, Rainbowman. See you at eleven.'

'I look forward to it. Goodnight.'

Lester watched her walk up her garden path, making sure she was safely inside with the door closed before driving off. That was one reason for holding back. The other was to see if she would look back before going into the house. She did not disappoint. He drove away feeling a warm glow, as if the aura surrounding him was radiating heat. His cheeks were burning, and he wasn't sure if that was Lauren or the heater. Either way, it felt good.

20:57

Gray Warren sat in the centre of the sofa in the darkened lounge of 17 Braithwaite Drive, a tyre lever laid across his lap. He stared at the porch door, which was visible from the streetlight filtering in through the front door's glass panel. On a small table beside him, an empty bottle of Budweiser stood in a pool of condensation. He contemplated helping himself to another, not knowing how long he would have to wait for Lester to come home. Waiting was not a problem, he had nowhere to be; getting caught for drinking and driving was.

The February cold seeped in through the back door, which clattered constantly against the frame. The wooden structure had fought valiantly against the steel tyre lever but eventually splintered and cracked. Smashing the toughened glass would almost certainly have drawn attention on the quiet estate. It felt like a neighbour watch zone. He had sensed curtains twitching in windows as soon as he'd driven onto the estate, a hole in his exhaust unceremoniously announcing his arrival. For that reason, he decided to park two streets away.

In twenty years of breaking into houses, this had been one of the least challenging. No security, and no one home. He never knew for certain whether the house was occupied or not when he broke in. If it was, one of two things would happen: fight or flight. The occupant would either back away, hands aloft, or they would come at him. That's when the tyre lever came in handy.

Warren got up, walked over to the fridge, and opened it. He grabbed another Budweiser and scanned the fridge's contents, but there was nothing he fancied. He would grab a bite on the way home. Instead, he put the bottle cap against the edge of the work surface and hit it with his fist. The metal cap fell to the floor with a piece of Formica and he headed back to the sofa, stopping halfway when he saw lights coming towards him. A smile crept onto his face as the Ford Fiesta pulled up in the driveway, and he picked up the tyre lever again, adrenaline beginning to course through his veins.

After a minute, the lights reversed out of the drive. With a sigh, he finished his beer and left. He'd get David Lester later.

Chapter Twenty-Two

The swirls of Artex were barely visible as Lester lay in the darkness, staring at the ceiling. Not wanting to give in to Hayley's unspoken demands, he'd gone back to his mum's house. Hayley would be beside herself by now—he always chased her when she ran away. Not this time. She had to get used to life without him. His decision was made.

It felt like he had been awake for hours, and he questioned if he had slept at all. The past week had been so exhausting that he was left physically and mentally drained, and despite struggling to keep his eyes open, sleep seemed a luxury beyond his reach.

Lying there, looking at his old pictures on the wall, Lester was transported back twelve years to when he moved out to buy a house with Hayley. The sadness washed over him like wave. Life was a bit like Snakes and Ladders. You can progress through it, climbing ladders here and there, but landing on one of those snakes could send you right back to the beginning and then you had to start all over again. It wasn't quite that bad, he hadn't lost everything, but he had decided to walk away from the house and leave everything to Hayley, still feeling as though he owed her.

Had he been too impetuous in leaving Hayley? *For better or worse!* Those words reverberated inside his head, and he closed his eyes tightly. How many times had he criticised other couples who had divorced without really trying, and here he was throwing in the towel when he should have been getting back on his feet and preparing to go a few more rounds?

In truth, he felt sorry for Hayley. A broken marriage was the latest in a string of failed relationships courtesy of cheating partners. No wonder she had trust issues. All he had done was confirm her belief that all men were the same. Did she deserve to be abandoned for a younger woman, like her mother before her? It was a cliché that felt as though it was about to repeat itself.

He pushed Hayley from his thoughts, but his mind still whirled. His attention moved from Lauren, to Frances, to the man who'd pursued them last night, to his faltering career. For an instant, he considered taking sleeping pills, to make it all go away, but that was just a reminder of his sister's painful demise. It seemed there was no escape.

When he heard his mum pottering around downstairs, he knew that it was at least six o'clock and decided to get up.

'So what was the straw that broke the camel's back?' his mum asked as they sat at the kitchen table eating muesli.

'Sorry?'

'What was the final straw? What made you leave the witch?'

Like mother, like daughter, he thought. 'Nan called her a witch as well. Did you know?'

'Where do you think I got it from? I take it you've been to see Lauren then?'

Lester nodded. 'Yes. Like you said, she's very good.'

'So Nana came through?'

'She did. In fact, she was probably the wake-up call I needed.'

'So what did she say that I haven't said a million times?'

'Just that I shouldn't have to put up with it and that I don't owe her anything.'

'So how come you don't listen to me when I tell you that?' she asked, reaching over and slapping the side of his head.

He flattened his hair where her hand had ruffled it. 'I don't know. It was probably because it came from the other side. Ironically, it seemed more real, if that makes sense?'

His mum stared down into her bowl, unable to hold his gaze any longer.

Frowning, another thought came to him. 'You didn't tell Lauren to say what she said . . . did you?'

She looked up at him sharply. 'Of course not, David. I didn't even think you would call her. You've never shown an ounce of interest in that sort of thing before.'

'Perhaps Nan's blunt delivery is exactly what I needed. I don't know really, except that something suddenly clicked and I knew what I had to do.'

'Better late than never, I suppose.'

'I actually feel sorry for Hayley, Mum. She can't help the way that she is any more than I can or you can. She's become that way because of the things that have happened to her during her life.'

'Nonsense.'

'It's not nonsense. The things that happen to us throughout lives mould us, make us who we are. For instance, your fear of mice.'

His mother shuddered and grimaced.

'Have you ever come face to face with a vicious mouse?'

'I know they're not vicious, David. I just don't want them running up my legs and disappearing who knows where.'

'A mouse isn't going to run up your leg in a million years. It will always scurry away in fear.'

She shuddered again. 'Don't say that word!'

'Nan was always terrified of mice. I think you got your fear from her. I doubt if you've ever actually seen one in the fur.'

'Can we talk about something else please?'

'My point is, Hayley thinks all men cheat because her dad cheated on her mum and several of her boyfriends cheated on her. She expected it from me and, possibly, drove me to stray in the end.'

His mum raised an eyebrow at him. 'You had nothing to do with it, of course.'

Lester looked down at the empty bowl before him, unable to escape the guilt that hung on his conscience, no matter how he spun what happened. His mother had probably worked harder than anyone on their wedding, organising the caterers, the cake and doing the flowers herself. She deserved better.

'So what else did Nana say?' his mother asked.

He toyed with the end of his spoon until it clattered noisily against the side of the ceramic bowl. 'I don't know actually. Lauren hasn't filled me in on everything as yet.'

'She's a nice girl that Lauren. A bit cheeky, mind, but you could do a lot worse. And you have.'

'Yes, she's very nice, Mum, but the last thing I want to do is jump out of the frying pan into a bigger one.'

139

'Nice girls like that don't stay single for long.'

'What did I just say, Mum?' Lester asked, tilting his head forward. 'Anyway, what makes you think she's single, even if I was interested?'

'Just a hunch,' she said with a knowing smile as she got up and walked over to the sink with their empty bowls. 'Would you like egg on toast, dear?'

'Better not. I'm having lunch with Lauren later.'

His mum looked round, her eyebrows high on her forehead.

Lester kept from rolling his eyes, barely. 'It's just to say thank you for helping me this week. Don't go buying a hat just yet.'

11:27

'It looks much more impressive during the day,' Lester said, marvelling at the ancient monument. They stood at the summit of Pendlebury Hill. The wind swept unimpeded across the open fields, flattening the tall grass. A few sporadic trees stood hunched, their foliage permanently swept to the west, like crooked old women with hair a flow.

'Shame about the vandalism,' Lauren added, her finger slowly tracing the grooved letters George + Alice that were carved into the standing stones. 'At least paint can be removed.'

Her comment made him smile; they were on the same wavelength. 'The weird thing about vandalism is that sometimes it can be interesting.'

Her glare cried out for elaboration.

'There are some names and dates carved into the masonry in St. Paul's Cathedral, some going back to the eighteenth century. 1709, I believe. I've seen the same at Stone Mountain in Georgia going back to the nineteenth century and even some more recent markings from soldiers in the First World War in Dover Castle. I don't agree with it at all, but I find that more tolerable, if that makes sense?'

'It does, but only when it's a man-made structure.'

'Absolutely. I can't stand to see names carved in trees.'

'Really? I expected you to be more romantic.'

Lester opened his mouth, but he found he didn't have a ready response.

'I'm just kidding,' she giggled. 'I hate that too, although there is one place I find it acceptable.'

'Cave painting?'

'Exactly. There's something romantic about them. Ancient civilisations painting matchstick men and animals. That I can live with.'

'And aliens!'

She frowned, but he just smiled and shook his head. That was a conversation for another time.

'What about Mount Rushmore? Graffiti or a work of art?' Lester challenged.

'It's not graffiti, certainly. Graffiti is usually personal. Someone conveying a message, like this one with George declaring his love for Alice, or just leaving their mark. As much as I would love to see nature left alone, I can't help being in awe of sculptures like Mount Rushmore.'

'I'm with you on that. Mind you, we don't know how old this is, there's no date,' Lester said. 'Would it make it any more acceptable if it said George + Alice 1726 rather than 2024?'

'It would, somehow. Maybe because it would be about a couple who were long since dead.'

'I think you're right. The same is almost true of murders. We romanticise Jack the Ripper and some of the Wild West gunslingers, but if they happened today, they would be horrific.'

Lauren nodded, the bobble bouncing back and forth on her hat. 'I guess it's true what they say, time is a great healer.'

'It's weird to think that there are probably two bodies buried beneath those rocks.'

'Two?'

'At least. Frances and whoever the tomb was originally built for. There could be multiple bodies in there. Who knows what's happened here the past thousands of years!'

'Shall we get started?' she asked.

'Whenever you're ready.'

Lauren opened her handbag and began rummaging around inside. She pulled out a square of material, which she opened into a blanket, placing it on the ground just in front of the dolmen. Next, she took out a candle and forced it into the hardened earth. Lester watched with amusement as she lit it, expecting the flame to go out immediately in this wind, but to his amazement, it merely swayed, like an erotic dancer, shielded from the easterly breeze by one of the stone pillars.

Lauren sat down on the navy blanket and crossed her legs, placing her hands on her knees and closing her eyes. He watched her chest gently rise and fall for a moment, then the calmness in her face seemed to ebb away before his eyes. Those dimpled cheeks that he found adorable appeared to expand and sink into her skull, leaving her looking gaunt. The colour drained from her skin, and the shadows around her eyes darkened, making them appear deep set. When they blinked open, he swore they were green.

'Fran is here, inside me,' Lauren said, but her voice seemed higher, strained. 'She's letting me see through her eyes, showing me the past. Her life as it was.'

Slowly her eyes closed, and Lester frowned, transfixed by the subtle change in Lauren's face. She was still Lauren, but somehow she no longer looked like herself.

'This is beautiful,' Frances said, gazing out over the valley, her eyes drawn to the deep blue river that twisted and turned its way through the lush landscape. 'Can we not venture down there and sit by the water? We could get a boat and just float away somewhere . . . away from all this?'

'You know that is difficult for me at the moment, my darling. That is why we need to keep this love we share between us. The rest of the world is too naïve to understand what we have. The people are not forgiving.'

'Your wife wouldn't understand, you mean?' she said, pulling free from his embrace.

'No. That is why we need to be careful. Until the time is right.'

'But when will the time be right? I keep waiting and waiting until I feel I could burst.'

'Soon, my darling. That much I promise you.'

'And then we can announce it to the world?' Frances asked, her eyes wide and bright once more.

'Of course. Then you can shout it from the clifftops, my darling.'

He grabbed her hands, and they spun around in a circle, and then another, Frances throwing her head back and screaming with joy as they went faster and faster. After several rotations, they dropped to the grass laughing, eventually lying back and enjoying the sun's warmth on their faces.

'Actually, Alfie, we only have about six months more that we can keep up this pretence,' Frances said once she caught her breath.

'I'm not sure we can put a deadline on something of that importance, my darling.'

She sat up and looked down at him, reaching over to brush his silvery curls away from his eyes. Then she brought her hand back to rest on her abdomen, rubbing it in a circular motion. 'We will not have a choice.'

Alfred Dering sat up, his mouth and eyes wide. He stared at her for several moments before asking, 'You are with child?'

'Yes,' she beamed.

He glared at her stomach as though he could see through her flesh. 'How could you allow this to happen?'

'Some things are meant to be, my love,' she said, her hand cupping his chin and tilting his head so that their eyes met. 'Is this not the most wonderful thing imaginable? Is this not what we have been talking about all these months?'

He continued staring back in silence.

'Are you not overwhelmed with happiness?'

'What we spoke of were mere dreams.'

'Is this not then a dream come true?'

'No, Frances! It is too soon. I am not ready. We are not ready,' he said, getting to his feet, his fists clenching as he looked down at the ground. 'How could you do this to me?'

Frances looked up, her mouth agape, her head beginning to shake. 'Alfie? I don't understand. This is all we have ever talked about. Our future together . . . with our family.'

'I have a family. I have a wife and two boys. I have a career! Do you not see how this will ruin me?'

She stood up and walked towards him, her arms reaching out, but he pushed her away.

'You need to get rid of it, Frances. As soon as possible.'

'It?' She shook her head slowly. 'This is our son or daughter, Alfie. Why would you say such a thing?'

'It will be my undoing!' he said, backing away from her. 'Get rid of it, and we can continue as we have been. No one need ever know.'

Her arms crossed in front of her stomach, as though she could protect her child from his words. 'I would know! I don't understand. I thought this is what you wanted?'

'You are no more than a child yourself, Frances. I am old enough to be your father. It is scandalous, do not you see that? It will be the end of my career. My marriage and my family. I will face financial ruin. Public humiliation! You must get rid of it!'

'Please,' she said, stepping towards him once again, but he lashed out, the back of his hand swiping her across the face and making her cry out. She dropped to her knees, tears streaming down her face. 'This was supposed to be one of the happiest day of our lives,' she managed to say.

He squatted down beside her and turned her head to face him. 'We can still be happy together, Frances, but only you and I. Come back and see me when you are rid of that little bastard, and we need never speak of this again.'

Without another word, he stood up and started walking away, not bothering to respond as she called after him.

Lauren's eyes blinked open, and tears trailed down her cheeks.

'Are you okay?' Lester asked. She seemed to look beyond him. 'Lauren?'

Her raised index finger silenced him. 'She's still showing me something,' she said, wiping the tears from her face. 'Another man is comforting her. A big man with a chubby face and long, messy hair. She's lying face down on the bed, and he's sitting on the edge of it, stroking her hair. "Who is he, Fran?" he's asking her over and over. He's agitated. He's getting up and pacing the room, and when she doesn't answer, he starts pounding the wall with the side of his fist. He's threatening to kill him.'

Lauren's head was shaking. 'Fran tells him no and tries to grab his arms, but she accidentally scratches his face. He looks at her as though he's been mortally wounded. His fingertips touch his cheek where her nails raked across his skin. He sees blood and then he turns and leaves.'

At that, Lauren's head slowly dropped forward, her chin almost resting on her chest.

'Lauren? Are you okay?' he asked.

When she didn't answer, he walked over and reached out, his hand hovering above her shoulder.

'Lauren?'

Finally, she looked up, her eyes narrowing at the sight of his hand.

'Sorry. I was about to shake you, but I wasn't sure if you should be disturbed. Are you okay?'

She nodded, a smile gracing her lips.

'You look, dare I say it, as if you've seen a ghost.'

'These interactions really take it out of me. I feel like I've run a marathon,' she said, her voice weary.

'Is she still here?'

Lauren closed her eyes momentarily. 'I can't sense her anymore. Maybe because I've run out of steam.'

'I'm not surprised. Your whole face changed. You didn't look like you anymore.'

'She literally took over my body.'

'Isn't that dangerous?'

'It could be if I wasn't trained to control her.'

'How does that even work?'

'Think of her as a learner driver, controlling the car, steering etc. I have dual control, so I can slam on the brakes if I need to.'

'So what did she say or show you?'

Lauren sighed, seeming to gather her strength, then told him all she'd seen.

'I think it's clear how this must have panned out,' Lester said after she'd finished.

'It's not conclusive yet, but I think you're right. This baby changed everything. From the emotions I felt, I'm almost certain that Fran would have no intentions of getting rid of it. That's probably why he got rid of her.'

'And the big man at the end there, I assume that was her brother, George?'

'Most likely. There was a resemblance.'

'And we saw how he got his face scratched. Not from attacking her, as it was suggested at the time.'

'No, the feelings I got towards this man were just about protecting her.'

Lester was thoughtful for a moment. 'So, Mayor Dering the first is now suspect number one, I would say.'

'Unless he didn't want to get his hands dirty, of course. Men like him seldom do.'

Lester nodded, feeling a sense of anticipation overcome him. They were so close to solving everything. He wanted to continue on but noticed Lauren swaying slightly as though drunk. 'Perhaps we should call it a day?' he suggested.

'I would argue with you, but I don't have the energy.'

He laughed. 'I think you've earned yourself a good meal.'

'I should think so, although you might have to spoon feed me.'

'I don't usually do that until the fifth date,' he joked, but immediately regretted his words.

'You might have to make an exception. I'm dead on my feet . . .' She looked down and clearly realised she was sitting. 'Okay, I'm dead on my arse.'

'Come on,' he said, extending a hand to help her to her feet, 'let's go and eat.'

'Are you sure about this.' Lauren grimaced as she tried to stand, quickly sitting back down again. 'Sorry, my legs have gone to sleep,' she said through gritted teeth, rubbing her legs. 'As long as you're sure it's okay. I don't want you to get in trouble with your wife.'

Lester smiled down at her reassuringly. 'She's no longer an issue. We've kind of split up.'

Lauren's hand covered her mouth as she gazed up at him, her eyes wide. 'I'm sorry. Your nan may have mentioned something, but I didn't want to pry. Wait, it wasn't anything to do with me, was it?'

'No,' Lester said, considering how much to reveal. 'Well, not directly.'

'How then?'

Lester closed his eyes tightly and sucked in a deep breath. He hadn't expected this line of questioning and wasn't prepared with an answer. 'The message you gave me from my nan, telling me that I don't have to put up with it and that I don't owe her anything, made me realise that I *am* just her punch bag. Also, being with you has made me realise how a relationship should be.'

'But we're not together, Dave.'

'Yes, I know that. Of course I know that. What I mean is, just being in your company is so easy, so natural. There's no treading on eggshells. It's nice. Comfortable. I can be myself. With you, there's no pretence. That's how our marriage should be.'

'Oh, so you mean I'm like an old pair of slippers?'

'No, that's not what I mean,' he said, burying his head in his upturned palms. 'This is not going well at all!'

Lauren laughed, and he felt her hand on his ankle. 'I'm just messing with you. I know a little bit more about your situation than I let on.'

His face appeared from behind his hands, his brow furrowed. 'How much more?'

'Put it this way. Your nan's a real chatterbox.'

'She *was*.'

'She still is, Dave,' Lauren said with a knowing smile.

Lester closed his eyes, dreading how much more she knew about him. 'What exactly has she told you about me?'

'Now that would be telling. Come on,' she said, raising her hand for him to take. 'You promised me dinner.'

'I'm pretty sure I only said lunch. A sandwich and a packet of crisps, if you behave, which doesn't seem likely.' He grinned and hauled her to her feet, resisting the urge to pull her in close and kiss those lips. Her pained expression killed the moment, and she danced around on the blanket.

'Is this some sort of bizarre psychic spirit dance?' he asked, amused by her less than graceful moves.

'No, pins and needles,' she replied, stooping to gather the blanket and folding it in half before rolling it up and putting it back in her bag.

As they started back to the car, she reached down and took his hand. 'Just for support, you understand. I'm not trying to hit on you. Your bed isn't even cold yet!'

Cold doesn't even begin to describe it! 'If you say so,' he replied with a wink.

They headed towards the gap in the fence and followed a well-worn path across the field that they hadn't managed to find the night before.

It was cold, the relentless breeze taking the temperature below freezing, but somehow he failed to notice. It was with reluctance that he let go of her hand when they reached the car and divided to go either side of the vehicle. *I've got it bad*, he smiled to himself as he unlocked the car and opened the door.

'How about the Pilgrims Plight in Gatherford?' Lester asked when they were both seated and waiting for the blower to clear the misted windscreen.

'Sounds perfect.'

Lester reached to fasten his seatbelt when the driver's door was pulled opened. His head snapped round, but before he knew what was happening, he was wrenched outside, his feet scrabbling to get a hold on terra firma.

'Wh-what the hell are you doing?' Lester stammered as he was thrust up against the back door of his Fiesta.

Dark, deep-set eyes glared at him from a gaunt face. An ugly circular scar on his cheek, just below his right eye, suggested he had been glassed at some point. It was hard not to stare, but Lester quickly averted his gaze.

'Why are you asking questions about Alfred Dering?' the man asked, his foul breath a nauseating mix of tobacco and alcohol.

Mind racing, Lester looked back at him, his eyes blinking repeatedly. When he didn't immediately answer, the man tightened his grip on his jacket, close to his throat, making speech difficult. He could see the man's right fist clenched by his side, ready to strike.

'Just research,' he managed to say, his face red. He could hear Lauren shouting incoherently as she came running around to intervene, but he raised his hand to stop her. 'It's okay, stay there.'

'Research for what?'

'For me. Only me. It's my own investigation into ghost sightings in this area.'

'Ghost sightings?' The man laughed. 'What, do you think I'm fuckin' stupid or something?'

Lester shook his head as vigorously as the restraint on his neck would allow. 'No, honestly, that's all it is.'

The taller man leaned in closer, his wide eyes locked on Lester's, searching. Cloud after cloud of his vile breath drifted into Lester's face until he felt physically sick.

'That's all we're doing, right?' he said, turning his head as far towards Lauren as he was able.

Lauren nodded under the thug's scrutiny. He studied her momentarily, his eyes looking her up and down, before turning back to Lester. 'I don't give a shit what you're doing,' he snarled. 'Just keep your fuckin' noses out of our business, okay?'

Even though Lester nodded in agreement, the man just kept staring, not letting him go. Then he drove his fist right into Lester's stomach.

The wind knocked from his lungs, and Lester doubled over, dropping to his knees.

'Leave him alone.' Lauren advanced on the man, her hand rising instinctively.

'You leave us alone, or next time I won't ask so nicely,' the man threatened, glaring down at Lester.

He managed to nod his head, still struggling for air.

The tall man grinned, his top lip curling to bare nicotine-stained teeth. Then he kicked Lester in the side of the head, sending him toppling onto the concrete.

As the man walked away, Lauren ran over to him and knelt down. 'Are you okay?'

Lester winced, clutching his stomach. Slowly, he nodded.

'Can't you talk?'

He shook his head, writhing in pain as he fought to breathe. After several seconds, he was able to draw air into his lungs and open his eyes. 'Sorry,' he wheezed. 'I couldn't breathe. I haven't been winded like that since I was at school,' he said with a grimace. 'Looks like we're getting too close for some people's comfort.'

'Time to call it a day?' Lauren asked, her face etched with concern.

'No way! I'm more convinced than ever that there's a cover-up going on here.'

'I'm sure you're right, but is it worth it?'

He looked into her eyes, noting that they glistened with tears. Either she was scared for her own safety or for his. They *had* both been threatened. He wondered if he should continue alone, although he wasn't sure he could without her help.

'I'll totally understand if you don't want any further part in this investigation, Lauren. You don't have to stick around for me.'

'I don't want you to have any further part in this investigation either. Do you know who that was?'

He shook his head. 'One of the Mayor's henchman, I assume.'

'Try Gray Warren.'

Lester looked back at her blankly, wondering if that name should mean something to him.

'You've never heard of him?'

'Should I have?'

'My dad said he's the worst piece of scum he's ever been responsible for. Beyond rehabilitation.'

'Your dad?'

'He's a prison officer at Maidstone. Warren told my dad, off the record, that he's killed people.'

Lester stared at her, wide-eyed. 'He's scared. That's what they say about bullies. They're more scared than the people they pick on, who are usually smaller and weaker.'

She shook her head, the worry in her eyes giving way to determination. 'I'm not sure that's true in this case. I'm not going to let you go up against him. I don't want you joining Fran.'

'It won't come to that. It was just a shot across the bows, to scare us off.'

'Well, it worked!'

'I can't just walk away from this and let someone get away with murder.'

Lauren reached across and took his hands in her own, squeezing them hard as the blood-red Capri shot past them noisily. 'Even if it ends with you getting murdered?'

Chapter Twenty-Three

Lester lay on his old bed, his eyes closed and his hands tucked behind his head. Lauren had pushed pasta around her plate for the better part of twenty minutes during their lunch. She'd clearly been traumatised after their confrontation with Gray Warren. She wondered if they should drop the investigation, but he had no intentions of giving up.

He was blessed, or cursed, with his dad's determination. Whether it was on a challenging DIY issue, a problem at work, or a life decision, he couldn't just walk away as Lauren had suggested. He was genetically built to live by his dad's code: 'accept what you can't change and change what you can't accept.' He could not accept an innocent man's good name being tarnished any more than he could allow someone to get away with murder.

After dropping Lauren off at her house, he wondered if he would ever see her again. There was no 'see you later, call me, or let's catch up next week,' it was just goodbye. A parting handshake that had a finality to it that left him sad. Surely, fighting for justice and sticking to his guns was a good quality, but all he could hear was his nan saying, 'You stubborn fool, you're just like your father.' His nan was probably the stubbornest person he had ever known. She should be proud of him!

When his phone rang, his heart skipped a beat. Despite his bravado around Lauren, he was wary of Gray Warren. He hadn't been aware of him or his reputation but just by looking at the man, he could imagine what he was capable of. He reached for his mobile, hoping it was Lauren, but it was Hayley's name on the display.

'Hello,' he answered.

'David, thank God! Are you okay?' she asked, her words stuttered.

'Yes, why? What's the matter?'

'The house has been broken into.'

Lester sat up quickly, his thoughts immediately turning to Gray Warren. His knuckles turned white around the handset as he envisaged that man invading their home. 'Are you okay?' he asked, listening to her sniffling.

'I've called the police. They're sending someone round. Where are you?'

'Didn't you get my note?' he asked.

'Yes, I read your little note. You didn't expect me to take it seriously, did you?'

He refrained from responding. He had turned over the Post-It Hayley had left him and written, *We're over.*

'I'll be there in half an hour,' he told her, before hanging up.

Lester lay there a moment longer, wondering if he should call Lauren. What if Warren had followed them to her house? From what she'd told him, the man was capable of anything. He thought about it for a moment but decided against it, not wishing to worry her unnecessarily. She was clearly already shaken after their confrontation.

'I'm just popping to see Hayley,' he told his mum with the front door handle in his grasp.

'You're not getting back with her, are you?' she asked, momentarily distracted from the reality show she was watching. 'Don't be taken in by her, David. She's very manipulative.'

'We've had a break-in,' he said, opening the door.

'Gracious! Is she okay?'

'She wasn't at home at the time.'

'Thank heavens for that. She's not exactly my favourite person but I wouldn't want her to come to any harm. So what time do you think you'll be home?'

'I'm not sure. I'll text you.'

He left quickly, knowing that the conversation would continue indefinitely otherwise. He could hear her call, 'Drive carefully, dear,' as he walked to his car.

Lester rubbed his forehead and then massaged his eyes. His headache had been a dull annoyance all afternoon. He squinted as the lights around the room seemed to burn into his pupils. His stomach turned over every time he thought of that man in their house, on the sofa, the centre cushion indented where he had sat. The living room was still hazy from the three cigarettes he had smoked and discarded in an empty beer bottle on the side table. It left a white circle on the varnished surface, reminding him of the scar on Warren's face, as though it were his calling card.

The police forensic team had just left after nearly three hours. He had watched as they took photos and fingerprints while another officer questioned him and Hayley. Nothing had been taken, and the constable had told them there wasn't much they could do without any security footage. Her expression had seemed to suggest that the break-in was their own fault.

As he stood staring at the sofa and envisioned Gray Warren sitting there smirking, he could sense Hayley's eyes boring into him. 'What?'

'Do you know who might have done this?' she asked.

Lester exhaled through pursed lips. 'No,' he said, repeating what he'd said to the constable.

She continued to stare. 'I know when you're lying. You always delay, like you're concocting some bullshit story.'

'I think that's my cue to leave,' he told her and started walking towards the door.

'Don't,' she said, her voice suddenly soft, like her hand on his arm.

He stopped and turned to face her. Her eyes showed a vulnerability that he hadn't seen since they'd lost Carla.

'I don't want to be alone,' she told him.

'I've fixed the back door. Tomorrow I'll get a bolt for it and one for the garden gate.'

'Please, David. I'm scared.'

His nostrils flared as he inhaled, and he held his breath for a moment. 'Okay,' he said against his better judgement.

Her hand glided down his arm to his hand, and her fingers weaving with his own. 'Do you want to come up to bed?' she asked.

Don't be taken in by her, David. She's very manipulative. His mother's words rang in his head, and he pulled his hand away.

Big round eyes glared back at him.

'I think it's best if I sleep on the sofa,' he told her.

'Really? I offer you sex for the first time in four years, and you turn me down?' Her smile was ironic. 'You're fucking someone, aren't you?'

'I'm not doing this, Hayley,' he told her, moving towards the door again. He decided it'd be safer to sleep in the car. There was no telling what she'd do in this mood.

'Who is it? The woman who waited for her husband to go out the other night? Don't tell me, the landlord of the pub was really a landlady? Perhaps it's this ghost you've been obsessing about for the past week? Is that it? Some dead girl is more interesting than your wife?'

Her eyes welled with tears, and Lester thought for a moment before responding. 'There's no one else! It's all in your head, Hayley! That's where it's always been!'

'Was Harmony all in my head?'

'No, she was real enough, but she was the culmination of these arguments. Of you constantly accusing me of cheating.'

She scoffed, swiping the tears from her eyes angrily. 'I might have known it would turn out to be all my fault.'

'I'm not blaming you. Not at all. I have always taken responsibility, even for Carla, but give a dog a bad name . . . After seven years, I just ended up doing what you expected me to.'

'So now you're saying it was the seven-year itch? Shame you couldn't help scratching!'

'It was the very last thing I wanted, Hayley, but it was just so nice to be with someone who wasn't constantly picking a fight or accusing me of God-knows-what.'

'Don't you talk about her in my house.'

Lester held up his hands. 'It is your house,' he said calmly. 'That's one of the things I wanted to discuss with you today. I will sign everything over to you, but I won't continue paying the mortgage. I'm not a complete mug.'

'That's very big of you, David. Is that so you can walk away with a clear conscience?'

'Because it's the right thing to do. The breakdown of our marriage is on me. I'm not about to leave you high and dry.'

'Breakdown? What are you talking about?'

He took a deep breath when he saw the confusion in her eyes, then he walked over to the breakfast bar and picked up the pink Post-It Note and held it aloft. 'Which part of *We're over* don't you get?'

Her head shook as she stared at the note. 'You don't mean that. You're just bluffing.'

'I've tried so hard to make it work, Hayley, but I have to accept that it never will. We're damaged, and that's because of me. And I'm sorry for that.'

'But why? I've forgiven you for what you did. I took you back.'

Lester stifled the urge to laugh, but the twisted smile that formed on his lips was beyond his control. 'You may have taken me back but you've never forgiven me, Hayley. I fucked up and I'm sorry. I'm sorry that I hurt you but if you'd truly forgiven me you wouldn't keep punishing me for it. The constant jibes, the accusations, the suspicion. I can't live with it anymore. It's too hard.'

Hayley's unblinking eyes stared beyond him. 'What if I changed?'

He smiled. 'I don't think it's something you can simply turn off and on. There's no magic button. It's who you are, Hayley.'

'But what if I got hypnotherapy or something? What then?'

Lester shook his head, wondering why she cared so much when she was clearly as unhappy as he was. 'Do you even love me anymore?'

'Yes, of course.'

He looked down at the Post-It Note in his hand, a mix of frustration and sadness swirling inside him. 'You've spent eleven years trying to change me.'

'To make you a better person.'

'Make me a better person?'

'That's not what I meant. I just wanted us to have a better life. You needed a push, David. You lack ambition.'

He nodded. 'Has it made us any happier?'

Black tears continued to stream from her eyes, and she smeared them across her cheeks with the back of her hand. 'I think so.'

'Actually, the last four years have been the worst. Not just because of Carla or what I did, but the new job with more responsibility and longer hours has just led to more questions. More arguments.'

'I'll stop. From now on. I promise.'

'It's too late, Hayley.'

'It's not! If we both try, we can make it work. That's what couples do, right?'

'I've been trying. For eleven years.'

'We owe it to ourselves, to our marriage, to give it another chance, surely. If we love each other, we'll find a way to make it work.'

Lester maintained eye contact but remained silent, realising that this was probably the most pivotal moment in their relationship.

'You do still love me, don't you?' she asked, reaching for the breakfast bar worktop for support, as though the question was a physical burden she couldn't carry.

'I wish I did, Hayley.'

The weight of his words forced her to her knees, and she began sobbing as she knelt there. He had to stop himself from putting his arm around her and telling her it would all be okay, like he had countless times in the past.

'I'm sorry,' he said, but he doubted that she even heard him over her crying.

Pinching his own tears away, Lester turned and reached for the door handle. Before he could open it fully, Hayley rushed over and slammed it shut. She pushed him back against it and started unbuttoning her blouse.

'I know how we can make things go back to the way they were,' she said, slipping her blouse over her shoulders to reveal a white lacy bra. 'Remember when we couldn't keep our hands off each other?'

Lester's gaze lowered to her chest, and he felt a tightness in his jeans. He went to speak, but her hand brushed his thigh and cupped him, and his words were lost. He closed his eyes, enjoying her touch, that familiar squeeze, the way her hand glided up to his zip and toyed with it.

'No,' he said, his eyes glaring back at her. He grabbed her wrist before she could unfasten his zip and pulled it away. 'That's not the answer.'

He grabbed the door handle again, but she threw herself against the door, shaking her head and gazing at him through red-rimmed eyes. 'There must be something I can do?'

Lester looked down at the light grey carpet. The black tear stains around her feet would usually have sent her into a rage, but now they were inconsequential. 'I'm sorry. Please don't make this any worse,' he said, reaching for the door handle, but her weight against it was too much for him.

She folded her arms across her chest.

'Come on, Hayley. We need to let go of each other so we can both move on. Neither of us are happy. Why would you want to prolong this?'

'I still love you,' she whispered, black tears trickling down her cheeks.

'I don't feel loved. I haven't for a long time.'

Hayley closed her eyes tightly, her face twisting as tears flowed uncontrollably. Then she began to sob. With her resolve waning, Lester tried the door again. This time he was able to move her out of the way. He stepped into the porch and immediately opened the front door and out into the welcoming cold.

Slowly, he turned back, expecting further resistance, but Hayley hadn't followed him. He leaned into the porch and called, 'I'll call you in a couple of days to sort things out.'

There was no response, so he closed the door and started walking to his car. When the front door opened again, he turned around in surprise. He saw a flash of light and then felt a searing pain on his forehead.

'Go off to your fucking whore, whoever she is. She's welcome to you!' Hayley screamed from the doorway.

Lester blinked in shock as warm liquid dripped into his eye. When he wiped it away, the tips of his fingers were painted crimson with his blood. At his feet, shards of a shattered Budweiser bottle glinted in the outside light. He looked up incredulously at his wife, but the front door was closed.

The bitch is back, he thought to himself as he staggered over to his car and unlocked it. As he reversed off the drive, the blood seeped from the gash above his eyebrow. It was too dark to see the true extent of his injury, but he could feel the swelling all around it and expected it looked and felt worse than it really was. It was a first for Hayley. She had thrown things before and kicked, punched and even spat at him, but this was by far the most violent she had ever been.

Five minutes from his mum's house, his phone rang. Expecting it to be Hayley, full of remorse, or his mum, wondering where he was, he was totally unprepared to see Lauren's name on the Fiesta's display screen.

'Hi, is everything okay?' he asked.

'It's not too late, is it?'

'No, it's fine. I'm just driving back to Mum's.'

'I'm sorry about lunch. I just got spooked by Gray Warren. I know what a nasty piece of work he is and that he wouldn't have any hesitation in putting either of us in the ground.'

'You don't have to explain, Lauren.'

'But there's something you should know.' Lester thought her voice sounded oddly eager suddenly. 'I called my dad this evening to ask him about Warren. Obviously he doesn't know what we're up to, otherwise I'd never be allowed to talk to you again, but he did tell me Warren used to brag to Dad that he was the mayor's son.'

Lester was shocked silent.

'Dave?'

'Sorry, I wasn't expecting that. I've already been hit by a few curve balls today . . . and one bottle.'

'What?'

'Never mind, it's not important. His involvement makes a lot more sense now.'

'That's not all.' Lauren's voice was almost shrill. 'I've thought a lot about what you said, and I think you're right. We can't let these people get away with murder, and we can't let an innocent man take the blame for it. Even if the Coldwell family aren't around anymore to worry about it.'

'What are you saying?'

'I'm saying that I'm with you on this. We have to complete this investigation. It's our duty. Plus, I like spending time with you.'

Lester couldn't help the grin that lit up his face. 'Sorry, what was that last bit?'

'I said, I like spending time with you,' she repeated in a raised voice.

'I heard you the first time,' he laughed. 'I just wanted to hear it again.'

'You bugger!'

Still laughing, he managed to say, 'Sorry. In all seriousness, as much as I love working with you, I don't want to put you in harm's way.'

'Surely that's my decision.'

Though she couldn't see him, he shook his head. 'Things could get very dangerous going forward, particularly if we are getting too close for the mayor's comfort. Not that I've any intention of speaking to him again, but with Warren on my tail, he'll know anyway. Still, he can't stop me going back to Raghlan Coe, even with threats.'

'Us. He can't stop us,' Lauren insisted.

'Are you sure?'

'It's the right thing to do.'

Lester couldn't help the relief he felt in hearing that. 'So, are you free tomorrow?'

'I have readings most of the day, but I'm free in the evening.'

'Shall I pick you up around seven?'

'I look forward to it.'

'Until then. Sweet dreams, Lauren.'

'Goodnight, Rainbowman.'

Lester swiped the disconnect button and smiled to himself. It had been a monumental day. Breaking up with Hayley, getting Lauren back on his side, and learning about Warren's connection to the mayor were huge wins. It wasn't all positive though. He gingerly touched the wound on his brow, wincing as it throbbed uncomfortably. Glancing in the rear-view mirror, he saw shadows shifting in the darkness, and it occurred to him he might have concussion. *What if I pass out while driving?* He turned up the volume of the MP4 player so that the pulsating bass kept him conscious.

As he turned onto Crawley Lane, he thought he saw something behind him. He leaned forward, squinting into the rear-view mirror, but the night was devoid of all light except the red glow of his taillights. He increased his speed through the ancient woodland, recalling the local myth of how the trees along this stretch of road supposedly closed in on unsuspecting drivers, earning the nickname Creepy Crawley Lane.

Lester's full beam pierced the path ahead, revealing the crooked and gnarled branches that hung down like elongated skeletal fingers, clawing at the roof of his car. The thought made him shudder, and he pushed down harder on the accelerator. He was not easily spooked, but he couldn't shake the sensation that the road was growing narrower. The trees on either side of him seemed to loom closer, almost within touching distance.

Bright white light exploded inside the car. Lester glanced at the rear-view mirror and winced. The vehicle behind was just a few feet away, its full beam illuminating the inside of his Fiesta. *Warren!*

When the intensity of the light diminished slightly, Lester stole a glance in the mirror again. The moment he saw the silhouette of the driver, there was a loud thud, and he was thrust forward, the seatbelt locking and catching him. He floored the accelerator, but Warren matched his speed relentlessly. Another crash threw him forward. This time he felt his car accelerating on its own. Warren's Capri was pushing him from behind. He tried to race away, but the vehicle stuck to him like a trailer. He looked at the dashboard. Seventy-four miles per hour through a dark, country lane.

Hoping to slow Warren down, Lester took his foot off the gas. Sixty-seven miles per hour, sixty-five. His plan appeared to be working. He could see the end of the lane up ahead, his mum's house less than one minute away. Sixty-one miles per hour. His mind whirled as he considered his next move. Warren's engine roared above the sound of Survivor's 'Burning Heart.' Sixty-six miles per hour. His speed was increasing.

When Lester felt his car being forced to the right, he jerked the steering wheel to the left, away from the three-hundred-year-old oak in his headlights. But it was too late. He shut his eyes and braced himself just as he was thrown forward, the crash ringing in his ears.

Then there was darkness.

Chapter Twenty-Four

1:13, Sunday, 4th February

'David? Can you hear me, David?'

Lester felt a firm hand on his shoulder, trying to rouse him. Then he heard his name being called for a third time.

Time to get up already? I can't face school today, Mum, I've barely slept.

'David?'

He vaguely heard the chatter of voices and the crackle of a radio. Through the veil of his eyelids, he could see swirls of blue and red lights. An acidic burning smell was so overwhelming that he could taste it. It made him nauseous.

How much did I have to drink? Is that petrol I can smell?

'David?' The hand on his shoulder shook him more vigorously.

Slowly, he opened his eyes, but the dazzling blur of lights made him turn away. Directly ahead, he could see a tree, a big wide oak, where his bonnet should be. He blinked rapidly, but it failed to clear the image.

'David, we need to get you out.' The woman's voice was calm but assured. 'Do you have any pain any-where?'

He pointed to his forehead.

'Can you move your legs?'

Lester looked down, but he couldn't see them beneath the steering wheel and the deflated airbag, both of which rested on his lap. He wiggled his feet and nodded.

'Good. We're going to try to move your seat back so that we can slide you out.'

He could smell her spicy perfume and see her tattooed wrist, but as he tried to turn to face her, stabbing pains shot through his neck and shoulder. He grimaced.

'Is it your neck?'

He nodded, his teeth still clenched.

'It looks like you hit that tree pretty hard. It's lucky you didn't hit it square on, otherwise I don't think we'd be having this conversation. The engine would have been in your lap.'

Is she allowed to say things like that?

He looked to his left to see that a section of the engine filled most of the passenger side. *She may have a point!* He could sense the woman rummaging around under his seat.

'Gavin, can you pull the seat from behind?' she called.

The backdoor opened, the cold air suddenly noticeable, and then he was aware of hands on the back of his seat. He hissed in pain as his chair was hauled backwards several inches on the metal rails.

'Okay?' she asked.

'I felt that,' Lester told her.

'We should be able to get you out now. I'm just going to lower the seat as much as possible.'

She reached down the side of his seat and started to pump the lever, and he felt the pressure of the steering wheel ease as his seat lowered. 'Gavin?'

Her colleague wandered over and grabbed Lester's upper arm. 'Can you slide towards me, David?'

How do they know my name? Lester gritted his teeth and pushed himself towards the door using the edge of the seat. Strong hands pulled him into the cold night air, where he was able to stand and stretch. His legs felt shaky, threatening to buckle beneath him, but they took his weight.

'How do you feel?' the female paramedic asked.

'Like I've been in a car crash.'

She smiled. 'Let's get you to A&E so that they can give you the once over. Do you need to get any possessions out of your car?'

He shook his head and allowed her to lead him over to the ambulance.

'Mr. Lester?'

He stopped and looked round. It was the same officer who had breathalysed him a little over a week ago.

'Trev?'

The officer frowned momentarily but then came the recognition. 'Right,' he said, pointing his finger at Lester, 'the phantom guy. What was it this time, a werewolf?'

Lester turned away as the policeman mocked him.

'So what happened?' the officer persisted, looking past him to survey the damage to his car.

He was thoughtful for a moment, knowing that ratting on Gray Warren would be like signing is own death sentence. 'A deer,' he replied eventually.

The policeman nodded slowly. 'And how fast were you going?'

'Less than sixty. It's national speed limit down this road.'

The officer's eyes narrowed slightly as he studied Lester. He slowly walked to the rear of the vehicle. 'How did you get those dents in back?'

'Someone rear-ended me in the week.'

'Wow, you've had a busy couple of days, Mr. Lester. You'll understand if I give you another breathalyser test?'

'We can take a blood test at the hospital,' the female paramedic told him. 'We need to get him checked out.'

'It's okay,' Lester told her, glad he declined Hayley's offer of a drink earlier.

05:47

The morning was a blur. Having passed the breathalyser test, the police officer had leaned in and asked, 'So tell me, what really happened?' clearly not buying his 'deer' story, which he simply repeated. So much for 'the truth will set you free.' In this case, the truth will get you killed!

All Lester wanted was to sleep, his mind and body were battered and fatigued. He tried to convince the paramedics that he was fine and that he could walk home, but they persuaded him that he needed to get checked out as he might have internal injuries.

Lester regretted backing down as he sat in A&E. It was almost four hours before they saw him. They took blood samples, x-rays, and a CT scan before giving him the all clear. Apart from some bruising on his chest, where the seatbelt had restrained him, and a sore face from the airbag inflating, his worst injury was the gash on his forehead where the bottle had hit him. He declined stitches and discharged himself, agreeing with the attending paramedics that he was lucky to be alive.

After getting a taxi to his mum's house, he had snuck through the front door and up the stairs just before she got up. Then, fully dressed, he climbed into bed and surrendered to the enticing embrace of sleep.

18:29

'Hello again, Lauren,' his mum said as she opened the front door. 'Perhaps you can talk some sense into him? Has he told you what he's been up to?'

Lauren frowned when she saw him standing there with a torch in his hand and a plaster on his forehead. 'Ouch,' she said, her head tilted slightly. 'How big was the bottle?'

Lester put his finger to his lips until his mother turned around. 'What bottle?'

'I thought it was an animal in the road, but it turned out to be a bottle,' he explained to his mum before turning back to Lauren. 'I crashed my car last night, hence my text.'

Lauren put her hand to her mouth. 'Are you okay? We can postpone.'

He grabbed his jacket and scarf and put them on before shoving the torch into the front pocket of his jeans. 'I'm fine, honestly,' he replied, glaring at his mum. 'Are you sure you're okay to drive? I know you don't like driving at night.'

'I'm okay if someone's with me.'

His mother stood, shaking her head. 'Just like his father. He couldn't be told either.'

'I'm fine, Mum. Please, stop fussing.' He leaned in and kissed her on the cheek. 'I'll see you later. I won't be late.'

'Good. After last night, I won't sleep a wink until you're home.'

He rolled his eyes as he stepped outside and closed the front door behind him. 'It's so much harder the second time around.'

Lauren looked at him with quizzically.

'Living at home. Perhaps it's because you get so used to your independence and doing things your own way that you just feel . . . smothered.'

'Ah, it's nice to have someone worry about you.'

'It's stifling,' he said, before opening the passenger door of her Mini and getting in. It felt strange getting back in a car so soon after the accident. 'I didn't tell her about the bottle because she'd probably report Hayley to the police and I don't want things to get complicated.'

'Lucky it wasn't a couple of inches lower. You could have been blinded.'

He nodded, following her gaze down to the bulge in his jeans.

Lauren giggled. 'Wow, looks like someone's pleased to see me.'

He pulled out his flashlight. 'Sorry to disappoint. This thing's like a portable floodlight. Much better than our phones.'

'We'll be like Mulder and Scully!'

'Definitely. And I brought some tunes, as requested,' he said, handing her his USB memory stick.

'Good, I like those old classics you've been playing.'

Old? I should be offended, Lester thought, putting on his seatbelt and grimacing at the sudden pain in his neck. 'I don't think I've ever been this close to my knees before,' he joked.

'You can put the seat back, silly! My friend Muriel was the last one to sit there. She's five foot nothing.'

He searched around under the seat for the adjustment lever. When he found it, he lifted it up and pushed the seat back as far as it would go. Then he was able to force the torch into his front pocket.

'How's your head,' she asked, wiping the inside windows with her mitten covered hand.

'It's hard to tell at the moment with the swelling.'

'Did you have stitches?'

'No. I think stitches will make the scar more visible.'

Lauren smiled sympathetically. 'Are you sure you want to do this?' she asked, her hand on the gearstick.

Lester thought about her question for a while. After last night, he also had doubts if he should continue investigating, but he was not about to be dictated to by another bully. Lauren had no idea that Gray Warren had broken into his house and run him off the road, and he decided to keep it that way. He was certain she would end her involvement in the investigation if she knew, and he needed her.

Mum's right, I'm just like dad.

'Doing the right thing isn't always easy. It takes courage and conviction. Only a small minority of people stand up for what they believe in, some even giving their lives for their cause, but it's those people who truly make a difference. We've seen it with Martin Luther King, Rosa Parks, and Emily Pankhurst. Where would we be now without these campaigners? Stuck in the dark ages.'

'Wow! I never realised you were so political.' She raised an eyebrow at him. 'You're not planning to give your life for this particular cause, are you?'

'Only for family, which is basically just Mum now.'

'What about friends?'

'I don't have any . . . apart from you, of course.'

'Whoa, let's not get ahead of ourselves.'

Lester looked round in surprise.

'I'm only kidding,' Lauren said, slapping his thigh playfully. 'You're so easy to wind up.'

Lester let out a relieved chuckle. 'I'm not used to all this joviality. And I'm not political. I just have this thing about fairness and justice. Like, is it fair that George Coldwell will forever be condemned for murdering his sister? Is it fair that Frances lies restless for all eternity, and is it fair that her real killer gets away scot-free?'

'That's already the case. Whoever murdered Fran is long gone. We are literally digging up the past here, and I think we just need to be sure that we understand the repercussions of our actions. Are you willing to risk your life for fairness and justice for two people that no one either knows about or cares about?'

'Dering cares, otherwise his bastard son wouldn't have paid us a visit.'

'And that's my concern. I just want you to think seriously before we head off, while there's still time to back out,' she said, her mitten-clad hands grasping the steering wheel.

'I can't, Lauren, but there's no pressure on you. Honestly.'

'I'm with you a hundred percent. I just had to be sure that you were all in. Gray Warren is not someone to be messed with.'

Lester gave an assured nod, and she started the engine, her smile disingenuous as she pulled away. They drove in silence for several minutes until they reached the dual carriageway and began to ascend Pendlebury Hill.

'Is this our first fight?' Lester asked.

'It's not a fight. It's an adult discussion. Probably your first?'

He looked round and caught her smirking.

'You don't know how to take me, do you?' she said.

'I'm still trying to figure you out. It's a big adjustment after Hayley.'

'She really did a number on you, didn't she?'

He nodded. 'I must have done something really bad in a past life. Perhaps you could tell me?' he said with a grin. 'Anyway, we're just going back to Raghlan Coe to communicate with Frances. We're not there to ask questions about the Dering family. Not unless we find out that they buried her there.'

'Even if she is buried there and even if we convince the police to dig her up, it's unlikely there'll be any evidence linking the Dering family to her murder. Not after a century.'

'Who knows what they can do these days with forensics and DNA. Even if we only manage to arrange a proper Christian burial for Frances and allow her to rest in peace, that's something.'

'True,' Lauren agreed.

'In case we do have another run-in though, you did bring a baseball bat, didn't you?'

'Don't even joke about it! I'm terrified, but like you, I'm on a mission. Besides, it looks like you've got a baseball bat in your pocket,' she said, her eyes twinkling.

'You wish!'

They continued up Pendlebury Hill with 'More Than Words' playing on the MP4 and Lauren singing along, often with the wrong lyrics, which Lester found endearing. At the roundabout, she took the first left to head back down the old road. A little over a hundred yards further on, she indicated and pulled into the empty layby. Although neither of them said anything, they were both relieved that Warren's Capri was not waiting for them.

They got out of the car and stepped into the darkness. The temperature was 2 degrees courtesy of dense cloud covering. Lester pulled out the Youngtrend flashlight from his pocket and switched it on.

'Wow! That is bright,' Lauren said.

'It needs to be,' he said, dropping back slightly and shining the torch on her bottom.

'What are you doing?'

'Just admiring the view,' he said with a grin.

She brought her leg up behind her, the heel of her boot just missing him.

'What was that?!' he said, jumping back.

'I call it "the kick back." You never know when you're going to need it.'

'Some kind of martial arts move?' he asked, continuing to back away.

'No, just something I came up with after three years of dance lessons and five years of gymnastics.'

Lester stopped dead. 'You're a gymnast?' he asked.

'Was,' she replied, frowning at his grin.

He looked skywards, put his hands together and cried, 'thank you, God!' for which he received a punch on the top of his arm. 'Ouch! How do you manage to hit the same spot every time?'

'Practice!'

He took her hand, his intention to make her feel safe although it was now evident that she was quite capable of looking after herself. If nothing else, her mitten helped to keep his own hand warm. He was also able to guide her through the gap in the fence and onto the well-worn path that they had missed on their first visit, which led them directly to Raghlan Coe. Lauren was still quieter than usual, and he suspected that she was more worried than she let on.

'How are you doing?' he asked as they started heading downhill through the long grass.

'Okay, just starting to channel spirit.'

'Can you just turn it off and on whenever you like?'

'Pretty much. I have to otherwise they would be around constantly, and I'd never get anything done.'

'How do you do it?'

'It's a bit like when you're watching TV and someone is talking to you; you focus on that person and what they're saying and you block out the TV. Or vice versa if you're a guy!'

'Oi!'

'I'm sure that doesn't apply to you, though, Dave.'

'Sorry, what was that? I was listening to the traffic on the dual carriageway.'

She squeezed his hand, and he laughed. 'I hang on your every word, my dear.'

'Yeah, you all do to begin with, but it never lasts.'

'It sounds like you're talking from bitter experience?'

'No worse than anyone else, I suppose, and nothing like you've had to endure. I bet that's put you off relationships for life?'

'You'd think so, wouldn't you?'

'So it hasn't?'

'Well, who knows what could happen if the right girl came along,' he said with a teasing smile.

He felt his fingers being squeezed again although more gently this time. The mood had changed in that instance, and as they continued down the hill, they began swinging their arms back and forth again like children. He felt a smile reach his face.

He and Katie used to do the exact same thing when they walked to and from the car. It felt like she was there with him. He thought about asking Lauren if she was there, butthe grey stones of Raghlan Coe appeared in the beam of his flashlight, distracting him. They stepped up their pace as though there was a sudden urgency to get there.

'I can sense her already,' Lauren said as they came within fifty yards of the monument. 'She seems to get stronger every time I talk to her.'

'Can you ask her if she's buried here?'

'I'll try. Quick, she's trying to show me something.'

They jogged for the last twenty yards. In the clearing around the stones, Lauren opened her bag and took out her blanket. She laid it on the ground and sat down.

'She's saying, beneath the capstone.'

'What does that—'

Her raised hand silenced him. 'She's walking me through a hospital,' she said, crossing her legs on the blanket. 'We're walking through a narrow corridor with a high ceiling and a shiny polished floor. I can almost smell the disinfectant. She's coming to a big open area with glass doors. It's the reception. She's passing by it, but a voice is calling her back . . .'

'Fran, wait! I have something here for you,' the receptionist yelled after her.

Frances stopped and looked around. 'Something for me? What is it?'

The receptionist handed her a letter and looked up at her expectantly, but she ignored her. It was Alfred's handwriting. With the letter in her hand, she headed to the hospital entrance and slipped out into the warmth of the autumn evening. Several of her colleagues loitered around the entrance, so she walked around the corner, away from prying eyes.

Her heart pounded as she ran her finger under the seal flap and opened it. Surely he was writing to apologise. 'My darling, Frances, I am so sorry for the atrocious way that I reacted. It is, of course, the most wonderful news imaginable.' But what if it was the opposite?

With her heart beating furiously, she slipped the letter from the envelope and unfolded it. She took a deep breath and held it as she read his words.

My darling, Frances, I throw myself at your mercy. My behaviour yesterday was unforgiveable, although I hope that you can find it within your kind heart to do just that. I was naturally surprised when you announced that you were with child, and I fear I may have panicked and reacted monstrously. I would understand if you never wanted to set eyes on me again, but I sincerely hope that you will come tonight to the usual place and give me the opportunity to make amends. I have had time to think, and now I see, as you already knew, that we could have the most glorious future together. Our lives can be blissful once again if only you would have the good grace to forgive my terrible reaction.

Yours eternally,

Alfred.

Frances's hand trembled as she re-read the letter. Tears streamed down her face as she folded it into three and put it back in the envelope.

Concentrating during two surgeries that afternoon was almost impossible. Twice, Dr. Kemper stopped operating to check if she was all right, having handed him the wrong surgical instruments both times, but she managed to contain her excitement until the end of her shift.

Margaret Winter put her head around the door of the operating theatre and waved to her. Frances looked up and whispered something in Dr. Kemper's ear before walking over. He rolled his eyes.

'Are you nearly done?' Margaret asked.

'I'm afraid I could be a while yet. We have a young lad in this evening who was hit by shrapnel in a bomb blast. We have to amputate his leg.'

'I admire your dedication, Fran. In that case, I'll call for you in the morning as normal?'

Frances smiled. 'Goodnight, Maggie. See you tomorrow.

The smile faded as soon as her friend's back was turned. She hated lying to her. It had become a habit over the past three months since the start of her whirlwind affair. Alfred had sworn her to secrecy from the very beginning and even though they had been best friends through school, college, trained at nursing school together, and even ended up working in the same hospital, discretion was paramount. No one could know, at least for the time being.

She returned to the operating theatre and continued assisting the surgeon for a further ten minutes until a relief nurse arrived. In the toilets, just by reception, she removed her nursing cap and quickly applied some makeup before hurrying to her rendezvous. The nights were becoming increasingly darker, and she dreaded the four months that lay ahead, walking to and from work in darkness. The only advantage was that she could stop en route to be with the love of her life.

'Why will you not allow me to change before I come and see you?' she had asked him many times. 'I feel so unattractive.'

'As if that were even possible, my darling. I simply do not wish to arouse suspicion unduly and you coming to my house, all dressed up and looking ravishing, would just get tongues wagging. People around here could not begin to comprehend our love for each other. They are mere peasants with small minds. A young

slip of a thing like you and a family man in my position, I guarantee that they will only jump to vulgar con-

clusions. Let us just maintain the professional pretence and stick to the story that you are simply providing

aftercare treatment following my episode three months ago. I'm sure you understand. I simply cannot be in-

volved in a scandal.'

'As you wish,' Frances replied, her disappointment evident.

'We will be together one day. Our happiness is all that matters.'

It was a promise that he had made many times and reinforcing it regularly was enough to make her

smile, enough to make her forget he was married and had two adult children, both older than she was. None

of that mattered, the age difference, his ailments, his standing in the community. She just wanted to be with

him and, so it seemed, the feeling was mutual.

Pendlebury Manor was situated halfway down the hill. It usually took her about forty minutes to walk

from the hospital although, such was her desire to be with him that she often found herself hurrying down

the hill once she could see the red terra cotta roof tiles through the tops of the perimeter of Thuja trees.

Soon he would tell his wife about them and then she could have him all to herself. She could barely wait.

Breathless and excited, Frances eased to a walking pace. It was then that she became aware of footsteps

behind her. Glancing over her shoulder, she saw the silhouette of a tall, broad man, just visible in the glow

of a street lamp. Her heart raced, and a chill ran down her spine, He seemed to have materialised out of

thin air. There had been no one behind her just a few minutes earlier. She continued down the hill, a grow-

ing unease gnawing at her. She looked round again. He was getting closer, much too close for comfort. She

quickened her pace, her own footsteps suddenly echoing in the silence of the night.

The tempo of the footfalls behind her increased, becoming louder and more urgent. She was running

now, her breaths coming in short, panicked bursts. She resisted the urge to look around, imagining him clos-

ing in on her. When she turned her head, her heart leapt in her throat. He was mere few feet away. She

could see his wild, glaring eyes and flared nostrils. Cars passed them on the road, but no one stopped to

help her. She was on her own. Running for her life. Fear pumping adrenaline into her veins to aid her es-

cape.

Pendlebury Manor loomed ahead, a beacon of hope on the opposite side of the road. She could see the opening of the gravel driveway up ahead. She looked round to make sure the road was clear and stepped off the pavement. Just as her foot hit the concrete, she felt a rush of air from behind as his hands grabbed her shoulders. She screamed, her legs collapsing beneath her, and she fell heavily to the ground, his weight pressing down on her. Despite her pain, she threw back her elbows with all her might, connecting with bone and freeing herself of his grasp.

She scrambled away on all fours before getting to her feet and running to the manor. The pain of her badly gashed knees as the gravel crunched nosily beneath her feet made her wince. It wasn't long before the sound of heavy footsteps began to pound in her head in time with her own heartbeat. The man was relentless. Her legs felt weak, shaky, but the sight of Pendlebury Manor at the end of the driveway drove her on. She willed herself to keep going.

Up ahead, she saw her beloved Alfie waiting for her by the front door. The sight gave her the boost of strength she so desperately needed.

She rushed up the steps to the house, grabbing the handrail for support, and fell into his open arms. As her legs gave way, she felt his strong arms come around her. Finally, she felt safe. Relief washed over her as she wept. She could have stayed like that forever, but he released his hold on her and pushed her away. She stepped back and looked up at him, her eyes questioning.

'I am sorry, my darling. This is not how I intended things to end between us,' he said as she gazed back at him, the word 'end' reverberating inside her head.

'Alfie?' she said, shaking her head as she searched for that familiar loving look in those cold grey eyes.

He looked past her and nodded solemnly. As she turned around, she found herself staring into the face of the man who had chased her. There was a familiarity about him. Her bewildered mind tried to place him but, as she turned back to Alfred, the man's hand swung quickly towards her, hitting her in the side of the head with a wooden object. The instant oblivion was a welcomed relief to her turbulent thoughts as she crumbled to the ground in heap.

'Oh my God!' Lauren's eyes flickered open, her hand covering her mouth.

'What is it?' Lester asked.

She remained quiet, her eyes darting back and forth. It was a few moments before she allowed her hand to fall away and was able to speak. 'It was the man she loved . . . Alfred. He was behind it.'

'What did you see?'

'I saw her running across the road and looking round in fear, probably as you did last week. That's probably the emotional part that is recorded into the fabric of this place, the concrete, the earth, the trees, and played over and over like a video.'

'What was she running from?'

'A man. She seemed to recognise him although she didn't seem to know him.'

'What happened? Did this man kill her?'

Lauren shrugged. 'I don't know. He hit over the head with . . . well, it looked like a truncheon, but I don't think it killed her.'

'That would make sense actually. I told you about my theory, that the policeman who framed her brother actually killed her? Alfred Dering.'

'She called her lover Alfie.'

Lester nodded. 'Father and son. The older Alfred was the first Mayor Dering and the son went on to become the second Mayor Dering, ironically because he supposedly solved the Frances Coldwell murder?'

Lauren took a breath. 'So this whole thing is one big cover up? Even now, over a hundred years later, the Dering family are still trying to cover their tracks.'

'So it seems. I guess after a century has passed, you can assume you've gotten away with it. What they didn't count on was us showing up.'

'I think you really ruffled some Dering feathers. But you're right, we can't let them get away with it. I still don't know exactly what happened to Fran, but I have a feeling it happened further down the hill near where you first saw her. Did you know there was a manor house there?'

Lester shook his head. 'Not that I've heard of. It's so overgrown there, though, that it's impossible to see anything on either side of the road.'

'Maybe it's no longer there, but that's where Fran was running to when you saw her.'

He looked over at the stone monument, his thoughts distant. 'Did you manage to ask her if she's buried here?'

'I didn't get a chance. She just took control and showed me that day in her life. I saw it all as though it was happening to me. I could hear her thoughts, feel her emotions, feel her lungs aching as she ran.'

Lester listened in wide-eyed wonder as Lauren explained all she had seen.

'So, we don't know if it was that knock on the head that killed her?'

'No, but that's when I lost the connection. My instincts are telling me no. We need to find this manor house.'

He nodded. 'And did they look alike, father and son?'

Lauren closed her eyes for a moment. 'I suppose. The younger Alfred had black, slicked back hair and a moustache. Her lover had grey hair and was fuller in the face, but I guess there was a resemblance. The eyes maybe. She did seem to recognise him.'

'Perhaps there was a photo of him in the manor house.'

'Did they have photographs back then?'

He laughed, extending his hand to help her to her feet. 'Yes, Lauren, but not mobile phones.'

'I know that, silly,' she said, punching his arm in exactly the same place once again. 'Although they probably didn't have them when you were born.'

'Hey, I'm not that much older than you,' he said, leaning in until his face was just inches from hers. His eyes locked onto her lips, full and inviting and there for the kissing. It was the perfect moment, but his head urged him to stay focused. He pulled back. 'Should we go and check out this manor house?'

'Okay,' Lauren said with a frown. Was it his imagination, or did she seem disappointed? 'I think we're done in this place. Fran's presence is no longer here.'

Lester picked up her blanket and folded it before handing it to her. They walked back up the hill hand in hand, both lost in thought. *That* moment played over and over in his mind, and he wanted to kick himself for pulling away. He had to find a way to lighten the mood.

'Was it only Frances who came through tonight,' he asked before the silence became awkward.

'Yes. She kind of dominated so no one else got a look in. I didn't even have to meditate to pick her up, she was right there, waiting.'

Lester looked down at the ground, kicking out at some long weeds.

'Were you hoping for a message from your dad or Kat?'

'Or Nan. She seems to like talking to you.'

'She certainly does.'

'It must be like having a super power. Is it?'

Lauren stuck out her bottom lip. 'I've never really thought of it that way, but that's a fun way to look at it.'

'And seeing auras. That's pretty aurasome!'

She groaned.

'You can tell a lot about people before you even speak to them. You know, if they're having a bad day, for instance.'

'I guess so, but, again, I've never even thought about it. I see them all the time but, at the same time, I don't really see them. Do you know what I mean?'

'Sure. You have to focus, right?'

'Exactly!'

'But you noticed mine.'

'Yes, but it was hard not to. It was so gloomy. Probably the same colour as Eeyore's.'

'You know Eeyore's not real, right?'

Lauren raised her fist to punch him but Lester immediately covered the bruised area of his arm with his own hand.

'So what colour is my aura today?'

'Pink.'

'You said that without looking.'

'It's just hard not to notice after the blues the other day.'

'When was it blue?'

'Stop it! You know what I mean.'

He stopped and held her back as she tried to continue walking. 'Remind me, what does pink mean? Am I starting to get in touch with my feminine side?' he joked.

Lauren turned to face him and shrugged.

'Come on.'

'I don't remember,' she said, pulling away from his grasp.

She carried on walking and he hurried to catch up, realising that his signals were confusing her. *I have to put this right*, he told himself as he drew level with her. He went to speak, but as her Mini became visible in the layby, she raced ahead.

'Lauren?' he called after her, struggling to keep up.

She stopped and bowed her head, pausing momentarily before turning to face him. Her sigh was heavy, expelling in a thin white stream cold night air. 'Basically, it means love.'

Chapter Twenty-Five

20:11, Sunday, 4th February

'So, are we going to talk about the elephant in the car?' Lester asked as she drove down Pendlebury Hill.

Lauren's giggle changed the atmosphere instantaneously. 'Do you want to know what colour my aura is?'

'Absolutely!'

'It's also pink.'

Lester turned towards her, his eyes becoming narrow slits.

'Don't look at me like that. It's complicated. You've literally just left your wife, and she sounds like a bit of a psycho. There's already one psycho after us, and I've only known you for a week, Dave. That's a lot of psychos to deal with!'

'But . . . you like me?'

'Yes.'

A feeling he hadn't felt in a long time threatened to overtake him. He couldn't contain the smile on his face. 'Do you love me?'

'What? It's only been a week!'

'I know, but you're all pink.'

'So are you. Does that mean that you love me then?'

'Lauren, until yesterday, I thought you might even be bald underneath that bobble hat.'

'And?'

'And I still couldn't stop thinking about you.'

Lauren grinned. 'And now that you know I've got hair?'

'It's a bonus. When I saw you yesterday, I thought you were stunning. I was lost for words.'

'I thought you were quiet,' she said, dimples appearing in her cheeks. 'By the way, it's the only place I have got hair.'

Lester's lower jaw opened, and he shook his head slowly. 'Don't tell me things like that!'

She giggled while he continued shaking his head. His smile soon faded when he noticed that her speedometer had clocked up two miles.

'Slow down, we're almost there,' he said, looking around to see if anything looked familiar. He pointed to a grass verge on the opposite side of the road. 'Let's park over there?'

Lauren checked her rearview mirror and steered over to the side of the road. She pulled up the hand brake, killed the engine, and then turned to face him. 'Should we just talk about this before we go?'

Lester nodded. 'Okay, cards on the table. I like you, Lauren. Maybe too much, as my aura suggests, but my head is all over the place right now. It's not a rebound thing, that much I do know, but I do need to get my head straight before I start something new. I'm not one of these modern guys who sleeps with you for three months before deciding to date. I was brought up the other way around. I want to get to know you first.'

Her eyes glistened as she smiled softly back at him.

'You are so easy to be around. You make me laugh. You make me smile so much that my face aches. I just don't want to rush into something when everything is so unsettled. It wouldn't be fair to you. Once this investigation is over and once I find a place of my own, then I think I'll be ready to move on, but I don't think it would be a good idea to start anything before then.'

'Thank you,' she said, taking his hand and squeezing it.

'For what?'

'For being honest with me. For not taking advantage of me. Most guys would have swooped in and had their wicked way with me in your shoes.'

'I'm not most guys . . . unfortunately.'

She managed to find that sensitive area on his upper arm with her fist once again.

'Ouch! Every time!'

'That's what comes of having three older brothers,' she said with a wink.

'So, will you wait for me?'

'I'll wait for you, Rainbowman. According to your nan, you're one of the good ones.'

'She can be a little bit biased,' he said, reaching over and taking her other hand. 'I'll make you glad you waited.'

The urge to kiss those lips was so overwhelming that he was almost shaking, like a recovering alcoholic locked in a pub overnight. After what she had just said, he knew she wouldn't have minded, but he didn't want to undermine his whole speech about waiting. It was going to be torturous, but he knew it was the right thing to do.

'Shall we go and crack this case then?' he asked.

'If it means being a step closer to us being together, count me in.'

She squeezed his fingers gently, and he squeezed them back in return. It wasn't on the same level as a kiss, but it was more affection than he'd been shown in years, and it was enough for now.

They both got out of the car through the passenger door and zipped up their jackets simultaneously.

'Where did you see her exactly, can you remember?' Lauren asked as she illuminated the area around them with her mobile phone flashlight. 'I know I've just seen the whole thing replayed in my head, but I was paying more attention to her and the guy chasing her.'

Lester walked off down the hill, shining the flashlight at the road, his eyes scanning the concrete until he saw black tyre marks. 'Over here!' he called to her.

Lauren wandered down to join him, more slowly than usual.

'Are you okay?' he asked, sensing that she was spent.

She nodded, but with a lack of conviction. 'That session up at the rocks really took it out of me. Fran zapped all my energy.'

'We can come back another time. She's been dead over a hundred years. A few more days won't hurt. Honestly, Lauren, there's no rush.'

'We're so close now. I just want to see it through to the end,' she told him, her smile even less convincing.

'Okay, if you're sure,' he said. 'Hopefully this won't take long.'

'So is this where you saw her the other night?'

Lester shook his head. 'I thought so, but these skid marks curl the wrong way to mine. This is probably someone braking for a fox or badger. Let's keep going.'

They walked down the hill, looking along the right-hand side for the gravel pathway that Lauren had seen in her trance, but there was nothing obvious. After almost twenty minutes, he could see that she was struggling.

'Was it definitely on that side?' he asked, pointing to the opposite side of the road.

She nodded. 'Yes. She walked down this pavement to a certain point where she could see the house. That's when she looked back and saw the guy following her.'

'And she continued running?'

'She didn't run, but she was definitely hurrying. Then I could see his gravel driveway over the road and that's when she crossed over and looked back.'

Lester shivered, but not with the cold. It was the thought of what had happened there in 1916.

'Well, it must be around here somewhere. I was watching your speedometer, and it registered two miles right about where we parked.'

Lauren's hand covered her mouth.

'What's wrong?'

'You were going by my speedo?'

'Yes, so?'

'That thing's been broken for ages.'

'Ah. So we have no idea where we are? That kind of makes sense because it felt like we'd travelled too far. I think we have to head back up the hill.'

He could see from Lauren's expression that her mind was willing but her limbs were not. 'Does that mean that the house will be back up the road past where we parked?' she asked, her shoulders sagging when he confirmed with a nod. 'Okay, well, you can give me a piggyback because my legs are done in.'

'That sounds fair.' He stooped down and lifted his arms up from his sides.

'I'm just kidding, silly,' she laughed, swinging her scarf against his head.

'No, you should let me do this for you.'

'Hmmm, I'm not sure I'm that brave.'

'Come on, live a little.'

Lauren was hesitant but eventually came up behind him, put her hands on his shoulders, and jumped up onto his back.

'Jesus!'

'What?'

'You're a lot heavier than you look!' he said, quickly adding, 'just kidding,' when there was no reaction. He handed her the flashlight. 'You're in charge now.'

They began the slow ascent back up the hill, with Lauren occasionally kicking her heels into his thighs and shouting 'giddy up!' This motivated him to run for a few yards, but the novelty quickly wore off, and after half a mile, he was struggling, although he refused to admit as much. The relief of seeing her car up ahead as they rounded the bend was enough of a boost to keep him going.

He crouched down and allowed her to jump down onto the pavement. 'That'll be £20 please, madam,' he said, holding out his hand.

She slapped it, and they laughed. 'You should be paying me.'

'I should be paying you?'

Lauren nodded.

'I should be paying you to let me carry you five miles up a steep hill?'

'Five miles! I doubt if it was even half.'

'It felt like five miles.'

They continued walking up the hill, their hands brushing against each other several times before he took hold of hers. Just five minutes from where they had parked, Lester pointed to the skid marks he had left in the road over a week earlier, the wavy lines signifying the start of his journey.

'The entrance to the manor should be along here somewhere,' Lauren said, shining the flashlight at the dense foliage flanking the road.

Lester followed her back the way they had come, his eyes fixed on the edge of the concrete after discovering that there was a pavement running alongside it hidden beneath the undergrowth. After several yards, he stopped when he noticed a drop in the kerb.

'Over here!' he called, pointing to the pavement. 'I think I've found it.'

She hurried over and handed him the flashlight, which he aimed through a parting in the trees. The area lit up like a football pitch. On the other side of the trees and bushes, there was a narrow clearing and further on a ragged mound, which he estimated to be up to twelve feet high.

'There,' he said, stepping aside so that she could see the area he was illuminating through gap in the foliage. 'Does that look like what Frances showed you?'

'I don't see any manor. It should be right about where that hill is,' Lauren said.

'I suspect that hill was the manor. Now it's just hard core.'

'Hard core?'

'A pile of rubble.'

She stood on her tiptoes for a better look. 'Can we get closer?'

'We might be better coming back during the daylight,' he said, watching as her smile ebbed away. 'Even with this torch, it's still too dark. And too dangerous.'

'But that means waiting until the weekend. I don't think I can wait that long.'

He thought about it for a moment. He was just as keen to solve the mystery, but he knew it wouldn't be easy on the other side of the wall of vegetation.

'Please?'

'Are you sure you're up to it? You were dead on your feet a little while ago.'

'I feel better now. I think I've got my second wind.'

Most of the left side of Pendlebury Way was overgrown with foliage, hiding the chalk cliff face that Lester knew was there, complete with a sheer drop to the quarry two hundred feet below. Because of natural erosion, there were no longer any occupied residences on the hill, apart from the Bridal Falls pub.

'Okay,' he said, shining the torch beam into the foliage to see if they could find a way through.

Even though he was freezing, his body trembling, Lester was grateful that it was winter and that many of the trees had no leaves. It made things a little easier, although finding a gap in the hedgerow was proving challenging in the darkness. The undergrowth was so dense in places that no light was able to penetrate it. He decided to crouch down to find a way through the tree trunks. As he shuffled sideways on his knees, his torchlight gleamed off something. He leaned in closer, brushing dirt and debris from the surface. It was a stone plaque.

Sarah Jane Kendall

Our beloved Princess

14th May 1949 – 14th May 1970

Lester looked up at Lauren. 'This is the exact spot where Sarah Kendall was killed as well.'

'The phantom bride?'

He nodded. 'I know they're related somehow. I just haven't figured out how yet.'

'She died on her twenty-first birthday,' Lauren pointed out. 'What are the odds of that?'

'Three hundred and sixty-five to one,' he replied. 'Actually, I read somewhere that there is a greater risk of dying on your birthday, but I can't remember why. Is it just a coincidence that both Fran and Sarah were exactly the same age when they died here?'

Lauren stared pensively at the memorial for several moments and he wondered if she was trying to connect to Sarah.

He gave the plaque one last look, resolving to help Sarah Kendall when he could. He'd gotten so caught up with Frances, he'd almost forgotten there were two phantoms.

After crawling around on his hands and knees for several minutes, he managed to find a gap big enough for them to squeeze through. He shuffled his body to find the right angle, cursing as gravel dug into his knees, but he knew those stone chippings meant that they were in the right place.

'We can squeeze through here,' he called to Lauren, who was looking for her own gap in the undergrowth.

She walked over and crouched down beside him, looking doubtful. 'Seriously?'

He grinned and gave an affirmative nod. Then he began edging through the narrow gap between two Thuja trees. She giggled as he swore, sharp branches and blackberry thorns scratching at his face and snagging his clothes, but her amusement quickly diminished when it was her turn. She grunted and moaned as the foliage clawed at her woolly hat, pulled her mittens from her hands, and tore her jacket. When Lester laughed at her angry rant, she slapped him hard on the backside.

'Ouch! What was that for?'

'For not talking me out of this,' she growled.

'I tried to, but you are one determined young lady,' he replied, still laughing.

'And what's so funny?'

'You're cute when you're angry.'

They continued crawling a few more yards until they were finally free of the foliage. As soon as they were standing again, Lauren punched him on the arm, managing to find the same spot even in the dark.

'Ouch! I've already got a massive bruise there!'

'Still think I'm cute?'

He nodded. 'Are you okay, though?'

'I'll survive,' she replied, 'although you might not.'

He laughed and shone the beam of his flashlight around the immediate area before highlighting some sandstone chippings to their right. 'I'm guessing this was the gravel driveway, once upon a time.'

'Yes, it looks like it, although a lot less pristine than how I saw it. It's green with algae and overgrown with weeds.'

'That's what a hundred years of neglect can do,' Lester said, raising the light towards the mound of rubble. 'Come on, let's take a closer look.'

She took his hand, and he guided them along the gravel driveway, their footsteps crunching noisily as they navigated their way around large weeds, bushes, and trees that continually blocked their path.

'It's like an obstacle course,' Lauren observed.

Something scurried through the vegetation behind her, and she screamed. 'What was that?'

Lester shone his torch in the direction the noise had come from, but there was no sign of whatever caused it. 'Probably a rabbit or a rat.'

Lauren shuddered. 'Remind me why we're doing this?'

'Not for fame and fortune, that's for sure!'

A few feet ahead, the huge pile of rubble rose before them. It was larger than Lester had first thought, almost twenty feet high in places, much of it covered in ivy, as though Mother Nature was trying to reclaim it. Sections of beige stone wall remained, none more than six feet high, whilst terra cotta roof tiles were visible throughout the mound. As they drew closer, Lauren pointed out the stone steps that Frances had shown her.

'That's where Fran was hit on the head,' she said, letting go of his hand and running up them, almost stumbling in her haste. 'Alfie was waiting here for her, and she came running up and fell into his arms. Then he told her he was sorry but this was the end and pushed her away. That's when his son whacked her on the head. That was the last thing I saw.'

Lester surveyed the area, shining his light slowly around the rubble. He could see remnants of furniture, paintings, crockery, kitchen appliances, and everything that probably would have been in the manor at the time it was destroyed.

'What do you suppose happened to this place?' Lauren asked as he continued to illuminate the debris.

Within the ruin, there was evidence of charred bricks and blackened remains, which he assumed was caused by a fire, but there was no structural shell remaining. The amount of damage suggested something more devastating happened, and judging by all the foliage, including several large trees growing sporadically within the mound, it was some time ago.

'My first guess would have been a fire, but now I wonder if it was bombed in one of the wars. Somewhere at the end of the back garden, there's a hundred to two-hundred-foot drop. It's strange that no one has ever rebuilt it or even looted the place. It looks like there are still some treasures buried in there. Maybe because the cliff will eventually claim the house, they decided not to rebuild and just took the insurance money. If it was even insured to begin with. I doubt we'll ever find out.'

'What about Frances?'

'She might well be here, somewhere. This is where you saw her getting knocked out. It's also where I first saw her. There's a reason we're here. Are you sensing anything?'

'There's a lot of activity around here, but I'm keeping them at bay for now. Let's see what else we can find before I begin.'

'Let's take a look around the back,' Lester said, taking her hand and leading her down the steps, his eyes darting around the rubble to see if there was anything of interest remaining.

A narrow path, a continuation of the driveway, ran all the way around the back of the garden through a mass of overgrown grass and plants that dwarfed them. In some places, the path was impassable, and they had to walk in the field beside it. Lester did his best to suppress his amusement at Lauren's less than graceful strides through the muddy undergrowth. She was definitely a 'girly girl,' with her love of pink, sparkles here and there, and touches of faux fur on her coat sleeves and hood. At least she wore boots, even if they weren't designed for walking through the harsh terrain in which they'd found themselves.

'We need Indiana Jones,' Lauren joked between grumbles about the state of her boots and green marks appearing on her coat. Her loud scream when a bird suddenly shot up into the sky beside her made Lester jump and grasp his chest as though his heart was trying to escape through his ribs. 'Sorry, she said, 'but it's like a jungle out here.'

His heart was still racing when they reached the back garden—an impassable wall of dense foliage that blocked their way forward.

'We're not getting through that,' he told her, his flashlight failing to penetrate the mass of greenery.

Lauren was quiet. He turned around to face her and saw that she was standing with her eyes closed.

'Lauren?' he said.

She held her hand up to silence him, her forehead furrowing in a frown as she concentrated. She remained like that for several minutes, her expressions suggesting pain and anguish. 'Fran's back,' she said eventually, easing herself down into a sitting position.

'Do you want your blanket?' he asked, already anticipating her response and reaching for her handbag.

'There's no time. She's taking control of me again.'

Lester's eyes were instantly wide as Lauren's arm rose up and her finger pointed straight ahead of her, into the undergrowth.

'That's where I died.'

Chapter Twenty-Six

20:43, Sunday, 4th February

Frances woke with a sudden jolt, startled by a thunderous noise. What was that? *Opening her eyes made no difference. It was so dark that she couldn't even see her hand in front of her face. Desperate fingers clawed to remove whatever blindfold or covering was over her eyes, but all she could feel was skin.* Why can't I see?

She began to panic, her breathing coming in short, sharp spurts. Then the sound came again, like a clap of thunder right above her, making her cower into a ball as the ground shook beneath her. Dust and rumble fell onto her head, and she coughed as she inhaled it. There was no siren, but it was reminiscent of the air raid on the All Saints Hospital last year. She remained there, frozen with fear, until the rumbling and the sound of falling debris all around her stopped, and everything became still once more.

Where am I? *The air was dank and suffocating, its earthy scent invading her senses. She felt the ground beneath her where she lay. It was cold and unyielding, a smooth surface littered with gritty fragments, like solid compacted soil. Summoning her courage, she stood up and tried to walk, only to be met with a jarring clank of metal as a sharp tug on her left wrist stopped her. She was cuffed and chained to the wall. Her fingers traced the cold surface of the steel bracelet, rough in places where it was starting to rust. She tried to make her hand as narrow as possible in order to ease the band off, but the metal dug into her flesh just below her thumb. She followed the chainlinks to the wall, splaying her fingers out to brush against the rugged texture of bricks. Then she grabbed the chain and pulled, and then she pulled some more, but the chain stayed as it was.*

Frances sat back down and propped herself up against the wall, her eyes straining in the inky blackness for the faintest trace of any shapes or a sliver of light that might be a doorway. But she couldn't see anything. She had no idea if it was day or night, or if the blow to her head had blinded her. It throbbed, and when she dabbed the area tentatively with her fingertips, she could feel it was swollen. Her left eye also ached and wept constantly, so she suspected her cheekbone was broken or fractured.

How did I end up here? Chained up like . . . a prisoner! *Then she remembered the joy and excitement of reading Alfie's letter, the fear and panic as that man chased her, and then the heartbreaking betrayal of the man she loved. Realisation hit her like a truncheon blow. Alfie had used her and discarded her like some worthless rag doll.* How could he do this to me? To our child? Locked up in the dark like a criminal. *Tears stung her eyes, and she lay down on the earth, sobbing into her folded arms. Her only escape from that cold, dark prison was the oblivion of sleep.*

When she awoke, it was with startled panic. There were no obvious changes in her surroundings, but something had caused her to sit up abruptly. As she listened carefully, she could hear the occasional drop of water echoing through the darkness. But there had been something else. She closed her eyes and concentrated. Even though it made no difference visually, she felt as though she had locked down one of her senses to focus on another.

Then it came, the tiniest patter. Her skin erupted with goosebumps, and she instinctively huddled into a ball, drawing her knees to her chest and holding them there. Rats! *She had attended numerous operations and treated all manner of injuries, bomb victims with limbs hanging by tendrils and gangrene, but the one thing she could not abide was rodents, especially with their freakish hairless tails. Their sounds grew louder until she could hear them scurrying all around her, hundreds of them. The thought of them climbing all over her while she slept made her retch.* I dare not ever close my eyes again!

Still, she couldn't keep her eyes open forever, and eventually Frances faded in and out of sleep, finally awaking to the rumble of her stomach. She was sick with hunger. She had no idea how long she'd been there, or even what day it was. She had already urinated twice. The first time she was in tears, crying with the pain of her bladder threatening to burst. Still she strained to fight it, despite the pain that eventually spread to her lower back, but there was a sudden lapse and she lost control for a second. Moments later she surrendered to the excruciating pain, warm liquid spreading in a pool beneath her. The relief was instantaneous.

Most of her urine soaked into the earth beneath her, but it turned the hard surface into a slushy mess, and her uniform was quickly sodden with mud. The second time, she held back until it was so uncomfortable she had no choice but to relent, doubting that anyone would come for her in time.

The longer she remained there without food and water, the more she realised that she was being left to die. It was not so much the need for self-preservation but for that of her unborn child that she crawled around on the floor, searching for anything that could help her to free herself of those shackles. There was nothing other than tiny round pellets that made the bile rise in her throat. Rat droppings!

She scoured her nurse's uniform, hoping for something, anything. There had been a watch in her pocket, but that was gone, and she doubted it would have done much good anyway. Her shoes, though, brought a spark of hope. She remembered that she had worn the last pair until they had literally fallen apart. There was a thin strip of metal in the sole to provide support. Maybe that was enough to unlock these shackles.

Feeling a small glimmer of hope, Frances removed her right shoe and started bending it back and forth. After several minutes, she realised that this was having no effect and fell back against the wall, frustrated. Her head was spinning from the effort. Even so, she tried again, this time bending the shoe almost in half before bending it back the other way. She tried again, and again, thirty or more times until she felt something give. Her fingers ran across the sole, and she felt a crack in the leather. With renewed vigour, she doubled her efforts, bending and pulling until she felt it coming apart. This time when she checked, she could actually sink her fingers into the tear and feel the smooth, shiny metal within. She grabbed it and pulled, whooping with excitement when the thin metal strip slid out easily.

Immediately, her fingers felt around the cuff for the lock and carefully guided the metal strip towards it. Working blindly was difficult and frustrating, but she remained calm and patient as she tried to force it into the lock. No matter which angle she tried, it would not go in. It was too wide. She tried folding it with her fingers, but it was too sturdy. Even hammering it with the heel of her other shoe made no difference. Overcome with complete and utter hopelessness, she fell forward on the ground and curled into a foetal position.

How long can someone survive without water? *Frances woke with that single thought in her head. She was still unable to assess how long she'd been there but guessed, purely from the number of times she'd needed to defecate, that it was probably around two days and nights.*

She believed the answer to her question was three days. Shorter if walking through a scorching dessert or exerting energy. Longer if she was motionless or cold. At least she had that in her favour.

She estimated that she only had a day left to live then. Two at the most. If no one was coming for her, and she already knew they were not, then she had to take drastic action, make sacrifices in order to survive for the sake of her unborn child. The only solution she could think of was to cut off her hand, but being a nurse, she knew that was not possible. Even if she could saw through the radius with the strip of blunt metal and endure the excruciating pain, she would bleed to death in a matter of hours.

Frances sat back against the wall and licked salty tears from the corners of her mouth. As she sobbed, her chest heaved, and she felt her uniform catch on the rough texture of brick. She turned around and touched it and then immediately began moving the metal strip back and forth against it. After a few moments, she stopped to run her finger along the edge. It was hot and rougher than before. Feeling that spark of hope reignite within her, she rubbed the strip vigorously against the wall until it became too hot to hold. It dropped into her lap, and she waited a few minutes until it was cool enough to pick up once more. The third time, she tore the hem off her dress and wrapped it around her fingers for protection. She had already scraped her knuckles along the brickwork twice and holding the metal strip was making her hands sore.

Hours passed, but Frances persevered. She was getting used to the darkness and was aware that her senses had developed. Her hearing had become more acute, although it only heightened the sound of scurrying rodents. The other negative was that her sense of smell was now overwhelmed with the stench of her own faeces. She had used the same area each time, stretching the chain as far as it would allow so that she could put as much distance between it and her, but it was simply not far enough.

Every so often, Frances would stop and try the metal strip in the keyhole. There was a moment of jubilation when the end fitted for the first time, but she knew she had to keep going. She needed more length before it could trip the lock. Just knowing that she was making progress was enough to keep her motivated. She continually swapped hands and changed the bandage when the old ones were soaked with her blood, but she was running out of hem. She would have to tear up her uniform at some point. That was if she could even move her fingers. They were aching, sore, and bloody from her endeavours. Embedded with thousands of tiny steel splinters that stung like metal thorns.

By the time the metal strip was able to be inserted all the way inside the keyhole, Frances was exhausted. The adrenaline rush drove her on against her body's desire to shut down and rest. She twisted the metal strip back and forth, moving it around inside, but nothing was connecting or catching. Undeterred, she repeated the action over and over, searching for the internal mechanism to open the lock, but it was no use. Frustrated and feeling defeated, she collapsed on the sodden earth and wept herself to sleep.

She was jolted awake from the excruciating pain in her hands. Frances screamed in agony and jumped to her feet, shouting at the rodents that had been gnawing at her bloody fingers. She clenched them into fists and closed her eyes tightly against the searing pain. She wiped away the tears before they reached her mouth, having realised that they did not quench her parched throat but only made her thirstier. Earlier, she had resorted to drinking her own urine, but as she attempted to bring her cupped hands to her lips, the chain on her shackled hand pulled tight and her hands separated. The warm, acrid liquid seeped through her fingers, and she quickly licked her hands, cringing as she did so.

Her legs quivered beneath her, and she moved back against the wall and sat down. She could feel her body shutting down although she knew she couldn't afford to fall asleep again. The rats had tasted her flesh now, and they would be back. She had to get out of that prison of darkness.

After patting the ground to recover the strip of metal, she guided it back into the lock and began twisting and turning it. For more than an hour, she tried it, but eventually she gave up. Her second option was to try and wear down the chain in the same way that she had worn down the metal strip. They were thick, heavy links, and she knew it would not be easy, but it was much better than the alternative, which she tried desperately not to think about.

She worked diligently for over an hour, taking regular breaks and swapping hands whenever she could no longer endure the pain. Her fingers touched the area on the chain that she'd been working on, and her whole body sagged. The surface was scratched, but there seemed to be no reduction in its thickness. It would take days to wear down, and she didn't have that much time. The sense of hopelessness was overwhelming, and she closed her eyes and wept, her thoughts turning to the third and final option.

Frances rested her hand on her stomach and allowed it to circle several times. With only a matter of hours left to live, Frances accepted that she had no other choice. 'I have to do this, for you,' she said, her raspy voice echoing in that empty enclosure.

The simple act of shifting her weight to her right buttock and placing her shackled hand beneath her left buttock took all her energy. She sat upright once again, evenly distributing her weight, and relaxed. It would take between ten and twenty minutes for her hand to go numb, then she would have to perform one of the most difficult tasks of her short life. For once, she was grateful for the darkness—it would shield her from seeing what she was about to do.

Time had lost all meaning. Frances counted up to five hundred, but even that was an effort, and several times she forgot what number she had reached. Delirium was starting to set in. She could no longer feel her hand beneath her, so she knew that her circulation had been cut off. It was a dead weight that she placed palm up on her lap, and with tears streaming down her face, she took the thin metal strip between her thumb and forefinger and rested it at the base of her other thumb. Abductor Pollicis Brevis, *the name suddenly popped into her head. Ironically, it was a question that she had failed in her nursing exam and now she had total recall, not least of all because of the relevance of the word 'abductor.'*

She tried to steady her hand, but it was shaking more and more. Then, after taking a final breath and holding it, she dragged the rough blade across her skin. She was aware of the metal ripping through her flesh, but the pain was masked. Blood oozed from the wound, warm and slippery, as she pulled the metal strip back and forth and pressed down even harder, feeling it sinking deeper into the muscle. This time she could feel more, but it was still tolerable.

She continued cutting, deeper and deeper. By the time she met the resistance of bone, she was screaming from the pain. The sound of her desperate sobs echoed in the darkness. Still no one came. She could feel the throbbing in her hand and managed to slip it beneath her buttocks for another ten minutes. The next part would be the longest and hardest.

Frances's eyes flickered open, and she screamed, quickly standing and flailing her injured arm wildly until the rat let go of her thumb. The thought of those hairy beasts crawling all over her, eating her flesh, made her shudder violently and retch, but nothing came up. Her stomach was empty, as were her bladder and bowels. She had no idea how long she had been asleep, but her thoughts immediately returned to what she needed to do in order to survive.

Once she had found the metal strip at her feet, she began sawing through the bone. The throbbing around her thumb was intensifying with every passing moment, and she shouted through clenched teeth. After ten minutes, she could barely hold the metal strip in her bloody fingers. She could feel that she had made a groove in the bone, but cutting completely through it would take several hours, and she doubted she had that long.

Frances allowed the metal strip to fall from her grasp and then lay down on the ground. Her body curled back into a foetal position, like the child within her. The pain in both hands was slowly ebbing away. She shivered, although she could no longer feel the cold. She could not feel much of anything as she lay there with hundreds of tiny clawed feet crawling towards her. She simply mouthed a prayer to God, asking for divine strength and one more chance to free herself of that prison.

'Lauren?' Lester said softly, a gentle hand on her shoulder. He had stood and watched, a helpless bystander, as she had displayed a multitude of emotions, before rolling onto her side and curling up into a ball. Her eyes opened, red and swollen where she had been crying. 'Are you okay?'

She didn't respond but instead pushed herself back up into a sitting position.

'Lauren?'

'I never awoke,' she said, wiping the tears from her face. 'Those were her final words as she just faded.'

He stepped towards her and opened his arms, ready to embrace her, but she held up a hand.

'It's okay. These are her emotions, not mine. Well, partly mine. I can't help grieve for this poor girl. The suffering she went through in the end.'

'What did you see? You went into a trance and screamed a couple of times, but it looked like you were either in agony or the throes of ecstasy.'

'Unfortunately it wasn't the latter. Frances was chained up somewhere over there,' she said, pointing to the overgrown back garden.

As Lester looked across the thicket, he imagined Frances resting peacefully beyond, like Sleeping Beauty, although he didn't feel worthy of any comparison to Prince Charming astride a noble stead. The garden was almost impenetrable. They would need a chainsaw, strimmer, or machete, although he would have settled for a sword. As keen as he was to fit this piece of the jigsaw puzzle into place, he conceded that it would not be possible without the right equipment.

'I thought it was a cellar at first, but I got the impression that there's an air raid shelter or a coal bunker over there. Her first awareness was of bombs going off, at least that's the feeling I got, and that's consistent with what we saw back there.' She nodded towards the ruins behind them. 'I'm not sure that they intentionally left her there to die or if they were simply unable to free her because they were killed themselves. There were no sirens to warn them, if that's what it was, so they would have had no chance to run down here for cover.'

'Well, that makes things a little less sinister, I suppose. I can't imagine they would have intended to keep her locked up for any length of time in an air raid shelter in the middle of a war. The risks of getting caught would have been too great, and we know that Alfie was keen to keep his sordid affair quiet.'

'Yes, that did strike me as odd. I think they were just keeping her down there until they had decided what to do with her, otherwise they would have just killed her. Like you say, why risk his wife finding her in there? There would have been a huge scandal, and I'm sure he wouldn't have remained mayor too much longer.'

Lester nodded, his eyes transfixed on the undergrowth in front of them. 'It's unlikely that she's still down there, not if Alfie's son planted the chains under her brother's bed.'

'She's not here,' Lauren said, shaking her head adamantly. 'I really felt her strongly up at the top of the hill. She's a lost soul, desperately wanting to be reunited with her unborn baby, but that place is not hallowed ground, not for a Christian. I think the only way that she'll find peace is if we get her reburied in a church. Maybe then she can move on.'

'That's not going to be easy,' Lester said, wondering how he would explain any of this to the police. 'The police thought I was wasting their time before.'

'Can we go?'

He looked into Lauren's eyes. They were almost pleading. 'Of course. Sorry, I forget how much all this takes out of you.'

She smiled weakly. 'Taking on all their emotions is almost as taxing as the energy they use. At least I get to walk away from them when it's over. I just want to go home and have a long soak in a hot bath and a good night's sleep.'

'Of course. You've earned it.'

Sensing her legs might collapse beneath her at any moment, Lester took her hand and guided her back the way they had come while Lauren gave him a brief summary of what Frances had shown her. When they reached the section of undergrowth that they had to crawl through to the road, he reminded her about thorn bushes and other undesirable plants, pushing as many of them out of her way as he could to help make her journey back to the car easier.

'How are you feeling,' he asked once they were back in Lauren's Mini, fastening their seatbelts.

'Physically and mentally exhausted.'

'Do you want me to drive?'

'Thanks, but it took me six months to get my seat and the mirrors all lined up perfectly after the last service. I'm okay to drive. At least I can do it sitting down,' she joked.

She started the engine and wiped the inside of the screen several times with her mitten-covered hand until it was clear enough to see.

'I just want to say thank you so much for everything you've done over the past week. Hopefully I wasn't too pushy. I get a little over enthusiastic sometimes,' he said.

'You weren't pushy at all,' Lauren assured him. 'In the end, I was as keen as you were, although I think I may just have been a little too ambitious tonight. And you are entirely welcome, by the way,' she added, patting him on the knee. 'So, which way shall we go?'

'You might as well keep going down here now, especially if you want practice driving at night.'

'That was three hours ago. I'll settle for quick and easy now,' she said, putting the car in first gear and pulling onto Pendlebury Way.

Lester watched her as she sat forward in the driver's seat, squinting into the dark night and steering around the numerous potholes that turned several sections of the road into a slalom course. She frequently wiped the windscreen with her mittens, but the wool was either wet or non-absorbent as it just spread the moisture across the glass. His own view was impaired, and as they approached the bottom of the hill, he too leaned forward to peer through the windscreen, to get a better look at the object up ahead.

'Is that a car parked across the road?' she asked, automatically slowing down.

'Shit!' Lester said, recognising the vehicle and, as they drew closer, the owner standing in front of it. 'It's Warren!'

'What?'

'Stop the car!'

Lauren stepped on the brake and steered her Mini onto the grass verge flanking the road. They stared at the dark figure leaning back against his battered Ford Capri, a boot-clad foot resting against the driver's door.

'What do we do?' Lauren asked.

Lester thought for a moment. 'Turn around. Let's go back up the hill, and we'll drive back down the dual carriageway.'

She nodded, removing the handbrake and steering hard to the right before hitting the gas. Her Mini was almost able to make the turn in one go, but she stopped and reversed rather than risk scratching the bonnet in the hedgerow.

'Shit!'

'What?'

'He's getting in his car,' Lester said, looking over his shoulder as they started heading up the hill. He watched as the headlights illuminated and then slowly swung in their direction.

Aware that she was looking at him, he turned to stare into her wide eyes. 'Can you go any faster?' he asked.

She pushed her foot down hard on the accelerator pedal and looked into her rearview mirror. 'He's gaining on us!' she screamed, suddenly looking away as he turned on his full beam.

Lester sighed. There was no way they could outrun his Capri in her Mini. 'We can't let him get in front of us. He'll just block the road again.'

'There's not much I can do about that.'

'Drive in the middle of the road, that won't leave him enough room to get past.'

Lauren angled the vehicle to the right and straightened up, the long grass thudding against the underside of the car.

Warren drove right up behind them, so close that his headlights were no longer visible, although his silhouette appeared ominously in the driver's seat.

'Just stay there,' Lester said. 'There's nothing he can do about it.'

The sudden crash jolted them both forward in their seats, and Lauren cried out in surprise. 'My car!'

Lester glanced over his shoulder. The Capri was closing in on them again. 'Hold on!' he said.

The second impact was less severe, but Warren's car was now right up against the Mini's bumper. Lauren screamed again as Warren accelerated loudly and began pushing them up the hill.

'Just stay straight and ease off the gas a bit,' Lester said, his voice steady despite his nerves, 'otherwise he'll force us off the road.'

Again he was greeted with her wide-eyed glare. 'Why didn't we bring your car?'

Lester didn't respond; eleven years of marriage had taught him to bite his tongue, but he couldn't help but wonder, *Why didn't you see this coming? You're supposed to be clairvoyant!*

As she reduced speed, the sound of Warren's engine intensified as it worked harder to push the Mini uphill. Then the sound diminished as Warren dropped back. Soon he was fifty metres behind them. They both looked round, thinking they had won, only to see those menacing lights grow bigger and brighter as he closed in again. They braced themselves for another impact as they approached the top of the hill. If they could reach it, they believed they were probably safe, at least for the time being.

'Can you go any faster?' Lester asked, knowing how close they were to the top.

'I'm going as fast as I can,' Lauren said, her voice tense. 'My foot is flat on the floor.'

'You're drifting over. Try and come back into the middle,' he said, looking over his shoulder once more.

The roar of the Capri's engine rang in their ears seconds before the third impact. Lauren screamed again, ignoring Lester's directions for her to return to the centre of the road. Just as he feared, Warren came racing up on the inside of them. When the cars were side by side, foliage whipping the sides of both vehicles, Warren turned to looked at them. In the darkness, Lester couldn't tell if the man was snarling or laughing. Neither was good. Then he swung his car into the side of the Mini. Lauren's scream pierced the night once again, and Lester grabbed the steering wheel, guiding it to the right to avoid being run off the road.

'My poor car! I've just cleaned it!' she yelled.

Lester glanced beyond her to see Warren positioning himself far to the right, and he knew that he was preparing to ram them again.

'Get ready to brake,' he said.

She nodded vigorously, her eyes fixed on the road ahead, her knuckles turning white where they gripped the wheel. Lester focused on Warren. He could see his eyes darting between them and the road ahead as he geared up to try and run them off the road.

'Now!' Lester cried, pulling up the handbrake as he sensed Warren was about to make his move.

Lauren hit the brakes hard, the tyres screeching as they skidded towards the side of the road. The Capri careered across their path, clipping the front of the Mini and sending them drifting over to the grass verge. As they looked up the hill towards the Capri, Warren threw the driver's door open and came marching towards them.

'Quick, turn around,' Lester urged as Warren got closer.

Hands trembling, Lauren turned the key in the ignition and immediately stalled the car. The second time she was more successful. Warren was just a few feet away.

'Lock the doors!' he said, his eyes fixed on the other man as he headed towards the driver's side.

Lauren pressed the lock on the key fob just as Warren grabbed the door handle. He tugged it repeatedly, glaring in at her and baring his teeth. She screamed, fighting with the gearstick as he backed away slightly. Her shrill cry came again as his elbow shattered her window, showering them in tiny fragments of glass. His hand reached inside the door and opened it.

Without a second thought, Lester rushed out of the car and raced around to the driver's side. He stopped just a few feet away, his hands raised in surrender when he saw that Warren had Lauren pulled tight against him, one hand across her forehead, pinning where she stood, the other holding a knife against her throat.

'Please, don't hurt her,' Lester said calmly. 'This was all my doing.'

'You should've thought about that before you started fucking around in things that don't concern you!'

'We'll stop, right here and now,' he said, his eyes never leaving Lauren's. His mind raced as he tried to find a way out of this.

'I know you will.'

'We'll walk away, I promise.'

'There's only one way to make sure you two keep your mouths shut.'

'Kick back,' Lester said, watching as Lauren's wide eyes narrowed.

'What?' Warren's nose wrinkled like a cornered fox.

'Kick back!' he repeated.

Lauren suddenly brought her heel up hard into Warren's groin. He dropped to his knees, and Lester stepped forward and pulled her away from him.

'Get in the car!' he told her, pointing to the passenger side.

As Warren looked up, Lester raised his booted foot and kicked him in the head, sending him sprawling to the ground. 'That's for trying to kill me!' He stepped forward and stood over him. For an instant, he thought about stamping on the man's head, over and over until it cracked open like a watermelon. Instead, he kicked him hard in the stomach and watched as the man curled up in a tight ball. 'That's for breaking into my house!'

He backed away quickly and slipped into the driver's seat before starting the engine. As he adjusted the seat and pushed it back, he threw a glance at the wing mirror and saw Warren's silhouette in the red glow of the taillights. He was getting to his feet.

'Shit!'

The gearbox crunched in protest as he tried to put it in reverse without depressing the clutch. He tried again, spinning the wheel hard right as the Mini sped backwards. There was a loud thud, and he stopped.

'What was that?' Lauren turned to him.

'Warren,' he replied.

'We're dead!'

He hit the gas and swung the steering wheel hard to the left, mounting the grass bank briefly before straightening up. Then he floored the accelerator pedal as they raced back down Pendlebury Hill.

He checked the rear-view but didn't see Warren coming after them. Maybe he'd decided to let them go, like the first time he'd chased them.

They had travelled less than a mile when the twin beams of light dazzled him in the rearview mirror. Warren was right on them again.

'Fuck!' Lester muttered, flicking the switch beneath the mirror to dim the light.

'Warren?' Lauren asked.

He nodded. The man had snuck up on them.

'What are we going do?'

'Make sure he doesn't get alongside us.'

He pushed the accelerator pedal to the floor again. Seventy-four miles per hour.

'I'm scared, David,' Lauren said, her voice shaky.

'It's going to be okay,' he told her, a supportive hand on her knee.

The car jolted as they hit another pothole, causing Lauren to scream again.

'Sorry,' he said, gripping the wheel tightly.

Bright white light filled the car, and Lester glanced over at the speedometer: sixty-seven miles per hour. He knew there was no way they could outrun Warren. Their only chance was to block his attempts to draw level with them. The Capri was about ten feet behind them, the roar of its engine taunting them as it drew closer.

Seconds later, there was a jolt as the Capri bumped them. Lauren screamed as Lester's white-knuckled hands clenched the steering wheel, zigzagging across the road to cut off any attempt to pull up alongside them. The Capri's headlight shone in his wing mirror, so Lester swerved over to the right, only for Warren to swing across to the left-hand lane and pull up alongside them, glancing inside briefly to lock stares with Lester.

'Shit,' he spat the word, angry at how easily he had drawn level with them.

He watched, feeling helpless, as Warren's mouth curled into a grin. The cigarette that hung limply from one corner of his mouth dropped into his lap, and Lester saw his gaze drop down to find it.

Lester hit the brakes and pulled up the handbrake, his eyes widening as he looked from Warren to the road. There was Frances, stepping out onto the road, her eyes were wide with terror. Warren slammed on the brakes and turned the steering wheel hard to the right.

Lester watched in shock as the Capri cut right across the road in front of them, the right-hand side of the vehicle rising from the sharp angle. Everything seemed to slow down as the Capri flipped over. Thousands of glass fragments filled the air, like frozen raindrops in their headlights, as the vehicle rolled several times before ending up on its roof. It slid down the hill another fifteen yards before it finally came to a standstill, the wheels still spinning.

Lauren's hand covered her mouth as she stared at the crumpled car before them. Lester was equally stunned as they turned and faced each other.

'Did you see her?' he asked after a long silence.

'It was Fran.'

Lester nodded.

'Should we call an ambulance?' she asked.

He was silent for a moment, until the smooth skin on her forehead rippled. 'Of course,' he said, grabbing his phone and dialling 999. It was answered quickly, a woman asking which emergency service he required. 'Ambulance, police, and fire brigade, please. There's been a crash about a mile and a half down Pendlebury Way, between Greyton and Gatherford. One man. No, we haven't checked yet. It has literally just happened. To be honest, the guy was trying to kill us. My name is David Lester, 17 Braithwaite Drive, Gatherford. Thanks.'

He hung up the phone and turned to Lauren. All colour had drained from her face. Unfastening his seat-belt, he sidled across his seat and put his arms around her. He wasn't sure how she would react, but she nestled into him and then burst into tears, sobbing into his shoulder for several minutes before finally coming up for air.

He kissed her forehead and moved back into his seat. 'I'm really sorry,' he said as she continued staring at the battered Capri.

'What for?'

'For getting you into all this. Endangering your life. Getting your car smashed up. Shall I go on?'

'It was my choice,' she told him, her eyes transfixed on the Capri. 'Why hasn't it exploded?'

Lester allowed himself a smile. 'They only do that in the movies. It's for dramatic effect. I don't think we need any more drama tonight.' With a sigh of resignation, he grabbed the door handle and pushed it open.

'Where are you going?'

'I'd better go and check on him. How would it look to the police if we didn't at least appear to have done something?'

'Be careful,' she warned, her eyes unblinking as she stared at the Capri.

Lester grabbed the torch and got out, pausing momentarily to check the damage to her Mini before heading down to the overturned Capri. His steps were measured. He couldn't help but feel apprehensive as he approached. What if Warren had some weapon and was just waiting for him to come to his aid? At that thought, Lester remained cautious as he circled the vehicle, illuminating the area before him with the flashlight.

Gray Warren's head protruded through the driver's window, blood dripping from multiple cuts on his face, a cigarette dangling from the corner of his mouth. Lester started walking towards him but stopped almost immediately. In the beam of his torch, he could see a pool of liquid glistening around the roof of the car. He sniffed the air, and his jaw dropped open as though in a silent scream. That same smell had overwhelmed his senses earlier that morning, while he was trapped in his own car. As he started backing away, Warren's eyes opened. When he saw Lester standing there, he went to speak. The cigarette butt was stuck to his lip and dangled against his cheek. Lester could see it burning into the man's skin. Instinctively, he shouted for Warren to stop, but the man shook his head frantically, and the butt fell to the petrol-soaked concrete.

The road lit up in an instant blaze of amber light, causing Lester to stumble backwards with the sudden burst of heat. There was no love lost as he got up and watched Warren fight wildly to free himself from the shackles of his seatbelt. Hanging upside down and bleeding profusely, he thrashed about as flames engulfed him. There was muffled screaming from within the metal shell of the Capri, but to his surprise, Lester felt nothing as the man who had left him for dead burned before his eyes.

The explosion that followed lit up the night sky and sent Lester diving to the ground once more. He covered his head, only looking up when the intensity of the fire ten yards away died down.

'Are you okay?' Lauren was at his side in an instant, brushing his unkempt hair from his face as he sat up.

'I think so.'

She helped him to his feet, and they stood mesmerised by the raging fire before them.

'He'd better get used to those flames where he's going,' Lester said, his eyes fixed on the dark silhouette in the driver's seat.

Lauren punched him on the arm, again managing to hit the same spot.

'Ow! Com'on, the guy was going to kill us. I just wish we had some marshmallows.'

The top of Pendlebury Hill became a glow of flashing blue lights, indicating that the emergency services were on their way. Lester took her hand and led her back up to her Mini.

'How are you feeling?' he asked, once they were inside.

'A bit numb. I've spoken to more dead people than I can remember, but I've never actually seen anyone die before.'

'Me either,' he said with a sympathetic smile. He knew she didn't appreciate him speaking ill of the dead, but as far as he was concerned, the world had just become a better place without Gray Warren in it. 'I guess Frances got her revenge. Even if it was only her lover's great-grandson.'

She nodded, her face turning neon blue as a police car headed down the hill towards them at speed.

'I'd better move the car to let them through?' she said, realising that her Mini was blocking the road.

'I would just stay here until the police have checked the scene. Let them handle it.' He looked into the rear-view mirror and saw the car approaching behind them. 'I'd best go and deal with them. Sure you're okay?'

Lauren nodded, and he opened the door and got out, walking around to the back as the police car slowed and pulled up just in front of him.

It was going to be a long night.

Chapter Twenty-Seven

A little over a week ago, it had taken the police more than one hour to arrive at the scene. Tonight, it took slightly over five minutes. When the police car pulled up a few yards behind them on Pendlebury Way, Lester walked over and ducked down to talk to the driver. He looked across to the passenger seat to see the same constable he had spoken to that morning and the week before.

'This is becoming a bit of a habit, Mr. Lester,' Trev said.

The driver frowned and looked from Lester to his colleague. 'Do you two know each other?'

'Mr. Lester and I have met twice in the past ten days. I hear there was also a third call that I wasn't able to attend. A break-in, wasn't it?'

Lester nodded, his gaze shifting to the top of the hill where he could see two sets of flashing blue lights. 'I can explain everything, but, first of all, do you need us to move the car? We just left it where we stopped.' He could see Lauren watching them through the back window.

The driver craned his neck to look beyond the Mini. 'Is there someone in that wreck?'

'Yes. I went to help him, but it looks like the petrol tank must have been damaged, and the whole thing caught light and then exploded.'

'We saw. Are you hurt?'

Lester shook his head.

'Okay, back it up over to the side of the road to let the ambo get through, not that there's anything they can do. Do you know who the driver was?'

'Gray Warren,' Lester said casually as he indicated to Lauren to reverse over to the side of the road.

The two policemen looked at each other briefly. There was a hint of a smirk as the driver opened the door and stepped out. 'Detective Constable Harris,' he said, offering his hand.

Although he didn't believe it was customary, Lester shook the policeman's hand, his eyes fixed on Lauren as she reversed up the hill several yards and parked.

'I'm not going to lie, Mr. Lester, Gray Warren has been a thorn in our side for many years, hasn't he, Trev?'

'That's putting it mildly,' the other officer said, getting out of the passenger seat. He nodded his head at Lauren as she walked over to join them.

'Can you tell me what happened?' Harris asked while Trev headed towards Warren's vehicle, taking his mobile phone out.

Lester stepped aside and waited for the fire engine and ambulance to pass by before explaining to Harris the events of the past week, starting with his first encounter with Frances. The officer scribbled notes as Lester recounted how Warren had stalked them, assaulted him, broke into his house, and then run him off the road. When he turned back to Lauren, he saw her walking back to her Mini.

'Why didn't you report any of these incidents?' Harris asked.

Lester remained silent, wondering how best to answer.

'Mr. Lester?'

'My wife reported the break-in,' he replied, frowning as Lauren got back in her car.

'And the rest?'

Lester sucked in a breath and sighed audibly. 'With all due respect, I report Warren for threatening behaviour, you slap his wrists, and then I end up having to drink through a straw for the rest of my life, or if I'm really lucky, I get a blue badge so that I can park anywhere. I think, based on tonight's evidence, I did the right thing.'

Harris raised a single eyebrow and made a note in his pad.

Bright lights coming down the hill made them turn their heads in unison. The Audi kept coming, leaving Lester lost as to why the driver was not turning around and going back the other way. The vehicle pulled up behind the police car, and a man in a grey herringbone trench coat got out.

'Looks like they've sent in the big guns,' DC Harris mumbled.

'David Lester?' the man asked as he approached.

'Yes.'

'Detective Chief Inspector Fenny,' the man said. He was short and thin with a gaunt face and dark hair that was turning to steel at the sides. 'It sounds like you've had a lucky escape. Most people who've gone toe-to-toe with Graham Warren aren't around to talk about it. I can't tell you how long I've been trying to collar this guy, and now it looks like I never will,' he added, watching their colleague as he walked up the hill towards them. 'So, what's the verdict, Trev?'

The police constable shook his head. 'He's toast, guv. It's definitely Warren's car. At least it was.'

'Looks like you're the big hero, Mr. Lester.'

'I haven't done anything. This was all Warren's doing.'

'I've no doubt. I've been after this guy for almost ten years. He's clever for someone who never finished school, and he's got friends in high places. I can't say I'll lose any sleep over his demise, but for me, he'll always be the one that got away.'

'I'd never even heard of him until a couple of days ago.'

The DCI looked over at Lauren's Mini. 'We have a file on most bad guys. This guy's got his own cabinet. There are a lot of unsolved cases we believe he was connected to which look like they will remain that way now.'

'Sorry,' Lester found himself saying.

'Is she okay in there?' the detective chief inspector asked, squinting at the Mini. 'She doesn't look happy.'

'She's understandably upset,' he replied, only realising how true his words were when he caught her glare. 'I'd better go and check on her.'

The DCI shrugged and followed him over to her Mini. Lester bent down to talk to her through the open passenger window. 'Are you okay?'

Lauren continued staring at the firemen as they fought to extinguish the blazing Capri. 'How could you not tell me Warren broke into your house and ran you off the road?'

Lester closed his eyes, the smell of burning more noticeable in complete darkness. 'I didn't want to worry you.'

'Or is it because you thought I wouldn't help you anymore if I knew?'

'I tried to talk you out of it when you told me who he was,' he said with a shake of his head.

'You should have tried harder, like maybe mentioning he tried to kill you.' The disappointment in her voice was like a punch to his gut.

'I'm sorry.'

'You know, I thought you were different, David, but you put my life in danger because you couldn't be honest with me. You used me. I'm sick of guys and all their bullshit!'

Lester went to speak, but she held her hand up in front of his face to silence him. He stood up, not knowing what else to say, even if she was prepared to listen. When he looked round, he saw that the three policeman were huddled together watching him.

Fenny turned to his colleague. 'Do you have everything you need, Harris?'

'I need to speak to the girl and get statements from both of them. We need to check the car as well, take some photos of the damage Warren caused.'

'Are you both local?' the DCI asked.

Lester nodded. 'Gatherford. Lauren lives in Meadowhurst.'

'Would you prefer to drop by the station tomorrow to make statements? I'm sure you both just want to get home?' Fenny said with an empathetic smile.

'I appreciate that. We do.'

'Harris, get the girl's story. Trev and I will give the car the once over and then they can go.'

Lester watched as DCI Harris crouched down beside the driver's window and questioned Lauren while the other policemen walked around the Mini and took some photos of damage to the side and rear of the vehicle.

After twenty minutes, Fenny walked over to Lester. 'You guys can go,' he said before leaning in. 'Do you need a ride home?'

'I might,' he said, a sigh whistling through the corners of his mouth as he watched the Mini's headlights swing in an arc before them. Lauren then reversed back before heading up Pendlebury Hill.

'Sorry about that,' Fenny said.

'Not as sorry as I am,' Lester replied, worried that there was no coming back from this. He'd ruined the best thing in his life before it had even start. Maybe Hayley was right. This obsession had gotten him nowhere.

23:57

Despite feeling drained, both physically and mentally, Lester couldn't sleep. Too much had happened, and his mind wanted to relive it all. His mother, who was usually in bed by nine o'clock, had stayed up to make sure he was home safe and then quizzed him on what was going on. He had eventually fobbed her off, but the whole exchange had left him on edge. He hated lying to her, but there was no need to worry her on top of everything else.

Instead of sleeping, Lester decided to do some research on Pendlebury Manor, one of the many unanswered questions that whirled in his head. Finding out what happened to it would provide another missing piece to the jigsaw, he was certain.

After typing 'Pendlebury Manor' in Google, he found one relevant Wikipedia article. He read through the History section, noting that it was purchased by Alfred Dering in 1915. At the bottom of the website, there was an article entitled 'The Demise of Pendlebury Manor' with a section from the *Kent Messenger* newspaper dated 4th October 1916.

Greyton's Mayor Amongst 15 Killed in Zeppelin Bombing Raid

Fifteen civilians, including the Mayor of Greyton, Alfred Dering, were killed in the early hours of Wednesday morning during a surprise bombing raid. Greyton Town Hall raised the alarm when a zeppelin was seen heading towards the Kentish town. Despite the warning, twelve people were killed in the town centre when four bombs were dropped onto shops and houses. The zeppelin then headed towards Dover, where it dropped a fifth bomb on Pendlebury Manor, killing Dering, his wife, Elizabeth, and their youngest son, Richard. The residence was completely destroyed by the attack.

Lester rubbed his chin as he thought about the timing of the attack. It had happened just hours after Frances had been imprisoned by Dering and his son. No one would ever know whether the mayor intended to kill her or not. Why his policeman son had not freed her would also remain a mystery. He may even have been injured himself, although, having just lost his parents and his brother, it might not have been high on his list of priorities. It was almost certain that he had gone back to the ruins of Pendlebury Manor later to recover her body from the air raid shelter along with the shackles that she had tried to escape. He had ultimately profited by becoming chief constable and then mayor himself, almost as though he had engineered the whole thing.

Lester's thoughts jumped to Gray Warren and how Frances had exacted her revenge on the great-grandson of her lover. He wondered if she would continue to haunt Pendlebury Hill now that she had found justice. That they hadn't yet found her burial place weighed on him. That was something he intended to pursue with DCI Fenny when they met tomorrow evening. She deserved a proper Christian burial.

Finally, his thoughts turned to Lauren. He had done his best to push her to the back of his mind, feeling physically sick to think that he had screwed up a real chance of happiness. They had been getting on so well, as if they were destined to be together. The investigation made him feel alive in a way he had never done and to have someone like Lauren as equally interested had just made it so special.

Had he used her, in the way that she suggested? As he lay in the dark, he wondered if he was that cold and calculating. He convinced himself that he hadn't told her because he didn't want to frighten her. Should he have protected her and kept her out of it? Telling her about the break-in and the attempt on his life would surely have ended her involvement, and without Lauren, he never would've discovered what had happened to Frances. Without her, this case would never have been solved.

He shook his head at himself, realising Lauren was right: he had used her, and he deserved to lose her. He closed his eyes tightly, but he couldn't stop the tears. Grief had been a familiar companion throughout his life, but this was the first time he experienced it since losing Carla.

Chapter Twenty-Eight

17:51, Monday, 5th February

Lester sat in the empty waiting room of Greyton Police Station, his stomach churning as he thought about what he would say to Lauren when she turned up. He looked at the time on his phone and sighed. It had been more than half an hour since his arrival, and he wondered if the receptionist had even told Fenny that he was there.

Where's Lauren?

He checked his phone again. There were no texts or WhatsApp messages. Just as he was starting to wonder if something had happened to her, the door opposite where he was sitting opened, and DCI Fenny appeared with Lauren in tow.

He stood up, opening his mouth to say something, anything, but he could only watch in silence as Fenny thanked her for coming in. She turned and walked past him without making eye contact.

'Hello again, Mr. Lester. Thanks for coming in this evening,' Fenny said.

'Didn't you want to see us together?' Lester questioned, turning to watch Lauren exit the building.

'Ms. Miller rang this morning and asked if she could come in earlier,' the policeman explained. 'Hell hath no fury like a woman scorned.'

Lester frowned back at him.

'We would have interviewed you separately anyway,' Fenny said, opening the door he had just come through. 'This way, Mr. Lester.'

Lester followed the detective chief inspector along a narrow corridor to a door on the right. He opened it and stood aside. 'Take a seat. I'll be back in a bit. Can I get you something to drink?'

He raised his hand. 'I'm fine, thanks.'

Lester pulled the moulded plastic chair from under the table and sat down. He remained alone in the small white-walled meeting room for several minutes, staring at the large dark glass window beside him. For all he knew, he had an audience watching him. Maybe they were looking for signs of stress, like biting his nails or fidgeting anxiously. *Why would they though? Surely I'm not under suspicion?*

When the door opened, Lester was surprised to see a female police officer enter the room, and he found himself standing.

'Be seated, Mr. Lester. I'm Detective Constable Kumar. I'm just going to take a statement and then DCI Fenny has some questions for you.'

'Okay,' he replied, sinking back into the chair with a crumpled brow.

'So, can you describe the events that took place on the night of Sunday the 5th February?'

Lester recounted their evening from the moment they were driving home from Pendlebury Manor until the time the police arrived on the scene. He was amazed at how quickly and clearly the DC wrote down his statement, only once asking him to repeat himself. Once it was complete, she read it back to him and asked if there was anything further he wished to add. When he replied no, she asked him to sign and date it. Then she left the room.

Alone again, Lester checked his phone and saw that it was already seven-thirty. Moments later, DCI Fenny entered the room holding several files.

'Sorry for keeping you waiting, Mr. Lester. That took a little longer than anticipated.'

The policeman took the seat opposite and opened the top file, which contained his statement and some notes his colleague had made the previous evening. After a couple of minutes, DCI Fenny looked up with wide eyes that stared as though he had downed a dozen espressos that afternoon.

'I've been assigned to this particular case because, as I mentioned last night, I've been observing the deceased very closely for a number of years. Your statement and Ms. Miller's statement seem to corroborate with our notes from yesterday evening and the evidence taken from the scene. I also have the report on your accident dated 3rd February. Your break-in, also dated 3rd February, and the incident you reported on the 27th January. Looks like you have had a fun-packed week or so.'

Lester rolled his eyes towards the ceiling.

'I just have a couple of questions before we wrap things up, starting with, how did you come to know Graham Warren?'

'I don't know him. My first encounter was on the 2nd February, when he followed us from the top of Pendlebury Hill and tried to intimidate us with his dangerous driving.'

'Another encounter you didn't report.'

'It was nothing really.'

'And how do you know it was Warren?'

'There aren't too many Capris on the road these days. There's even fewer now.'

'So when did you first meet him?'

'I only met him once, before last night. It was the next day. He didn't make a great first impression. He was waiting for me in a layby at the top of Pendlebury Hill. He punched me in the stomach and kicked me in the head.'

Fenny nodded. 'Yes, the assault you mentioned last night. And you didn't report that incident because of potential repercussions?'

'Exactly. Once Ms. Miller advised me of who he was, I decided that reporting it would be detrimental to my health.'

'And the second incident?'

'Also on the 3rd February. Warren chased me down Crawley Lane and forced me off the road and into a tree.'

'So you're convinced that Warren was warning you off because you were asking questions about his family?'

'Yes, he said as much. I assume you know who is father is?'

Fenny nodded. 'And do you think Mayor Dering's involved?'

'It all happened after I visited him at his house.'

DCI Fenny paused a moment, then asked, 'And what did he say exactly?'

'That he would do whatever was necessary to preserve the Dering family name.'

'And why, exactly, are you investigating the Dering family?'

'I believe that the Mayor's grandfather, Alfred Dering, killed a nurse by the name of Frances Coldwell back in 1916 but pinned it on the deceased's brother.'

'1916?' Fenny laughed and sat back in his chair, grinning across the table. He wiped his palm across his mouth, his eyes remaining fixed on Lester. 'Do you have any proof?' he asked eventually.

'I don't have any proof, personally, but I'm pretty certain I know where you can find some.'

DCI Fenny stood up. 'I think I'm going to need another coffee. Can I get you one?'

'White, no sugar. Please.'

While Fenny left the room, Lester took out his phone and again checked his messages. Nothing. He was conscious of the dark glass windows beside him and wondered if the DCI had just gone into the next room to observe his movements. He reminded himself that he was innocent and opened a new WhatsApp message to Lauren.

Dear Lauren. I am so sorry. I thought about what you said, and I totally understand why you would never want to talk to me again. Please know that I never consciously meant to deceive you. I would never knowingly put you in harm's way. I hope you can forgive me, one day. Rainbowman.

He put the phone back in his pocket and rubbed his face just as Fenny returned with two coffees. He placed them down on the centre of the table and sat before taking the bottom file and opening it.

'So, this whole thing started on Friday, 26th January, when you claim a girl stepped out in front of you at exactly the same location as last night's incident? A girl by the name of Frances Caldwell?'

'Coldwell. Yes, a nurse who disappeared in 1916. She was having an affair with the mayor and became pregnant with his child. The mayor and his son, both named Alfred Dering, chained Frances up in what we think was an air raid shelter at the bottom of Pendlebury Manor, but the mayor and his family were killed when the manor was bombed that night. We believe the son came back at a later date and recovered Frances's body and pinned the murder on her brother. He was . . . mentally challenged,' Lester said after trying to remember the politically correct terminology.

Fenny sat back in his chair, his eyes fixed on Lester's. 'That's quite a story, Mr. Lester. How do you know all this? I'm pretty certain none of it's documented.'

'Some of it is. You can look up Frances Coldwell and her story, the history of the Greyton mayors, and the Pendlebury Manor bombing. I believe you also have several files on reported ghost sightings on Pendlebury Hill.'

'Indeed, we do. Maggie mentioned you asked to see them.'

'Maggie?' Lester asked.

'The duty officer. You believe this Coldwell girl is buried up at Raghlan Coe and that there may be evidence of her murder in an air raid shelter at the back of some ruins adjacent to the scene?'

'I'm ninety-five percent certain, although I don't know if it was an air raid shelter or if it's even still there. If it is, I'm willing to bet there'll be DNA evidence. She lost a lot of blood, and I doubt that Dering would have removed all traces of her being there.'

Fenny frowned at him, leaning back slightly. 'How could you possibly know that she lost a lot of blood or that she was even there to begin with?'

Lester took a deep breath as he thought about his response. 'I'm not sure if Lauren mentioned it but she's actually a medium.'

The smile on the policeman's face was inevitable.

'We were working as a team. My research and her spiritual abilities.' Lester wondered if he should go into more detail about how Frances was able to take over Lauren's mind, but he thought better of it.

The DCI was silent, the rhythmic banging of his chair legs hitting the tiled floor quickly becoming annoying as he rocked back and forth.

'It's impossible to know what their intentions were prior to the mayor being killed himself,' Lester continued. 'But if they were going to kill her, why didn't they just do it instead of chaining her up. Technically, she either bled to death or died of dehydration. I don't think the Derings actually murdered Frances, but they were ultimately responsible for her death.'

'I've got to say, Mr. Lester, that in thirty-two years in the force, this has to be the most fanciful tale I have ever heard. And that includes eleven years in the Met. That's not to say I don't disbelieve you. You both have clean records, your statements corroborate, and I'm pretty sure you guys didn't get together to get your stories straight as Ms. Miller clearly isn't speaking to you. The damage to her vehicle is consistent with your statements and contain traces of red paintwork, the same colour as Warren's Capri. I'm willing to bet we'll find similar evidence on your own vehicle, if they haven't scrapped it already,' the DCI threw him a chastising glare. 'I'm also pretty sure you wouldn't have intentionally picked a fight with Graham Warren, so all that side of it checks out. I'm just not buying into this story about Ms. Miller talking to the dead.'

'Nor did I,' Lester said.

Fenny patted the files on the table in front of him. 'So what exactly would you have me do, Mr. Lester? I'm not comfortable asking the National Heritage if I can dig up one of their ancient monuments. They'll want something concrete, and we don't have it.'

Lester bowed his head for a moment. 'I didn't believe in ghosts myself until twelve days ago when one stepped out in front of me. Last night, I saw her again, and so did Lauren. Ms. Miller. I believe Warren saw her too and that he swerved to avoid her, ultimately killing himself in the process. Many others have reported seeing her, including a policeman. You have the reports in your filing cabinets. The psychic thing was even harder to get my head around, but Ms. Miller has told me things that she couldn't possibly have known. Now, I'm a total believer. Sometimes you have to open up your mind just a little bit,' he said, holding his index finger and thumb an inch apart for effect.

He could see by the way the policeman sat back in his chair and glared at him that he did not appreciate Lester's comment.

'You may have a missing person file from 1916. If you can find the air raid shelter in the back garden of where Pendlebury Manor once stood, there might still be some evidence of where she was chained to the wall. She tried to cut off her own thumb, so she would have lost a lot of blood. There should still be traces of it on the ground. I've given you the location of where she is almost certainly buried, the motive, and the perpetrator. We've done all the investigation work for you. All you have to do is the official part.'

The DCI ground his teeth together as he studied Lester. He made no efforts to hide his contempt, and Lester couldn't tell if he was even the slightest bit intrigued enough to follow up on his statement. 'Okay, Mr. Lester, you're free to go.'

'Does that mean you'll dig up the ground beneath Raghlan Coe?'

'It means you're free to go.'

Lester stood up and rested his hands on the table. 'Please,' he urged, maintaining the policeman's glare. 'We risked our lives to solve this case. Don't let that be in vain.'

'What you're asking is above my pay grade, and even if I can get my superiors on board, nothing will happen fast. There'll be a lot of red tape to cut through and a lot of people to convince in order to get permission to dig around over there. I'm not even sure how I'm going to sell them the idea. I'm certainly not going to be telling them any ghost stories. In some ways, it would have been easier if you'd dug her up yourselves.'

'I was trying to stay on the right side of the law.'

Fenny nodded. 'I'm not making any promises, but I'll do what I can.' He stood up, allowing his chair to scrape noisily across the epoxy-coated floor.

'Can I ask a favour? Assuming you get permission, can I come and watch?'

The detective chief inspector frowned back at him. 'It's not a spectator sport. Why would you want to see a dead body being dug up? It's not a pretty sight.'

'It's the final piece of the puzzle. I don't expect you to understand, but I just want to see the conclusion to this particular story.'

'Don't we all! I'm afraid the area would be cordoned off to the public. At best, you could watch from the sidelines, but there won't be much to see. They usually shield these proceedings from the public. I'll let you know when I hear something. If I hear something.'

'Thanks,' he said, following the DCI through the door and back along the narrow corridor to reception.

Standing outside in the drizzle, Lester drew in a breath of cool, damp air before getting into his mum's car. Immediately his shoulders sagged as sadness engulfed him. Having grieved for Katie, his dad, and then Carla, losing Lauren would bring more heartache, although he wondered if the emptiness inside was partly for Frances or even the conclusion of his investigation. It meant returning to the routine of his mundane life, something he no longer had the energy for. Things had to change. He had already moved on from Hayley. Now he needed to decide what was next. In his career, in his life.

There was plenty to work on while he waited for Fenny to contact him.

Chapter Twenty-Nine

11:23, Friday, 12th April

It was three weeks before DCI Fenny finally called him.

'I have some news,' he announced after Lester had snatched up his mobile phone to answer. 'An extensive search of the area formerly known as Pendlebury Manor did uncover an air raid shelter. Due to its inaccessibility, we know it hasn't been opened in decades. It wasn't even visible, so I was at a loss to explain how I even knew of its existence. Between you and me, I made up some bullshit story about having found the manor blueprints online. Anyway, the forensics team found traces of blood in the soil within the air raid shelter, just as you suggested. There was also a chain hanging on a wall and an eight-inch piece of metal buried in the soil.'

Lester closed his eyes and allowed himself a smile.

'After you gave your statement, I spent some time looking through the archives at all the other statements from witnesses who claim to have encountered a ghost on Pendlebury Hill. They go back as far as 1919.'

'I know.'

'But what you didn't know is that we still have a missing persons file for Frances Coldwell. I found it in a box tucked away in our cellar. In that box was a set of bloodstained shackles.'

'And?' Lester prompted, his heart racing with anticipation.

'And the blood on those shackles is a positive match with blood samples found on the piece of metal and in the soil in the air raid shelter.'

'Yes!' Lester punched the air. 'That's great news! So now they'll excavate at Raghlan Coe?'

'Let's not get ahead of ourselves. I can't deny that the statement Ms. Miller gave us was incredibly accurate in relation to where Frances Coldwell was imprisoned. The investigation team confirm that someone was detained there. In addition to the metal and soil, there was also bloodstained clothing and human excrement. It's hard for me to get my head around all of this, but I'm starting to accept there must be something in it. Convincing the National Heritage of that, however, is an entirely different prospect.'

Lester sighed.

'I have nothing linking Frances Coldwell to Raghlan Coe other than Ms. Miller's conversation with her, and there's no way I'm going to them with that. But don't lose faith, Mr. Lester,' the policeman said after a brief silence, 'we're still pushing for the excavation. It just might take a little longer than you would like.'

Lester sent weekly texts to Fenny, enquiring as to whether there were any updates, until finally DCI Fenny told him, 'I thought I'd made myself clear. We have a continuous dialogue with the National Heritage about the possibility of excavating the earth works at Raghlan Coe but, as I told you last month, it could take some time before a decision is made. You need to be patient and stop contacting me. Okay?'

The following week, Lester couldn't help himself; he called Fenny again but the policeman didn't answer or reply to his voicemail. The week after, he tried a second time with the same result. After the third unsuccessful attempt, he realised that the policeman was ghosting him. He smiled at the irony and, only then, did he finally get the message and decide to take a step back.

His need to know how things were progressing in the background kept him awake at night. He tried to convince himself that he just wanted closure, peace for Frances and vindication for himself, but he knew that he was obsessed. He had been since Frances stepped out in front of his car on the 26th January. His need to understand why she had chosen him had cost him his relationship with Lauren, someone he truly connected with and believed he could finally be happy with. *Is this what it's like to be an addict? Didn't they press the self-destruct button in the same way that he had in the pursuit of their own selfish needs?*

He knew there was no way back with Lauren and he accepted that he didn't deserve her. She was more than just collateral damage. She was a winning lottery ticket that he had thrown out with the junk mail. It wasn't all bad though. He had ended things with Hayley, something that was long overdue, and he was determined to sort out his career finally and do something that he would find fulfilling, like solving the mystery of Frances Coldwell's disappearance. That's what he found rewarding and he had already decided that he would dig into the mystery of Sarah Kendall once he was finished. One phantom at a time!

By the second week in April, Lester had picked up his phone over twenty times to call Fenny, but each time he had resisted the urge. The not knowing was agonising. The last time his patience had got the better of him like this he was twelve and begging his parents to let him open one of his Christmas presents early. The trouble was, one was never enough. There were many other colourfully wrapped presents of different shapes and sizes underneath that tree, and he simply had to know what they were. The same was true of knowing if the National Heritage would allow them to dig at Raghlan Coe.

The past two months had been a series of ups and downs. After several meetings with Hayley, she finally seemed to accept that there was no way back for them. He had initiated divorce proceedings, and so far, it was amicable. Knowing Hayley, it would not stay that way for long. She had even apologised for throwing a bottle at him and appeared genuinely remorseful when she saw the scar on his forehead.

With no investigation or wife making demands on his time, Lester threw himself into his work. He didn't want to stay at his job, but he knew it was the best option until he found what he did want. Luckily, his hyper-focus on work repaired some of the damage he had done at the start of the year. Walker had even given him a pay rise, after landing a new client, which was a bonus as he needed to find a new place to live. He loved his mum dearly, but he was struggling to live with her the second time around after years of independence.

'How are things going with Lauren?' she had asked during dinner.

'They're not.' Lester immediately regretted his terse response.

'Oh dear. Is there any chance of reconciliation? She's such a lovely girl, David.'

'She is,' he said, instinctively rubbing the top of his arm where she had punched him several times, 'but I'm afraid there won't be any grandkids just yet.'

'Such a shame,' she said, shaking her head. 'Still, you know what they say. When one door closes, another door opens.'

During that first week or two, no words of wisdom or encouragement helped to boost his positivity. That came when he decided to write a story about his whole experience. After twenty thousand words, he realised that it was more like a novel and found that he was spending most of his time either working or writing. It was something he enjoyed, and although he wasn't about to give up his day job, it offered the hope of a way out of finance.

Despite certain areas of his life improving, there was still a void. He had a yearning that he hadn't experienced since Jane Benson dumped him at the tender age of fifteen. Most of that he attributed to Lauren. Not a day went by when he didn't think of her and wish things had turned out differently. Unlike his relentless pursuit of Fenny, he didn't try to contact her again after his last text message, to which she never replied. He decided to let bygones be bygones.

The DCI's call came as a complete surprise midway through April. Lester was in the middle of typing a letter to a client when his mobile rang. He thought it was his mum, checking what he wanted for dinner, so he let it ring. 'Don't call me at work unless it's an emergency,' he had told her repeatedly, having been disrupted in meetings with clients and Walker. When he later checked his missed calls, he was annoyed at himself for missing the policeman and immediately called him back.

'DCI Fenny, it's David Lester. Do you have some news for me?'

'I do, Mr. Lester, but it's not good news. Unfortunately, National Heritage have denied our request to excavate the land at Raghlan Coe. I'm really sorry, but without some evidence that Frances Coldwell is buried there, I'm afraid this investigation is over.'

Chapter Thirty

Sleeping seemed impossible. Lester's mind had churned all night as he relived the investigation. *How can I prove that Frances Coldwell was buried at Raghlan Coe?* The question kept coming back to him.

As he lay there, his thoughts kept returning to something that DCI Fenny had said while he was making his statement. He had replayed those words several times since, but it was only now that they resonated with him. 'It would have been easier if you'd dug her up yourselves.'

Lester sat up in bed, instantly alert. Had the policeman been hinting to him about what he should do or was it just a throwaway comment? Either way, he believed it was the answer he needed. If he dug and found nothing, then at least he would have done everything he possibly could. On the other hand, if he dug and found Frances, then surely the police would see him as a hero rather than the perpetrator of a heritage crime. It was a risk he knew he had to take.

He thought back to all he'd learned of Frances from his research and from Lauren. He could hear Lauren's voice as she told him how Frances told Alfie that she was pregnant. Her first words, 'beneath the capstone,' had come directly after he'd asked Lauren to find out where she was buried. He remembered that the capstone was the top stone of a dolmen. Frances had told them exactly where she was buried, but there was so much going on at the time that he had missed it.

He had set his alarm for seven o'clock, but he was awake at first light. His frantic mind wouldn't let him sleep and he wanted to be the early bird catching the worm. He grabbed a fork and spade from his dad's shed as quietly as he could and headed up Pendlebury Hill in the work clothes he'd worn the day before.

There was little traffic on the road, but even so, he was relieved to find that there were no cars in the layby at the top of the hill. He was able to walk across the fields with the gardening tools unchallenged for the twenty minutes it took him to reach the ancient monument of Raghlan Coe. His hunger pangs gave way to nausea as he looked between the three standing stones and the capstone that balanced on top of them. He shuddered when he thought about what he was about to do and even questioned if he could do it.

With a deep breath, Lester stepped forward and positioned the fork in the centre space between the stones. He put his full weight on it, but the fork barely pierced the hardened earth. He looked up at the capstone, sheltering it from the rain, and shook his head. His second attempt was more successful, but he knew it was going to be hard work.

It took him half an hour to dig a hole two inches deep. He continued slowly, knowing that he had to be careful to avoid damaging any evidence buried in the ground. The soil below the surface was moist, so he swapped to the spade as digging became easier. As he removed another spade full of earth, it occurred to him that Dering had likely dug a shallow grave. Anything else would have risked detection. Ironically, Lester found himself in exactly the same position over one hundred years later.

In his haste, he accidentally struck the standing stone behind him with the spade, and it clattered noisily. He looked up in surprise and saw an elderly couple and their dog walking nearby. Wondering if they'd noticed, he stopped digging and stepped behind one of the stones to hide. When he peered around the crystalline sandstone, he could see that they were looking his way. They were in deep discussion about something, their eyes fixed on the dolmen.

'Ringo!' the man called over to his dog, who was chasing a rabbit into the hedgerow.

When the dog ran back to them, the man put his lead on and started walking back the way they had come. Lester kept a watchful eye on them from behind the standing stone. The man kept looking back, and when he was fifty yards away, he took out his phone and made a call. It was obvious he was calling the police, and Lester estimated that he had about thirty minutes before they arrived.

Adrenaline coursed through his veins, and he started digging faster, although he remained cautious. Sweat dripped from his forehead into his eyes, stinging them, and he blinked rapidly to soothe them rather than waste time by stopping to wipe them.

After another ten minutes, he had dug down twelve inches, piling the soil in a heap behind him, but he still hadn't unearthed any evidence. *Was that a police siren?* Greyton was only five minutes away, so it was feasible. The thought of the police coming for him drove him to dig even faster. It would still take them fifteen to twenty minutes to cross the fields, but he knew his time was running out.

Moments later, he could hear the siren loud and clear, and he turned to see a police car on the dual carriageway. He was already digging as fast as he could, his white shirt dripping with sweat despite the cool breeze. When the siren got even louder, he looked round and his jaw dropped at the sight of the police car speeding across the field towards him. He hadn't anticipated that. His time was almost up.

Lester went to thrust the spade into the ground when something caught his eye. It was small and ivory in colour. It could have been a stone, he had unearthed many during the past hour or so, but his head told him no. He dropped to his knees and quickly started brushing the dirt away with his fingers, revealing more of the round, smooth surface. It didn't take him long to realise what he was touching.

As the police car pulled up a few feet away, he grabbed his phone and quickly scrolled through his recent contacts and pressed call. Two officers jumped out of the vehicle and started heading purposefully towards him as DCI Fenny answered.

He felt firm hands on either shoulder pulling him away, but he just managed to put it on speaker as they took his phone away. 'It's David Lester. I've found her.'

Chapter Thirty-One

DCI Fenny burst into the interview room in torn jeans and a T-shirt and began pacing back and forth. 'Congratulations!'

Lester sat alone at a table by the wall, watching him through narrow eyes, not sure if he was being sarcastic. 'I couldn't just let it go.'

'Clearly.'

'It was you who gave me the idea.'

At that, Fenny stopped pacing and raised his eyebrows. 'Me?'

'You said, and I quote, it would have been easier if you'd dug her up yourselves.'

Fenny gave a shake of his head and glared at him. 'Don't go blabbering that around. I meant, it would have been easier two months ago, before I spent weeks getting to know the National Heritage suits on a first name basis. How will this look to them now?'

'This shouldn't reflect on you. It was all me.'

Fenny sighed. 'Hopefully they won't press charges as there's definitely a body there. Or at least a skull. The question is, was it buried one hundred years ago or five thousand years ago. You'd better pray it was the former otherwise you might be getting banged up for this.'

Lester looked down at the table in front of him. He knew, from his research, that he had committed a heritage crime but hadn't even considered that he might end up in prison as a result of his excavation. Even if he escaped a custodial sentence, there was a chance he could lose his job if Walker found out. He had zero tolerance for his employees being linked to any negative publicity in case they lost clients as a result.

'It's Frances Coldwell,' Lester said calmly. 'A hundred percent.'

'Let's hope so. In the meantime, they'll probably charge you and then you'll be released on bail. I'll do my best to deter the National Heritage from pressing charges, but I can't promise anything. It depends how pissed they are and if they'll even talk to me after this.'

'Why did you have to go digging up the past?' his mum ended her long silence after Lester had explained where he had been and why his best clothes were sodden with mud. 'Your father will be turning in his grave.'

He sat back in his chair across the table from her with his favourite mug nestled between his hands. 'I don't think he would. In fact, I think he would have done exactly the same thing. I inherited my determination and need for justice from him.'

'Your father never broke the law. Not once.'

'I think he would have done on this occasion. Sometimes you have to do the wrong thing to force the right outcome. You'll see. Once they positively match the DNA of that body to the blood found at Pendlebury Manor, this will go away.'

'Or you will.'

'Thanks for the vote of confidence, Mum.'

'What do you expect? Getting in trouble with the police, car chases, and that poor man who lost his life.'

'Poor man? Don't feel sorry for him, Mum. He was a villain! He was trying to kill me and Lauren.'

'And getting that poor girl mixed up in all of it. No wonder she wants nothing more to do with you. She was a lovely girl and such a talented spiritualist.'

'Medium,' Lester corrected her and pushed away the guilt he felt about Lauren, focusing on the positive instead. 'She is! And that's the reason I'm so confident that the body I found today is the girl who went missing over a hundred years ago.'

His mother shuddered and pulled her shawl tighter round her shoulders. 'Digging up graves! What will the neighbours think when they read about this?'

Lester opened his mouth to retort but decided against it. *What's the point?* He was just glad that he hadn't given her all the gory details otherwise she probably would have disowned him.

When his phone rang, he was surprised to see that DCI Fenny was calling him.

'Hello?'

'I just wanted you to know that we've been in discussions with the National Heritage for most of the day, and they have agreed to a supervised dig of Raghlan Coe using our forensics team and their historians. The excavation will start on Monday. Meanwhile, the area remains cordoned off to the public.'

'That's great news. How did you manage to swing it?'

'The discovery of a body is always a game-changer. It becomes a police matter, so really they had no choice but to comply. They could have delayed things by tying us up in red tape, but they believe it's unlikely that a chief or dignitary would have been buried in such a shallow grave. They just wanted some proof, and you gave that to them, albeit illegally. If this proves to be the remains of Frances Coldwell, I doubt they'll pursue any action against you.'

'Thank you,' Lester said. 'I know you've put a lot of time into this.'

'It wasn't exactly how I planned to spend my weekend, but at least things are moving in the right direction now.'

'Is there any chance that I would be allowed to come and watch the dig?'

'No,' the DCI said bluntly. 'Considering you're still part of an ongoing investigation, you should stay well clear. They will be strict regarding who is permitted to be in attendance. Even I'm not allowed at the site, and it's now officially my investigation. Besides, these guys are slow and methodical. Be warned, it could take some time. Don't go calling me every twenty minutes like last time.'

Lester was silent for a moment, contemplating the torture of days, weeks and even months of not knowing. *How can I stay away? After all this time, I have to know what's going on!*

DCI Fenny sighed and, as if reading his mind, replied, 'do me a solid, Lester. If you do happen to find yourself in the vicinity of Raghlan Coe, stay behind the police line. Otherwise I'll arrest you myself.'

'I will. I've done what I needed to. Now I just need to wait.'

'Exactly. I hope you're right about all this. I've gone out on a limb for you on this investigation.'

'I'm right,' Lester told him before hanging up the phone.

Chapter Thirty-Two

17:21 Wednesday, 17th April

Lester sat in the long grass behind the yellow and black 'Police Line Do Not Cross' barrier for the third consecutive day, staring at the dig site fifty feet away. This was the closest he was allowed to get, which was disappointing, particularly as this dig was only happening because of him. All he could see was a large white canvass tent that completely consumed Raghlan Coe. He had scouted the surrounding area for a better view, but there was no higher vantage point anywhere around the perimeter.

When the sun shone from behind, Lester could see a hazy silhouette of the dolmen and the men working within the tent, but otherwise there seemed to be little in the way of activity going on over there. He knew these things took time. Extreme caution had to be observed to avoid damaging any findings, but it was frustrating just sitting there watching helplessly.

When his phone pinged, he quickly grabbed it and swiped the screen several times until he managed to unlock it. He hadn't realised how cold his hands were until his fingers refused to obey his commands. It was a text, and he held his breath in his lungs as he clicked on the icon to see who it was from. The optimistic part of him, small though it was, hoped it would be from Lauren. He believed that time was a great healer and that, maybe after all these months, she would be able to forgive him, but his shoulders sagged when her name did not appear on his screen.

Hello deat what time shall I do diner ?

He couldn't help but smile as he read his mum's text. *One of her better ones*, he observed. He usually needed to read them several times to understand what she meant. Some messages needed to be deciphered, others were duplicated, and occasionally they would be completely blank.

He began to reply, *Hi mum, 6 pls. I would have had eno-*, when he heard shouting coming from the dig site. He stood up and watched with bated breath, struggling to separate the diggers from the dolmen as they huddled in a small group within the tent.

They've found something, Lester thought to himself as he began to pace back and forth.

It was over an hour later when DCI Fenny pulled up in the layby behind his car and a further fifteen minutes before he had trudged across two fields to where Lester stood watching with his hands deep in his pockets.

Lester turned around when he heard the policeman approaching. 'They've found something, haven't they?' he asked excitedly.

Fenny raised his hands, gesturing as though trying to slow down a speeding vehicle. 'They've unearthed an ulna and radius of a left arm. When they called me, I asked them to dust off her hand to see if we could make a positive identification, based on the statement Ms. Miller gave me back in February.'

'And?'

'They called me on the way here to confirm they've found scoring on the . . . proximal phalange, I think they called it.'

'In English, please?'

'The base of the thumb.'

'Yes!' Lester cried, punching the air with two raised fists.

'We still need to complete a DNA test to make a positive ID, but this injury is consistent with Ms. Miller's statement in which she claims Frances Coldwell tried to cut off her thumb with a piece of metal in order to escape her shackles. It appears that you've found her.'

Lester's cheeks were starting to hurt from smiling.

'You must be pretty pleased with yourself,' the policeman said, an eyebrow raised.

His head bobbed slowly. 'I'm not going to lie, it does feel good to solve a hundred-year-old mystery. Definitely better than landing a new client. To think that before the start of the year, I didn't believe in ghosts and spirits or any of that stuff, but now there's no doubt in my mind.'

'I'm still trying to wrap my head around it all, but I can't argue with the evidence,' Fenny acknowledged. 'I wouldn't hang around if I were you. They told me that exhuming her remains will take several days, especially if she's carrying a child. It means they have to be extra careful.'

'Thanks. I think I'll take your advice,' Lester said, trying to zip his jacket up a little further before realising it was already zipped up as far as it could go. 'There's no escape from that wind up here.'

'I'll keep you informed once they've recovered her body and done a DNA test. It'll take a week or so.'

Lester nodded. 'Thanks again,' he said, offering his hand.

The DCI shook it firmly. 'No, thank you.'

Chapter Thirty-Three

He often joked that he had been at the back of the line when they were handing out patience. Despite being told on several occasions to wait for a phone call, he had rung DCI Fenny several times since the discovery of the body at Raghlan Coe.

'You need patience,' the policeman's tone had grown colder with each call.

'Doctors need patients, I need confirmation.'

'I'll give you confirmation when I get confirmation, Mr. Lester. As I've told you before, these things take time. We just have to wait.'

How long does it take to dig up a body? Lester tried to research the subject, but the closest thing he could find was related to palaeontology. It wasn't until two days earlier, on the evening of Monday, 29th April, that he received the long-awaited call.

'Mr. Lester, it's DCI Fenny. I have some news, finally. The forensics team has positively identified the remains found at Raghlan Coe. The DNA matches blood samples found in the air raid shelter as well as blood found on the shackles located in our archives. They also found evidence of a skeletal foetus, which they believe was approximately ten weeks old. It's been confirmed that the body is that of Frances Coldwell.'

Lester opened his mouth to speak, but the words lodged in his throat.

'Mr. Lester?'

He swallowed hard and wiped his eyes, overcome with a mixture of emotion. Frances could finally be put to rest properly. 'Thank you,' was all he could say.

'You'll also be pleased to know that the National Heritage will not be pressing charges and nor will the Kent Police. Just try to stay on the right side of the law in future.'

'I will,' Lester said before releasing a long, drawn out sigh.

'You should also know that this story will break in the nationals tomorrow following our press release at noon. I thought you deserved to be the first to know, although someone appears to have leaked the story to the *Kentish Times*. They called me, hoping to get the scoop, and now they're keen to interview you. I didn't give them your details, GDPR and all that, but I have the name and number of the reporter that wants to speak to you. The rest is up to you.'

'Okay, thanks. So what happens now?' Lester asked. 'I'd like Frances to have a proper Christian burial. In the same graveyard where her mother and brother are buried.'

'I'll contact the coroner to find out if this can be arranged now that the remains have been identified. I'm sorry it all took so long, but you wouldn't believe how much protocol and red tape was involved. First they had to determine if the bones were of antiquity or of forensic importance. Then they had to get a license to permit the exhumation of the remains. The longest part, though, was unearthing the bones with tiny brushes to ensure they weren't damaged in any way.'

'I understand. It was just hard being a bystander after being so heavily involved for so long.' Lester hesitated a moment, then decided Fenny was used to him by now, so he may as well ask.'So what about the Mayor?'

'What about him?'

'He's not blameless in all this. He certainly involved Gray Warren after I visited him.'

'Proving that he ordered a hit on you and Ms. Miller might be difficult,' Fenny said, his tone suggesting he spoke from experience.

'To be honest,' Lester said, pinching his chin between his thumb and forefinger, 'I think he's already paid the ultimate price. He's lost a son in all this.'

The DCI gave him the reporter's name and number and promised to call him when he had spoken to the coroner. Having written the first draft of his untitled novel, Lester called the reporter from the *Kentish Times* and made a deal to promote his novel, once completed, if he submitted an abridged version of the events. It took several calls to the editor, but they eventually agreed to his demands as they were keen to cover the local story.

Chapter Thirty-Four

11:03, Friday, 10th May

David Lester stared up at the spire of All Saints Church, a prominent landmark in the bustling town of Greyton, and then down at its arched entrance. He had visited the church twice before, both times to attend a wedding. Today was a more sombre affair, although by no means a sad one. It was to celebrate a life that passed over a hundred years ago but which still lived, in a sense, until recently.

For the first time in a long time, Lester felt like he'd accomplished something good, but a sense of disquiet made it impossible for him to feel truly satisfied. Yes, Frances would soon be laid to rest, but there was still another phantom out there, and the prospect of trying to help her without Lauren by his side was inconceivable. With a sigh, he stepped from the bright spring morning into the dimly lit seven-hundred-year old building. It was Frances's day. He would worry about Sarah Kendall later.

Despite the story making national television news as well as the papers, Lester was surprised to find the church was brimming with attendees. There was standing room only, apart from the first pew on the left, reserved for family members, which he occupied alone.

'You're the closest thing Frances has to family,' Reverend Henley had told him when he had challenged why he was receiving special treatment. 'She wouldn't be here if it wasn't for you. None of us would.'

The church was silent, no one daring to cough or clear their throat as they waited for the service to begin. That silence was broken by the echoing of high heels on the encaustic tiled floor. A murmur rippled through the congregation. Lester wanted to look round, his mind conjuring up the image of Sarah Kendall, the phantom bride, walking down the aisle to complete her unfinished business.

The steps grew louder, accompanied by more whispers. People shuffled uncomfortably on their hardwood pews.

'Is this seat taken?'

Lester looked up and then rose from his seat. 'Lauren? I didn't think you'd come.'

'I couldn't stay away,' she said, moving to his left and sitting down beside him.

He could hear the white noise of numerous whispered conversations behind them. He went to speak, but Reverend Henley appeared in the pulpit, his presence silencing the congregation once more. He was glad because he didn't know what to say and that usually resulted in gibberish. Instead, he turned his attention to Henley.

Lester did his best to concentrate as the clergyman told the abridged story of Frances Coldwell's life, honouring his request not to mention his involvement. 'I don't want to take anyone's attention from Frances,' he told Henley when they had met a week earlier to discuss the service. 'This is her day.' Having declined television interviews and having his photo in the papers, Lester wasn't about to steal her thunder now.

He had first met with the vicar a couple of weeks earlier, as soon as DCI Fenny had confirmed that Frances's body had been released for burial. Greyton Borough Council had offered to pay all the costs as long as Lester made all the arrangements. He had arranged a proper Christian send-off for Frances, but only a service, no eulogies, biographies, or hymns since he didn't know what she would like. Anything they did would be speculative, and he just wanted her to be at peace. It meant that the service would be short and sweet, although to his surprise, the reverend ended the proceedings by reading a poem.

'I would like to conclude this service with a special poem entitled "An Ode to Frances,"' the reverend said, his gaze meeting Lester's quizzical frown.

Lester leaned over and whispered in Lauren's ear, 'I didn't ask for this.'

The world was full of conflict and chaos
It was a time of death and despair
But in you burned an ember of new life
Hope, like smoke, filled the air
But then flames burned and scorched you
Abandoned by the one you thought you could trust
Dreams were transformed into terrible nightmares
Foundations crumbled to dust

Your inner light was extinguished

And all you knew became a lie

Fighting valiantly for that life within

As mortality stared you in the eye

You gave everything you could

and never surrendered to the beast

Now we offer you to the Lord's embrace

In hopes that you may find eternal peace

'Thank you, Lauren, for those lovely words,' the reverend said when he had finished.

Lester looked round sharply. 'You?' he asked, louder than he would have liked.

She shrugged. 'I wanted to do something nice for her. I know this was your mission, but I felt her emotions as strongly as if they were my own.'

'This was *our* mission. *We* did this together,' he told her.

12:27

The churchyard was pleasantly warm, and Lester felt a peaceful calm come over him, surrounded as they were by colourful clusters of vibrant bluebells around the bases of several oak and elm trees. He and Lauren stood alone at Frances's graveside, looking down at the oak casket. Following Henley's committal, they had each emptied a shovel of earth onto the coffin and then several members of the congregation had stepped forward to do the same. Over the past twenty minutes or so, most of the crowd had dissipated, although there were a few people wandering around the cemetery reading headstones.

Now that his journey was over, he felt inexplicably empty, sad even, certainly not fulfilled as he had expected. He blinked away a tear and immediately wiped it away, although he wasn't quick enough to hide it from Lauren.

'It's ok,' she told him, as though reading his thoughts. 'They're ok.'

He turned to her, his forehead creasing.

Lauren smiled up at him and then looked back towards the oak casket, although her eyes looked above and beyond it. 'They're standing here right; Frances, her brother and their mother. It's the first time I've seen Frances looking happy. Truly happy.'

Lester followed her gaze, squinting as though it would suddenly allow him to see spirit. 'Really? They're here? How do you know it's her mother and brother?' he asked.

'I took a wild guess,' she said before hitting the top of his arm in that exact spot she always found. 'Of course it's them, silly! She's not going to just turn up with some randoms, is she?'

As Lester continued to stare his eyes suddenly widened. Perhaps it was a trick of the light, as the sun's rays stole through a gap between two clouds, but he thought he saw the outline of three people standing before him. Then they were gone.

'They're reunited. A family once more. That's because of you, David.'

Lester swallowed hard as a tear ran down his cheek. He wiped it away and managed to say, 'and you.'

'It feels good, doesn't it?'

He nodded, his smile lingering. 'Is this what it feels like when you release these trapped souls?'

'Kind of. I don't usually get quite as invested as this but there's a similar sense of reward, yes.'

Earlier, they had looked around the gravestones themselves to find where Frances's mother and brother were buried. The original plan had been to bury her with them, but Reverend Henley advised against it, explaining that the war graves were not deep enough for additional coffins.

'Strangely, there are no regulations about how deep a grave should be in this country. Just the recommendation of a two feet minimum depth,' he explained.

'Are we going to talk about the elephant in the graveyard?' Lauren asked, now that they were finally alone.

His head bowed for a moment and then he turned to her. He reached down and took her hands in his own and looked into those dark, fathomless eyes. 'I'm so, so sorry, Lauren. I really screwed things up because of my obsession to find out who Frances was and what happened to her. I realise how stupid and selfish I was putting you in danger and I just hope you can find it in your heart to forgive me some day. Losing you has been so hard. It felt like I was losing Katie and—'

She pulled her right hand away and put her finger to his lips, silencing him. 'Shhh. I have trust issues,' she said simply. 'I've been hurt so many times before that it just felt like déjà vu when I found out that you'd been keeping things from me. I thought you were like every other guy who'd let me down, but you're not. It took me a long time to realise that, but what you did for Frances was the most selfless act I have ever known. You didn't do it for fame or fortune. You did it because it was the right thing to do. It took me a while, but I realised I was right about you all along. Your Nan was right. You are one of the good ones, David Lester, and I forgive you.'

Lester pinched his eyes with his thumb and forefinger to stop the tears from falling down his cheeks.

'Hey,' she said, squeezing his hand tightly. 'How about we kiss and make up?'

He pulled her into him and angled his head so that his lips lined up perfectly with hers.

'Wow, good kisser,' she told him, her eyes wide and bright. 'Box ticked!'

'There's plenty more where that came from.'

'Promises, promises! Perhaps you can buy me lunch and then we can find out just how true that is.'

He took her hand and led her away, just glancing back one more time to that hole in the ground to mouth the words, 'Goodbye, Frances.'

As they headed down the narrow path through the graveyard, Lester spotted the former mayor standing in front of the church watching them. His black attire suggested that he was in mourning although he was a little surprised to see him there.

'That's the former mayor,' Lester told her as they followed the path parallel to the church.

'What's he doing here?'

'Guilty conscience, I expect.'

As they drew level with him, Dering walked over to them. 'Mr. Lester?' he called.

Lester had already made his mind up not to speak to the man, but his curiosity got the better of him. He stopped and turned to face Dering as he approached.

Dering stood closer than Lester found comfortable, locking eyes with him. For a moment, Lester wondered if the older man was about to strike him.

'I just wanted to say… sorry . . . for all of this. I don't expect you to understand, either of you,' he said, his gaze turning to Lauren, 'but my boy was just trying to protect the Dering name. It means something in this town, at least it used to. I was the last of four generations of Greyton Mayor, and I didn't want our legacy to be tarnished with scandal and corruption. Graham was a little overzealous, but he was doing it to protect me, and his grandfather and his great grandfather and his father before him.'

A little overzealous! 'Well, I'm sorry for your loss, Mr. Dering. I'm just glad that it's all over.'

Dering nodded, his eyes glistening with tears.

Chapter Thirty-Five

'It seems really strange driving up here again,' Lauren said as they headed up Pendlebury Way. They had one more phantom to put to rest.

'I was thinking the same,' Lester replied as he navigated the pothole-ridden road. 'It's a bit less stressful when some psychopath isn't trying to run you off the road.'

She smiled, although he could see in her face that it may have been too soon to make light of the incident with Gray Warren.

'Sorry,' he said, placing a hand on her knee. 'We'll laugh about it one day. I promise.'

She nodded. 'Maybe, but we'll have a flying car by then.'

As he drove past the spot they both knew so well, she turned to him. 'You missed it. It's back there,' she said with a flick of her head.

He smiled and continued up the road. A few moments later, he slowed and turned into the car park of the Bridal Falls Public House.

'Why are we stopping here?'

'You see that box of old files in the back?' he said, looking over his shoulder. 'I'm returning them to their rightful owner. Come on, there may be a drink in it for you.'

'But we've got work to do.'

He took out his phone and showed her the display. 'It's only twenty past ten. We've got time for one quick drink before we go.'

Reluctantly, Lauren got out of his new Fiesta and followed him to the front door. He pushed it open and was relieved to see several customers scattered around the pub. Paul Brotherton was behind the bar drying some glasses. When he looked up, Lester saw it took him a moment to recognise him. As soon as Brotherton's frown eased, he grinned and ushered them over.

'David Lester! I was not expecting to see you again,' he said, grabbing a pint glass and automatically beginning to fill it with lager. 'I read about you two in the paper,' he said, glancing at Lauren. 'This must be your sidekick?'

'She prefers medium to psychic,' Lester said with a wink.

'Paul Brotherton, pleased to meet you.' He extended his hand across the bar which she stepped forward to shake. 'Thanks for mentioning me and the pub in the press. It's done wonders for business,' he added, his hand indicating to the customers sat at various tables and booths.

'We couldn't have done it without you.' Lester lifted the Bankers Box of files up and then placed them on the bar. 'I know you said I could keep these, but our work is almost done, and I can see you still have a book to finish.'

'A book?'

'*The History of Pendlebury Hill*? I'm sure recent events must have got your creative juices flowing.'

Brotherton's gaze lowered momentarily. 'Actually, you guys did an amazing job, but it wasn't the outcome I was hoping for.'

Lester nodded. 'That's the real reason we're here. Do you have a moment to talk?'

'Sure.' Brotherton handed him the pint of lager and turned to Lauren. 'What can I get you to drink, young lady?'

'Prosecco, please.'

Brotherton reached for a glass from the overhead cabinets and filled it almost to the brim with sparkling wine before handing it to Lauren. He picked up his glass of red wine from the counter behind the bar and turned to the barmaid beside him. 'Amy, can you take over for me, please?'

They followed him over to the same booth where they'd sat almost four months earlier.

Brotherton sat down opposite them and immediately put the wine glass to his mouth and emptied half the contents. 'You said you're almost done? What more is there to investigate?'

Lester remained silent but held Brotherton's gaze until the older man eventually looked down.

'You know…don't you?' Brotherton said, unable to maintain eye contact.

'Why didn't you tell me?'

Brotherton shrugged and stared at his wine glass before finally looking up. 'Saying it out loud just brings it all back and I couldn't bear to relive the whole thing again. Not that I can escape it. I've been carrying this around for most of my life.' He picked up his wine and stared at the dark liquid swishing around inside the glass until it become blood. He put the glass down. 'How did you find out?'

'Even when I first started investigating it was pretty obvious from the files that there was more than one phantom, but your newspaper article and blogs only seem to be interested in Sarah Kendall. I knew that you would have realised this even before I found Frances Coldwell's name written in the back of your notebook. I'm not sure if you concluded the same as I did, that Frances was only appearing to men who had done something bad?'

Brotherton lowered his gaze once more.

'In my case, it was for cheating on my wife. I believe Frances appeared to you because of your drinking and driving.'

Brotherton's eyes homed in on his wine glass. 'To be honest, I never put that connection together, but the irony is that she caused the accident. When she stepped out in front of me, I instinctively braked, but the weight of my van took me across to the opposite side of the road,' he said, his eyes welling with tears, which ran down his face and disappeared into his beard.

'So, your real name is Paul Fenwick?' Lester said.

The older man nodded. 'I was getting so much hate mail once I was released. My car was vandalised. Windows in my house were smashed and graffiti sprayed on the door. I even received death threats. In the end, I changed my name and moved away.'

'But you came back and became the landlord of this pub?'

'More irony. My parents owned the Poacher's Arms. When they died, I inherited it. I was going to sell it, but I spent a bit of time sorting out their affairs and realised that I belonged here. No one seemed to recognise me. No one ever has. I guess the facial hair and glasses help.'

Lester nodded. 'I didn't either at first but the eyes gave it away. They have, dare I say it, a haunted look.'

'That's exactly what I am.'

'It can't have been easy coming back, living on the road where it happened.'

Fenwick shook his head, looking past them. 'It wasn't. There's a stone memorial where she died. People laid wreaths and flowers by it for years until they built the dual carriageway. It was a constant reminder. Not that I needed one. Sarah Kendall has never drifted far from my thoughts.'

'So when did you start investigating?'

'In June 1988. Two of the witnesses, Sandra and Bob Wren, called in for a drink one night and started asking me about a phantom bride. It seems they were doing their own investigation, but it was the first time I became aware of her. After that, I began investigating the paranormal activity along this hill, and when I read the reports about the girl who steps out in front of cars, I realised that's what happened to me. I relived that night with a clarity that I'd never had before. It was almost like I was watching a video of myself. I saw myself driving down the hill, listening to "Bad Moon Rising" on the radio, and then from nowhere, she appeared. Yes, I'd been drinking, and yes, I was over the legal limit, but I wasn't drunk. It's not something I'm proud of, but I used to drink a lot. I was immune to its effects, at least for the three pints I'd downed. Some people can have one beer and can barely stand up but still be legal to drive. I'm not trying to justify what I did, but when this girl suddenly appeared before me, I reacted exactly the same way that you did. I braked as hard as I could, and the van skidded and crossed the centre of the road. Tragically, there was a Mini with four girls coming in the opposite direction.'

Fenwick buried his face in his palms. Lester could see that he was sobbing and reached out to comfort him but held back. 'Did you tell the police about the girl?'

He nodded, his face still concealed. After a few moments, he lifted his head, removed his glasses and wiped his tears from the lenses. 'I did, of course I did, but I was ridiculed. "Wow, how much did you have to drink, Fenwick? So, where's this girl now then?" You can imagine the sort of comments they made.'

'I can.'

'After a while, my lawyer convinced me that I shouldn't pursue it, and I guess I blocked it out of my mind. Even when I was doing my investigations, I had this mental block around the girl stepping out in front of me, even though I'd read several witness reports saying the exact same thing.'

Lester took several mouthfuls of his beer before sitting back. 'It's not a coincidence that we're here tonight, Paul. Our unfinished business is to try and help Sarah Kendall cross over,' he said, turning briefly to Lauren. 'We just wanted to give you the opportunity to join us. Perhaps it will help you find some closure?'

Fenwick closed his eyes tightly. Lester was aware of people in the bar watching them but ignored them as Fenwick opened his eyes and looked first at Lester and then to Lauren, blinking away more tears.

Lester took a final swig of beer and stood up, placing a firm hand on the older man's shoulder. 'If you want to come, meet us at Sarah's memorial by eleven minutes past eleven,' he said. 'If not, thanks for everything, Paul.'

Once they were outside, Lauren grabbed his hand and stopped him, pulling him round to face her. 'That was a lovely thing to do, Rainbowman,' she said, standing on tiptoes and looking up at him with her lips puckered.

He kissed them, then pulled away slightly, lingering to gaze into her eyes. 'It's the right thing to do,' he said.

They drove slowly back down the hill for a mile and a quarter until they reached Sarah's memorial. The entrance to Pendlebury Manor had been cleared back in March to allow access for the crime scene investigators, and Lester was able to pull into the opening and park. He looked at the clock on dashboard before switching off the engine, 11:01.

He opened the car door and stepped out into the mild night air, aware of the huge contrast in temperature compared to the last time they were there. The silence between them was a mixture of respect and anticipation as he wandered over to the sandstone memorial and dusted it off.

The sight of bright headlights coming down the hill had filled them with dread during their last visit, but this time it was hope. The Land Rover flashed its lights at them and then pulled into the gravel driveway.

Fenwick stepped out of the vehicle and stood there for a moment before walking over to them.

'I wasn't sure you'd come,' Lester said, shaking his hand vigorously, 'but I was hoping you would.'

'I'd have come sooner, but my legs are like jelly. I don't think I've ever been this nervous in my life.'

Lauren shuffled sideways and slipped in between them before taking their hands in her own and squeezing them firmly. Silently, they stood and waited with tingling anticipation as she closed her eyes and tilted her head ever so slightly skywards. The hum of the dual carriageway was the only sound as she took slow, deep breaths, summoning the spirit of Sarah Kendall.

Even though he had seen a ghost twice and was now a firm believer, Lester was still sceptical that she would just suddenly appear before them. His stomach was tight as he continually checked the time on his phone. On the other side of Lauren, he could see Fenwick's hands were shaking. Years of guilt and self-torture could be ended if this plan worked, but it was a long shot at best, and even though Lauren always spoke to him of having positive thoughts, it was still too incredible to believe that it would happen. They watched her face as her expressions changed from concentration to frustration and then to jubilation.

Fenwick turned to Lester questioningly, but Lester shook his head, not wishing to disrupt the proceedings. He too had expected her to appear before them, as she was said to do every year on the anniversary of her death.

'I'm asking her what she wants,' the medium added. They watched her nodding as if she were listening. 'She wants her mother to know that she's okay. She was worried about them going out the night before the wedding, so now she'll be panicking because she hasn't come home.'

Lauren went silent again, and Lester could hear Fenwick's heavy sigh.

'I've told her that her mother has passed on and that she'll be waiting for her on the other side. I'm asking her if she sees a light. She's nodding. "They're always here. Car headlights, blinding. That's what killed my friends," she's saying. She doesn't realise she's dead too. She just associates the light as the headlights that took her friends. That's why she hasn't moved towards it.'

Fenwick hung his head.

'I've told her that she also died in the accident. She's processing,' Lauren said after a few minutes.

'Can you tell her I am so sorry for what happened,' Fenwick asked, his face twisted with the guilt and heartache he's carried for so long.

'She can hear you,' Lauren said, her lips curling in a smile. 'She says she forgives you.'

Fenwick closed his eyes tightly, and fresh tears ran down his cheeks. He took a few deep breaths before finally saying, 'Thank you, Sarah.'

'She's smiling and putting a hand on your cheek.'

'I can feel it,' he said, placing his own hand on his cheek.

In that instant, as car headlights illuminated the road, they stared in awe as she appeared, blonde hair, brilliant white dress, dazzling smile framed with pink lips. And then she was gone. They stepped aside as the car raced by, a couple of lads in the back shouting out the window, but they ignored them and continued to stare, mesmerised by what they had just seen.

Lester and Fenwick turned to each other and smiled.

'I've told her to walk towards the light. They're waiting for her.'

The two men turned to Lauren and watched her until a gentle smile crept onto her lips and her eyes flickered open. 'She's gone. She simply turned and waved just before vanishing into that brilliant light. She's finally at peace now.'

Fenwick stood tall, as if he'd been carrying Sarah around on his back for over fifty years. His face even looked different, less severe and intense, and the smile that lit his face glowed with inner peace. He turned to face the medium and hugged her tightly for several seconds while she looked at Lester with round eyes that started to show signs of panic the longer he held her. Eventually, Fenwick released his hold on her and instead took her hands and squeezed them. 'Thank you.'

'My pleasure. This is something me and the other mediums do frequently anyway, so that's one less to worry about.'

'You saw her too, didn't you?' Lester finally managed to ask.

He nodded. 'No offence, but I wasn't sure if any of it was real until she appeared. I did feel something on my cheek, but I still needed that visual confirmation. I take great comfort in knowing that she's finally at peace.'

'And you are too?' Lauren asked.

Fenwick nodded. 'I never thought I would be or even deserved to be, so I can't begin to thank you.'

'What will you do now?' Lester asked.

'Move on. Something I haven't been able to do for over half a century.'

'You're quiet,' Lauren remarked as Lester headed towards the bottom of Pendlebury Hill.

'Sorry. I was just thinking back over the past four months and how things have changed.'

'For the better . . . I think you meant to say?'

'That goes without saying, but I meant with the spiritual side of things. The journey we went through with Frances and Sarah. I kind of feel sad and empty now that they're gone. Does that sound weird?'

'Not really. They became a big part of your life this year. Focus on the fact that you've helped them both to cross over to their rightful place. You've done a good thing, Dave. You should feel good about it.'

'I do. To be honest, I got a real buzz out of helping them.'

'I know exactly what you mean. When we do the group sessions where we help lost souls find their way to the light, there's always a real sense of gratification. Maybe you could come along next time? I could even teach you how to do it if you like.'

'I'd love to. I've never had a hobby before. I wasn't allowed one. Perhaps that's why I let this investigation take over my life.'

As he turned into Lauren's driveway, he saw a dark figure sitting on the front doorstep.

'Who the hell is that?' Lauren said, squinting for a better view.

Lester looked at the clock on the dashboard. 'It's almost midnight!'

He parked on the drive and turned off the engine before getting out, both of them wary as the woman stood up to greet them.

'David Lester and Lauren Miller?' she asked.

They looked at each other and turned back to her. 'Who wants to know?' Lauren asked.

'My name is Tracy Shelldrake. I read the article in the *Kentish Times* about how you found that missing girl. I've spent weeks tracking you down. I feel you're my last hope.'

'Last hope for what?' Lester asked, concern etching his brow. 'What's happened?'

'My son, Nathan, disappeared nearly two years ago, and I know the police have given up looking for him. If you can find a girl that's been missing for a hundred years, I know you can find my little boy.'

Lester and Lauren slowly turned to each other, their smiles forming in unison.

Acknowledgements

I would like to thank my wife, Christine, for her unconditional love and support and for never giving up on me even when I did. For thirty years, she has been a writer's widow, never once complaining when I abandoned her to spend countless hours working on my projects. Hopefully, I can now reward her faith.

To my parents, Barbara and Brian, who have always been in my corner and never told me to give up my day job. This one's for you!

To my cover designer, SusanArts; my editor, Parisa Zolfaghari; and my proofreader, Monique Morgan: Thank you all so much for helping me get across the line!

About The Author

I've been writing since I was sixteen, quite some time ago now as you can see! First it was poems, then songs, a few short stories and, finally, novels. My first offering was Spirit, which I wrote on a little typewriter I bought with my first pay packet. It took several years to complete and I did go through the steps of trying to get it published but, inevitably, it got rejected by several publishers and agents. Nine books later and having studied the craft of writing in more detail I can understand why.

The idea for Spirit came from a visit to a tin mine during a family holiday to Cornwall. The site of these abandoned edifices around the county, some on steep inclines with tunnels stretching beneath the sea, resonated with me and the idea for the novel was born. Because I only had a hardcopy of Spirit in a world that was fast becoming digital, I decided to copy type the original manuscript into Word. Later, I found out about OCR (Optical Character Recognition,) which would have saved me weeks, if not months, of typing - not to mention RSI!

Spirit was followed up by Blindsight, the story of a man who is robbed of his site for doing a good deed but then develops a sixth sense of seeing visions when touching other's belongings. Soon he becomes involved in a police investigation to help find a number of missing teenage girls. My third novel, Tears of an Angel, was actually a different genre so I wrote it under the pseudonym of Christine Burney. There were two more offerings before I returned to the supernatural genre with Bear Claw Canyon. This is the tale of newlyweds who get lost in the Canadian wilderness with a mysterious 'ghost like' being pursuing them. Shadowman came next, which is about a boy who sells his soul to the Devil to kill off a school bully but then negotiates to buy it back in exchange for six lives! It took me years to write Disciples, which followed, and this is the one I am currently editing for what will end up being my second publication in 2024. It's the story of an American writer who buys an old church and unwittingly unleashes twelve dark souls into a small village with dire consequences.

As you may have gathered, there is a dark element to most of my novels. I'm not exactly sure where this dark side comes from, as I'm from a fairly normal family, but I've always had a passion for ghosts and anything supernatural. Hopefully, Phantom will be the first of many novels I am planning to release over the next five years or so. In addition to the nine I have completed and need to go back and edit, I have about twenty more books that I've started and need to go back and finish, so I have plenty of work ahead of me. Anyway, I must crack on, so I hope you enjoy Phantom as much as I enjoyed writing it.

Also by Shaun Sullivan

Disciples (2024)

Shadowman (2024)

Spirit (2025)

Blindsight (2025)

Bear Claw Canyon (2026)

Kill.com (2026)

Ravenbeck (2027)

By Christine Burney

Belle (2024)

The Tears of an Angel (2026)

www.shaunsullivan666.com

Printed in Great Britain
by Amazon

38741001R00145